SECOND CHANCES IN EVERSLEY VILLAGE

SUZANNE FOX

LITTLE ORCHARD PRESS®

For Dishie Trishie
Thanks for reading <3

CHILDHOOD MEMORY

Jaz walked into the Eversley Burrows estate. It was early summer. Her school tie was in her backpack and she held her blazer over her arm. She had a regular desk in the detention room and guessed Mrs Carter knew Jaz preferred doing her homework at school, as she had taken to giving Jaz a couple of biscuits, when no other kids were in attendance at the hour-long session. Jaz had to knuckle down if she wanted to pass her exams the following year. She needed support and a peaceful environment to study in, and she got none of that at home.

Turning into Rosemead Close, she heard the music of Britney Spears pumping from her house. *Stacey's on the bottle again*, she thought feeling a zap of fear in her chest. She had stopped calling Stacey 'Mum', as she resembled nothing like her friends' mothers, with her partying and the foul way in which she spoke. Taking a deep breath, Jaz passed a couple of neighbours who asked if she was okay. She gave them a silent nod and as they returned to their conversation in hushed tones, Jaz wondered whether they blamed her for the way Stacey had turned out.

Retrieving her key from her school backpack, she opened the door to the deafening sound of 'Toxic', which thumped through her mother's sound system. Stacey swayed from side to side, with a cigarette in one hand and a bottle of vodka in the other. Jaz stormed over to the CD player and pressed stop.

'What do you think you're doing you little ...' Stacey shouted abuse, the sort that Jaz had become used to. Jaz knew it was better to keep quiet when Stacey had been drinking and looking at the scene in the lounge with mess everywhere and discarded tissues, she guessed her mother had split up with her latest boyfriend. Jaz didn't have time for it. She was being picked up in half an hour.

Locking herself in the bathroom, Jaz had a quick shower and sat on top of the towel covered toilet seat. She opened her bag and took out the present Holly had given her at school. It was a top and jeans. She picked them up and pressed her nose against the soft material. They smelled fresh, unlike the usual smoke tainted clothes she wore. Although, they weren't the pretty colours that Holly dressed in, they were purple and black. Holly's mum knew exactly what Jaz liked.

Once ready, Jaz glanced in the mirror and smiled at her reflection. She was looking forward to the evening ahead.

Downstairs, she found Stacey sitting at the dining room table crying as she smoked another cigarette. Looking up, she frowned at Jaz 'Where d'ya think you're going?'

'Out. With Holly.'

'And what's with the clothes? You little wretch you nicked them, didn't ya?'

'No, Stacey. They're for my birthday. Which is today. I didn't expect you to remember.'

'Oh, that's it. Go on, attack me again. I've clothed and fed you for fifteen years, you cheeky little –'

'Stop it,' Jaz screamed. Feeling the tears prick her eyes, hoping they would not ruin her black eyeliner.

'As if I want to remember the day you were born,' Stacey shouted. 'My whole life was ruined.' She stabbed her finger at Jaz. 'You stole my childhood. I didn't get to be a teenager for long. I was a mum.'

'Stop blaming me for everything. It's not my fault.'

Jaz saw Holly's dad's car sweep into the cul-de-sac. Jaz marched over to the front door and opened it and stormed down the driveway. As she reached the car, she heard Stacey scream obscenities at her from the doorstep, ending with: 'And don't bother coming back.'

CHAPTER 1

'*A*re you ready for this, Tyrone?' Jaz dangled the key to the Lamborghini. Hesitating, she kept it just out of his reach. *He seems way too young to be buying such an expensive and powerful machine,* she thought as she handed the fob to her fresh-faced client. Her clients seemed to be getting younger and younger.

'Thanks, Jaz, but call me Ty,' he said, taking the key with a trembling hand. He was the new face of football at United and a rare home-grown one at that. Jaz had read up on him, as she did with all her clients, and knew he had come from humble beginnings. This she respected. She had chatted to him at a couple of corporate events, taking the young football star under her wing when he had appeared socially awkward. Frowning at her pocket, she felt her personal phone vibrate for the third time in fifteen minutes.

'Crystal's gonna go mad for this,' Tyrone said, referring to his girlfriend, a social media influencer, as he stared at the fob.

'It starts via the ignition switch,' Jaz said, pointing to an illuminated button. 'But don't start it yet. Get a feel for the car first.'

Jaz showed Tyrone how to adjust his seat. She realised the motor insurance on this car was going to cost a small fortune, but on a rumoured four hundred thousand a week – Tyrone could well afford it.

Jaz's phone buzzed yet again in her pocket. 'Make yourself comfortable, Ty and I'll be back in five minutes to answer any questions you have before we fire her up.' She swung her legs out and rose to standing, in a well-practiced manoeuvre.

Jaz headed outside where the air was cooler, for it was the first warm day of late May and the glass showroom was heating up like a greenhouse. Checking her smartphone, she saw she had three missed calls from her best friend Holly, who lived back in her home county of Somerset. Jaz had been living in Cheshire for a year, having been head-hunted by Hodges and Carter, a top car sales company in the north of England. *I hope everything's okay with the baby*, she thought. Jaz walked around the periphery of the showroom, stopping before the service garage, where the aroma of oil reached her nose. It was a smell she had become accustomed to over the fourteen years she had been selling cars. Comfortably in the shade and out of sight, she returned Holly's call, which was answered immediately.

'Jaz, long time no speak. Thanks for getting back to me,' Holly said.

Jaz's chest burned at the sound of her voice. She missed Holly so much it hurt. 'Is everything okay, hun? Is the baby alright?'

'Yes, all is fine with us,' Holly said over dog barks.

'Is there something wrong with Trixy?' Jaz asked as Holly's Shih Tzu yapped in high-pitched tones.

Holly laughed. 'No, she's on full form.'

'Is there a problem with the wedding?'

'No, all plans are on schedule.' Holly was planning a quickie wedding at the end of the month.

'You shouldn't be stressing yourself out with a wedding.'

'I'm not stressed out – I just want to get married, before I give birth.' She paused. 'Shh Trixy. Sit.'

'So everything's fine?'

'I've got some bad news.'

Jaz looked around to see if anyone was close by and lowered her voice. 'It's not Val, is it?' She gulped. Val was in her eighties and had been like a grandmother to both herself and Holly, and had been recovering from a stroke when Jaz left the village.

'It's Stacey.'

Jaz blinked, processing Holly's words. She hadn't thought of her mother for years, let alone seen her. 'Is she?'

'No, she's not dead, but is in a critical condition – in Frenchay Hospital. Her neighbour, Tina, has been over to the nursery trying to track you down.'

'Why me? I haven't spoken to her since she threw me out?'

'I'm not sure, but Tina asked for your number. I said I'd have to check with you before I gave it to her.'

Jaz sighed, as a multitude of curse words filled her head. 'I see.'

'I don't blame you if you decide not to make contact. There's certainly no pressure from me, considering how Stacey treated you.'

Jaz groaned. 'Why now?'

'Maybe she wants to make peace before she moves on?'

'Oh, chick. I hope not.'

'Or maybe there are tough decisions to make.'

'Like turning off life support?' Jaz swallowed. 'Do you know what's wrong with her?'

'A ruptured aneurysm. She collapsed in the street and the neighbours called an ambulance. They took her to Weston General but they transferred her to Bristol and had to operate.'

Jaz paced along the outside wall, not being able to remain still until she reached the showroom and the Lamborghini came into sight.

Tyrone started the engine with a growl.

'Look, hun, I'll have to call you back. I'm with a client.' She did not want him reversing into one of the other six-figure priced cars.

Ending the call, Jaz returned to the silver car with gold trim alloy wheels. The scene reminded her of herself, as a child, wearing her mother's shoes – wobbling in something that did not quite fit. A love of killer heels, she mused, was the only thing she had inherited from Stacey. Lowering herself into the bucket seat next to Tyrone, she knew her usual attire of skirt suit, wasn't practical for her chosen career, but it made her feel confident – Jaz the award-winning saleswoman, a far cry from the scrappy child she had been.

Tyrone beamed at her before asking a torrent of questions. As soon as she was convinced that he would make it home in one piece, she waved him off. Turning back to her office, she banged straight into Preston.

'Whoa. One more in the bag is it for the country girl?' Preston smiled as his impeccably groomed dark hair shone under the showroom lights, like a car bonnet. His work outfit always included a waistcoat – not only was he a petrol head, he was also a fan of the football manager look. And he wore his clothes well, with his tall frame of catwalk proportions. Jaz hated Preston calling her the country girl. It was one put down after another from him – all done to intimidate her, she assumed, but she had no intention of letting him know he got under her skin.

'I have you in my sights,' she said with a sweet smile.

'You wish,' Preston replied with a wink. He was Jaz's primary competition. She wanted to be top sales exec, and he was the only member of the team she had failed to pass since working at the premium car company.

Raising her eyebrows, she crossed her arms. 'I might have been here for less than a year, but I've been at this game for a lot longer than a babe like you.'

'I'm thirty and only two years younger than you.' He gestured at her. 'Half pint.' At six foot three, Preston towered over her.

'Leave it, junior.' Pushing past him, she flicked her dark choppy bob. 'I'll be top of the leader board by the end of the month.'

Preston laughed. 'You've only two weeks left.'

She looked over her shoulder, gave him a smug smile, then turned away.

Preston had been on her case as soon as she had arrived in Cheshire, calling her 'love' in his Manchurian accent. Forever commenting on the way she marched across the showroom like she owned the place. She guessed these manoeuvres were to put her off. She had been beating the boys in a man's world since she was eighteen. Preston had been top sales exec at Hodges and Carter, for the previous two years. *Not this year, pretty boy,* she thought as she approached the refreshments area.

Pouring a coffee from the percolator, which was kept topped up in the communal seating area for both clients and staff, she breathed in the fresh aroma of Brazilian roast and took the filled cup to her office. It was only semi-private with its glass walls.

Shutting the door behind her, she sat at her white desk and logged into her emails. But her eyes soon glazed over as she stared at the computer screen. Her mind was not on the job. A nervousness had crept into her bloodstream, as if she had been transported to her angry and troubled childhood. A picture of Stacey came to mind, with her shoulder length bleached hair and face red from drink, shouting, as she jabbed a finger at her. What had caused Stacey to be sick? She guessed it was more than likely to be alcohol.

Jaz sipped her coffee and shook her head as if to dismiss the memories. Checking her desk calendar, she saw it was two weeks until she was due to motor down to Eversley for Holly's wedding. Two weeks to smash her target and beat smug-faced Preston off the top spot. She couldn't afford to take any extra time off for a hospital visit, even if she had wanted to. No – Stacey was in her past and while they may be related biologically, no mother-daughter relationship had truly existed. She realised she had no reason to feel guilty.

Glancing at the clock, it had been well over an hour since she had cut Holly off. She took a deep breath, she knew she had to call her back and face the situation.

CHAPTER 2

'*H*i, hun. Sorry about earlier. I was selling a car to Tyrone Hart,' Jaz said to Holly as she spoke into her mobile phone, leaning back in her desk chair.

'Is that someone I'm supposed to know?'

'You really are out of the loop down there.'

'I take it he's a footballer?'

'Yes, he's been picked for England.'

'So, you've got your eyes on him?'

Jaz laughed. 'No. Not my type, way too young and way too rich. I've seen what those WAGs have to put up with and it's no life for me.'

'WAGs?'

Jaz tutted as she leaned forward in her chair. 'Wives-and-girlfriends – you need to get out of that village once in a while.'

'So, who are you seeing at the moment?'

'With all the corporate events and football matches, I've no time for a relationship of any kind.'

'What happened to Jaz the man-eater?'

Jaz giggled. She always felt much better speaking to

Holly. They had been digging playfully at each other since primary school. And while they were like chalk and cheese, with Jaz being brought up by Stacey on the local housing estate and Holly brought up by affluent parents on acres of land, she missed her desperately. They shared no blood, but Holly was one of the few people in the world Jaz considered family. When she had first set eyes on the small blonde girl at school getting picked on in the playground, being much bigger than her, Jaz had waded in and announced herself Holly's protector and bodyguard. It was always a source of amusement that Jaz stopped growing when she reached five feet tall and Holly grew up to be a willowy five eleven.

'So, you're doing well? Notching up the deals?' Holly asked.

'Yes, and funnily enough, I've been getting most of my sales from the wives. A couple of my clients go through cars like handbags.'

'Really?'

'Yeah, I sold a nice little Spyder to Amy Costa the other month. Now she's pregnant and wants to trade it in for a Range Rover Evoke – which she calls a mummy car.'

'Down here, a mummy car, is a dented Ford Transit.'

Jaz laughed. 'So how are the Lord and Lady of Eversley doing?' That was Jaz's nick name for Holly and her fiancé, Mitch. Holly owned a garden nursery with an arts hub attached, and Mitch owned the neighbouring farm. Since their coupling, they were considered the power couple of the village.

'We're doing very well, thank you. I'm hoping we'll finish the cottage before I go into labour. I can't wait for you to see it. We've managed to salvage some of the original features – the inglenook has cleaned up nicely.' Holly's buildings had burned down in a devastating fire two years before, and the cottage was the last thing to be restored.

'Are you still living on the farm?'

'Yes, we've decorated it, but I can't wait for us to move into our family home.'

'Very cosy.'

'Just wait Jaz, one day you'll fall for someone and want their babies.'

Jaz laughed and looked around her neat office. 'Honestly, this body was not made for childbirth. I'd look like a pumpkin. At least you carry it well with your tall figure.' Holly had texted Jaz a few pictures of her growing bump.

'I'm getting frighteningly large now. I can't wait to have baby cuddles. Just wait – you'll want one too.'

'I'll love being an aunty to your baby, but kids don't figure in my life plans.'

'So, are you a millionaire yet?'

'I'm on track. In two or three years, I'll be there. The bonus scheme here is amazing and there's the rent coming in from my apartment in Wells.'

'Wow. When you've made it – then you can settle down.'

'I'm not settling down material. You know that.'

'Things change when the biological clock goes tick tock.'

Jaz laughed. 'My clock doesn't go tick tock, it must be digital. Once I've made it, travelling will be the first thing I want to do. I've never had a trip abroad – can you believe that?'

'Yes, I can. I don't remember you ever having time off work – apart from the days you took to help me at the nursery.'

Jaz paused. It was true, life had been work, work and more work. No wonder she felt like she couldn't be bothered to go out in the evenings anymore. Maybe it was all catching up with her. It was fine when she was in her twenties, but if she was not careful, she realised she would burn out before she reached her goal.

'Have you had any further thoughts?' Holly's voice softened.

Jaz knew she was referring to Stacey. 'I can't afford the time to go to Bristol, especially as I'm coming down for a whole week before the wedding.'

'What should I say to Tina?'

'Don't give her my number. I'll call the hospital myself, to explain that I'm up north and that Stacey and me are not on speaking terms. Hopefully, her bloke has everything under control.'

Jaz had heard from the village grapevine that Stacey had hooked up with an old flame, fresh out of the forces, and they'd had a couple of children. She had only seen Stacey and her family from a distance. Stacey rarely ventured into Eversley village.

'Tina said Stacey's partner left six months ago.'

Jaz groaned. She knew Stacey's biggest alcoholic binges were after a relationship break-up. 'I'll call the hospital. Hopefully, if decisions have to be made, they can do it over the telephone.' She had no intention of making up with Stacey.

After ending the call, Jaz looked up the hospital's details and plugged the number into her phone immediately, otherwise she knew she would constantly put it off. After speaking to the switchboard, she was eventually passed through to the correct department.

'I understand you have a Stacey there? I'm Jasmine Swift, her daughter.'

'Thank goodness you've contacted us. Your mum has been asking for you constantly.'

'For me?'

'Yes. We fear she's fading and needs family contact, something to spur her on. Your brother and sister have been in, but it was too upsetting for them.'

It felt odd to Jaz, having someone refer to Stacey's kids as her brother and sister. She assumed their father must have visited with them, no doubt they were living with him. It sounded as if Stacey was after a reconciliation, rather than needing Jaz to make any health decisions.

'I'm hundreds of miles away, working and living in Cheshire. I've been here for some time,' Jaz said.

She heard the muffled voice of the nurse, who appeared to be covering the mouthpiece, before passing it on.

'I am Doctor Raj,' a man said down the phone. 'It is very important that you come to the hospital. Your mother is deteriorating and I cannot stress how essential it is for her to have contact with you.'

Jaz shut her eyes. 'But – '

'She was close to death, so please – we meet tomorrow? This is important for her recovery.'

'Er … I'll see what I can do.' Jaz ended the call and placed her head into her hands. She couldn't handle this right now. She'd have to call them back later to say she could not make the trip, ideally when the doctor was not around to make her feel guilty about it. She asked herself, why she hadn't explained immediately, that Stacey was her mother by blood only.

The door swung open and Giles Carter, director of the company, strode in. 'What's the problem?' His deep voice reverberated off the glass. 'Don't tell me you've lost that contract?'

Jaz looked up. 'No, of course not.' She had a three-car

deal in the pipeline for members of the board at City. 'It's family business.'

'I didn't know you had family. I thought you said your folks were dead?'

Did I? she thought, realising she had probably fobbed him off with that line, as she did not like discussing her past. 'My father's dead.' Stacey had told her he had emigrated with his family to Australia before her birth, but she had no intention of telling Giles that. 'My mother's alive, but only just. The hospital has been trying to track me down, because she's at death's door. But don't worry, I'm phoning them in a while, to tell them it's not possible for me to go back.'

'Blinking heck, lass, you'll have to go.'

'But I've the contract to sort.'

'You can do that on Monday. You haven't had a day's leave, to my knowledge, for eleven months. The amount of hours you graft, you're due a weekend off. Family is important, and we pride ourselves at Hodges and Carter as being supportive to staff. It would look bad on us if your mam was to die while you sold a Ferrari.'

'I guess ...'

'Mind you, missy, make sure your butt's back here this coming week to sign off that deal.'

Jaz felt as if she was sitting at the top of a death slide and Giles was pushing her over the edge.

'Well, off with you then,' Giles said as he left her office.

She clenched her fist and tapped the table. If she didn't go it would look like she was irresponsible. Not a good trait for a future partner. No-one ever told Jaz what to do, but she felt backed into a corner. Her mind scrambled as it threw up images of her childhood.

'I need to get out of here,' she said aloud.

The door opened and Preston strolled in. 'Anything up? I heard raised voices.'

'Cool it, tiger. I've not been sacked. I'm going down south to see my mother.'

'You got folks?'

'I know I'm pretty close to perfection, but I wasn't the immaculate conception.'

Preston laughed. His eyes shone as he looked at her. 'You're so funny, you make my day.'

'Well make my day and leave me alone.'

'Oh come on, you can tell me. What's up?'

Jaz wiped her brow, telling herself not to show weakness. 'My mother is sick, so I'm visiting her in the hospital this weekend.'

'Hey. Sorry to hear that. Where's it you're from again?'

'Eversley in Somerset'

'What's it like?'

'A biscuit tin village.'

'The way your nose is turned up, I'd have thought it was a hole.'

Jaz sighed. Preston had knocked it on the head, because she was really brought up in the Eversley Burrows Estate sat on the outskirts of the village.

'Is there a pub in the village?' He leaned back on the door frame, smiling at her, while blocking her escape.

'Yes, on the village green.' Jaz's ex-boyfriend owned it, and Julian was not someone she wanted to picture in her mind.

'Sounds great. Maybe me and the lads should come down.'

Jaz shuddered at the vision of the Cheshire team, steaming down to Somerset for a boozy weekend, invading her left-behind world.

'Anything else there?'

Jaz looked at the time on her phone. 'A corner shop, an antiques auction house, a garden nursery, an arts hub and a farm.'

Preston frowned. 'Maybe not then, love. What's your mam's house like?'

Jaz turned off her computer monitor. 'A pretty cottage,' she lied, picturing the shabby grey semi she grew up in. She wanted to go back even less now. 'As much as I love our little chats, I have to leave.' Jaz picked up her white Ted Baker handbag and walked towards him, smirking as she pushed past, then marched through the showroom waving and calling goodbye to the members of the team. Dread filled her as she stepped onto the street and walked towards her rented studio apartment to pack for the trip.

CHAPTER 3

*A*s Jaz reached Booth farmhouse, the motion sensor lights created a yellow hue, lighting up the drive. Parking her sporty, red, Audi TT, she looked at the dashboard to see it was just after eleven. She opened the heavy car door and got out, stretching her arms and flexing her hands. The front door opened to the sound of high-pitched yapping, which cut through the silence of the night. A bundle of white fluff bounded towards her.

She took a step back and leaned down, to avoid the dog jumping up at her. 'Hello Trixy, you haven't forgotten me then?'

The little dog with tan coloured ears yapped as if in reply. Jaz kept her face away knowing Trixy would lick the make-up clean from her cheek.

Holly walked towards the car.

Jaz rushed over and wrapped her arms around her. 'Wow, you're getting huge, hun,' she said feeling the pressure of Holly's firm bump.

Holly laughed. 'Thanks. Nice to see you too.'

Jaz squeezed Holly some more. 'I've missed you so much.'

'Sorry we couldn't come up and visit more than the once.'

Jaz released Holly and gestured around. 'I wouldn't have expected you to, hun. You've so much on here. I should have come down to see you.'

Trixy jumped up at their legs.

Over Holly's shoulder, Jaz saw Mitch striding towards them with his dark hair and ice-blue eyes. 'How's Eversley's most handsome man?'

Mitch laughed. 'Nice to see you, Jaz.' He planted a kiss on her cheek. Then stood behind Holly, wrapping his arms protectively around her. Jaz smiled at how perfect they looked together. They would not have looked out of place in Hello magazine under the heading, *Happy Couple Await Arrival of First Baby.* But neither of them would read it, unless they were in the doctor's waiting room. Unlike Jaz, who regularly leafed through the magazine and its counterparts, looking for background information on prospective clients.

Jaz smiled. She was so pleased for Holly, yet strangely sad feeling a little on the periphery now that Holly had moved on with her life. Yes, Jaz had moved on too, but was still doing the same thing she had done for years – selling cars.

'Sorry to arrive so late,' Jaz said. 'The traffic was a flipping nightmare. Then I felt tired so had to stop for food and caffeine.'

Mitch released his fiancée and walked to the rear of the car. 'It's a long way.' He lifted the hatch and reached for Jaz's luggage, and pulled a face as he heaved it up. 'How long are you staying for?'

Jaz laughed. 'I couldn't make my mind up what to wear. So I just threw most of my clothes in.'

Mitch groaned in mock pain as he lifted the heavy case.

'There may be a few pairs of shoes and boots in there,' Jaz said.

Once inside the farmhouse, it was much brighter than Jaz remembered.

Mitch shut the door behind them. 'You won't recognise the place. Asking an artist to move in with you has its benefits – she couldn't resist a house makeover.'

Jaz entered the lounge and could not believe the transformation into a clean, comfortable living space with an oak floor. 'Wow, it's smart in here.'

Holly ran her hand over the back of the modern sofa. 'We were a bit torn. This was such a traditional room, but we're taking the nicer of the antiques up to the cottage. The farmhouse will be used for work and staff accommodation, so we made it sleek, functional and easy to clean.'

Trixy jumped onto the sofa and settled down.

'We've decorated the bedrooms, so you can take your pick,' Mitch said.

'Mitch has an influx of students coming tomorrow.' Holly looked at her fiancé, smiling.

'What from Cirencester?' Jaz asked, knowing that Mitch had taken a weekly lecturing job at the agricultural college.

'Yes, he's recruited a team to help with the veg-box scheme. He hopes some of the graduates might stay on.'

'That's worked out well.' Jaz beamed at Mitch, always excited by business success stories.

Mitch nodded. 'It wasn't my intention to recruit anyone, but a few students showed an interest and asked if they could work here between terms.'

Jaz put her hand on Mitch's arm. 'I'm proud of you guys – you're doing so well.'

Mitch smiled. 'And so are you. I heard, you'll be a millionaire by the time you're thirty-five.'

'That's the plan.'

'I'll make tea for you two, then I'm off to bed. I need to be down at the sheds for five.' Mitch's farm was a mixture of cattle and vegetable crops. 'Come on, you,' he said as he scooped Trixy up and left the room.

Jaz turned to Holly. 'I feel sick in my stomach about tomorrow.'

'What time do you have to be at the hospital?'

'I'm leaving here at nine to get it out of the way. Then you and me can spend some time together.'

'Do you want me to come with you to Bristol?'

Jaz shook her head. 'I'll be fine. Just chill a bottle of white for my return.' She knew Holly had a phobia of hospitals and was even considering a home birth.

'We could go to the pub?' Holly bit her lip.

'No.' Jaz had no intention of going to the Eversley Arms – at all.

'So I take it you'll be avoiding Julian then?'

The mention of his name sent Jaz's stomach into a spin. She had spent the last eleven months pushing nagging memories of Julian, from her mind.

Mitch walked in with two steaming mugs of tea. 'Did I hear you say you were going to see Julian?'

Jaz crossed her arms. 'No, you didn't.'

Holly laughed. 'That's my fiancé with his size elevens.'

Mitch placed the teas on coasters set upon a glass coffee table. 'I thought you guys were the real thing. You were all over each other for months. Maybe you can pick up where you left off?'

Jaz shook her head. 'No, it ended.'

Mitch put his hands up. 'What do I know? I'm just a bloke.' He walked over to Jaz and put his hands on her shoulders. 'And good luck at the hospital.' He gave her a peck on the cheek, then turned to Holly. 'Are you coming up later?'

Holly shook her head. 'No, I'll stay in one of the twin rooms with Jaz.'

'Great.' He turned to Jaz. 'Since she's been pregnant, she's been snoring like a sow.'

Holly gave him a playful swipe. 'See you when you get back from the sheds.'

'THIS IS JUST LIKE OLD TIMES,' Jaz said as she got underneath the covers of the single bed and looked over at Holly laying against three pillows. Jaz had lived with Holly and her parents from the age of fifteen and they had shared a room. 'How many months are you again?'

'Seven.'

'You look quite big, hun.'

Holly grinned. 'Promise you won't tell?'

'What?'

'It's twins.'

'No way!' Jaz sat up.

Holly nodded. 'I've been worrying about it, though. Because Mitch's mum lost twins before she had him, so we've not told anyone.'

'I'm sure they're fine. That's amazing.'

'I'll show you the scan picture tomorrow. They won't let me have a home birth, though.' Holly bit her lip. 'I'll have to go to Bristol to have them.'

'I can understand that, chick.' Jaz cocked her head to one

side. 'But I know how much you hate hospitals.'

'We've been in a few times now for scans and appointments. I'm calming down on that front and telling myself, it's not only death that happens in hospital. If you want me to come to Bristol tomorrow ...'

Jaz shook her head. 'No, honestly, I'll be fine.'

'Are you going to see Julian at all?'

Jaz breathed in and laid back against the pillows. 'No. It wouldn't be right.' Julian's face flashed up in her mind, in particular the expression on it, the day she told him she was taking the job in Cheshire. She pushed it away. 'That relationship is over.'

'But you two were so cute. I've seen both of you in relationships before, but none of them were like the one you shared with each other. He'd fancied you for ages and when you two got together, I thought that was it – that it was a forever thing.'

'So did he. I feel bad about what I did. I can't go over there now, like nothing happened. I'd feel as if I'd have to apologise or something and why should I? It's my life?'

'What really happened? You never told me the full details, did you?'

Jaz took a sip of her now lukewarm tea and replaced the cup on the bedside table. It was true. She had not talked about it and she did not like to be reminded of it, because she was far from proud of the way she had upped and left the village. 'It wasn't right between me and Julian. It was too cosy, too Mr and Mrs.'

'I would have thought that was a good thing.'

'And then there was Noah. You know me, I'm useless with kids.'

'Noah thought the world of you. He asks me about you

every time I see him at the arts hub. He's taking lessons with a graffiti artist.'

'Graffiti?'

'Yes, we broke up the left-over boards from when the nursery was cordoned off after the fire. Rather than dumping it, they've been painting it with street art. Once completed, we deliver them to the budding artist's home, so they can display their creation in their back garden.'

'That's a great idea.'

'Yes, but there have been instances of graffiti appearing on houses in Eversley Burrows. And the village notice board recently had a splash of colour.'

'Oh no,' Jaz said with a laugh. But the mention of the estate brought Stacey back to mind, and while that was an unpleasant topic, she did not want to be quizzed any further on her split with Julian. 'I wonder if Stacey is close to the end?'

'Have you decided what you're going to say to her?'

'Not exactly, but I want to make it crystal clear. I will not rekindle our relationship if she's planning some sort of apology.'

'Right.'

'Obviously, I won't let rip when she's sick.'

'I fully understand. It's so hard for you.'

'I feel sorry for her, as I'd feel bad for anyone in hospital, but this is not the start of happy families.' Jaz yawned and reached over to switch off the bedside lamp. She didn't know what to expect, but knew tomorrow would come soon enough. 'Night, hun.'

CHAPTER 4

*J*ulian unbolted the front door of The Eversley Arms from the inside, pulling it inwards with a creek. It was a fresh day, and he filled his lungs with the morning air. He could not imagine a life where he did not start his day with this view over the village green. He had lived there for thirty-seven years – his entire life.

There were already three regulars waiting outside for their morning pint. Two were shift workers, and the third was Jim Kelly from Kelly's auction house, the pub's neighbour.

'Simon's got breakfast on the go,' Julian informed his waiting customers, as the smell of grilled bacon wafted from the kitchen.

Back inside, he poured their usual drinks. Jim settled in his favourite spot by the fire and the paramedic and nurse sat at the bar, chatting. Julian wasn't worried about the workers. This was the equivalent of their night time pint and supper. They would be asleep for most of the day. But he was concerned about Jim and his type. Those who would sit in the pub for most of the morning and get through a lot of alcohol. He knew business had not been great for Jim in recent years. That's what concerned him about the pub, facilitating unhealthy habits when he himself was fit, running around the rugby pitch twice a week, training the youngsters.

Having served his customers, he went back outside and set up the chalk board A-frame with the day's special offers.

Simon appeared in the doorway. 'Alright boss? I've served up the sarnies – you after one?'

'They smell great, but not today.' These days, he spent less time on the rugby pitch than when he played for Exeter, so needed a much healthier diet.

'What's on offer for the punters today?' Simon said, stepping back to look at the A-frame.

'That barrel of Canning's Stout won't last much longer. I've put it on offer, twenty-five per cent off. We won't replenish that with the next brewery order.'

Cutting through the peace was a vroom of an engine. Julian felt the hairs on his arms stand up. He looked ahead. Passing the edge of the village green was a red Audi TT.

'Ain't that your ex-bird?' Simon asked.

Julian followed the car with his eyes, spotting Jaz's personal number plate. 'Looks like it.'

'Has she moved back then?'

'I expect she's helping with Holly's wedding plans.' Julian tried to sound cool, as old feelings rumbled inside.

'Maybe you two?'

'No, she made it quite clear. She's not interested.'

'What happened then?'

'She got an offer she couldn't refuse.'

'What – from another bloke?'

Julian laughed. 'No, a job. Her career comes first.'

'Brutal.'

'Yep. You could say that.'

'To be fair, she doesn't look like she's from round these parts, does she? Looks more like one of those sex-in-the-city types.' He slapped Julian on the back. 'Well, plenty more fish, eh? And there's that right sort, you've got on your case.'

Julian didn't react, but he knew Simon was referring to Kimberly. Recently divorced, she had moved over from Surrey to live with her parents who were incomers to the village. Her son, Max, was in Noah's class at Eversley Primary and attended the rugby training Julian ran up at the local club.

A middle-aged couple walked towards them.

'I'll get back to the bar,' Simon said.

Julian nodded a hello to the husband and wife as they passed him. He arranged the tables with benches that spilled onto the village green. Looking skywards, he could tell it was going to be sunny and was hopeful for an increase in takings. He had been promoting the pub's soon to-be-opening bistro. Eversley was a lot more on the map these days, since Lovelands Nursery opened an arts hub. All sorts were coming, especially those with money to spend. He had taken advantage of that and had refurbished half of the pub and created the small restaurant. Some of the regulars had grumbled about losing the skittle alley, but they had rarely used it. He had kept the lounge bar with the bistro having a separate entrance.

Julian rubbed his hands together, the Eversley Arms was definitely up-and-coming, and he was pleased with how things were turning out. He had not looked back since Jaz left and he didn't intend to start now.

TAKING A DEEP BREATH, Jaz approached the ward reception as her heartbeat quickened.

She addressed the nurse behind the counter. 'Hello, I'm Jasmine Swift, Stacey's daughter.'

The nurse smiled, stood up, and came around the desk. 'You're in luck – Mum's awake.'

'Is the doctor here so I can have a word?' Jaz felt faint.

'Are you okay? You look quite pale.'

'Do you have any water?'

The nurse walked over to a cooler and poured Jaz a little paper cone of water and passed it to her.

Jaz steadied herself on the counter as the cool liquid filled her mouth. She looked towards the beds. 'I haven't seen Stacey for years. I just need to know what the situation is, so I can get back home to Cheshire.'

The nurse raised her eyebrows. 'She's always talking about you.' She smiled. 'People often want to make amends when they're ill. All you can do, in your mum's situation, is sit and rest, but the mind is forever thinking things over. I see it all the time. Patients go over their lives, what they've done, their regrets. Especially when they've had a life-threatening situation like your mum has. She probably wants to make peace.'

Jaz rubbed her forehead. 'I'm not sure I'm ready for that.'

'Dr Raj was quite keen for you to come. Honestly, it won't be as bad as you think.'

Jaz followed the nurse into the ward. There was a red-haired woman sitting up staring into space, with a man chattering away at her bedside. In the second bed, a lady with blonde hair and greying roots was propped up against pillows with an oxygen pipe underneath her nostrils.

'Stacey, you have a visitor,' the nurse said.

Jaz stopped short. She had not recognised her mother at

all. She had rehearsed a few lines in the car for Stacey, but now she could do nothing but stare.

'Jasmine has arrived.' The nurse touched Stacey's arm.

Stacey put her hand up to her mouth and her eyes filled with tears as she moaned. Various alarms sounded from the machinery next to the bed.

The nurse turned to Jaz. 'Mum's very emotional and because of the sensitivity of the brain, we can't use sedation.' She beckoned Jaz. 'Don't worry, she's here now, Stacey.'

Jaz trembled. Stacey looked much older. Jaz knew she was forty-eight, but skinny, with drawn cheeks and red watery eyes, she looked at least ten years older. While Jaz felt sorry for this sick person, she could not connect to her. She felt cold, as if ice was flowing throughout her body.

'I'm sorry.' Jaz turned and marched away, hearing the amplified click of her stilettos as she went. Seeing a chair just outside the ward, she sat down. Putting her head in her hands, she breathed deeply, fighting against the fuzzy feeling that consumed her to the point where she feared she would pass out. She sat in silence for a few minutes until the nurse approached her.

'Drink this.' She passed her another cone of water.

Jaz sipped it slowly.

'It can be a shock,' the nurse said.

'She looks so old,' Jaz whispered.

'Stacey's very ill. But the doctor hopes that she will regain her health and normal functions.'

Jaz finished the water and crushed the cup in her hand.

'We didn't realise you were estranged,' the nurse said. 'She's been asking for you for days. But she needs to relax and stay calm.'

Jaz nodded. 'It's going to be hard for me to have a normal conversation with her. I literally have not spoken to her since I was fifteen. I don't know her and trust me, the only memories I have are those she won't want to talk about.'

'Tough childhood?'

Jaz nodded but didn't elaborate, especially as she felt close to tears. She wasn't someone prone to crying in public, or alone come to that. The last time she had cried was on her fifteenth birthday.

'It will be a long and difficult road, but it's easier with family support,' the nurse said.

Jaz shook her head and stood up. 'I'm not the right person.'

'Dr Raj wanted to meet you today but was called to an emergency. He's taken a great interest in your mother's condition and asked me if you could go to her house and pick up some treasured items – like a photo album, soft toy, a favourite cushion and some of her own clothes. That will help her connect to the person she used to be.'

No way, Jaz thought. Why should they drag her into this when she owed Stacey nothing? 'I don't have a key.'

'We have one that Stacey asked us to give to you.'

'She did?'

'Yes, yesterday, when she knew you were coming. She's up and down. Unfortunately, today is a down day, but some days she can communicate quite well.'

'I'm not sure ...'

'I'll get the key from the desk.' The nurse went to her station.

Jaz breathed out and sat back – closing her eyes. *Why me? Why not her ex?* she thought. The bleeps and voices around her melded into one buzz. She didn't want to argue about it, she just wanted to get out of there.

The nurse handed her a set of keys. 'Doctor Raj is trying out new natural methods of rehabilitation. He wants to watch your mum interact with personal items, with an emotional attachment. He's preparing a paper on the subject, which he plans to publish. Stacey has given consent for her case to be included in any publication. I assume you're okay with that? It won't involve drugs, only natural methods.'

'It's up to Stacey.' Jaz stood up. 'I'll see what I can find at the house and will bring it in tomorrow, but I have to tell you – I won't be involved in this.' Jaz looked down at the keys in her hand not wanting to catch the nurse's gaze.

'I'll let your mum know you've gone. She had an increase in her blood pressure, so I'll give that as the reason. It'll give you time to get your head around the situation. I think it's great for you to have come here, under the circumstances. You're a lovely person, Jasmine.'

She doubted that. 'I'll drop the items in tomorrow, on my way back to Cheshire.'

'Any time you can come down and visit will be appreciated.'

Jaz left the hospital gulping in the fresh air, as her body trembled. Checking her phone, she saw it was already half past ten and called Holly.

'How's it going?' Holly asked when the call was connected.

'Absolutely awful, hun. Stacey looks so old. I didn't even recognise her. She started bawling her eyes out when I got there. Alarms were going off left, right and centre.'

'Did she say she misses you?'

'She couldn't speak today. It was so brief I literally saw her and left.'

'Maybe she feels sorry?'

'She should do, but that doesn't mean I can forgive her, just like that.'

'It must have been a shock.'

'It was awful, chick. I've built a whole new world for myself, without any help from her. And now she's sick – she expects me to come to the rescue.'

'Are you on your way back?'

'No, Holls – it gets worse. I've got to go to the house.'

'What? Stacey's place?'

'They gave me her keys to pick up some belongings.'

'Shall I meet you there?'

'No. I'm gonna go in, grab some bits, then get out, proper quick. As soon as I'm done, I'll be at yours for that wine. I so need it, hun, I really do. Are you at the nursery or the farm?'

'The farm.'

'Great. I won't be long, assuming the roads are clear.'

CHAPTER 5

*J*az reached the Eversley Burrows estate. Driving in, she instantly noticed the changes. When she had lived there, the houses were identical. With the same windows, the same front doors and the same drives – but not now. The residents had done their upmost to make their own properties individual. As she turned into Rosemead Close, her heart burned – there at the end was her childhood home. It looked slightly smarter, but still had the original features that the neighbours, who had clearly bought their ex-council homes, had spent time to disguise. The driveway was dotted with tufts of grass and weeds.

She killed the engine, remaining in her red Audi. *I could come back tomorrow?* she thought but noticing curtains twitching in nearby properties, she decided to get into the house and get it done, before she was bombarded with questions from her mother's well-wishing neighbours.

Opening the heavy car door, she got out, then closed it gently before approaching the front door with Stacey's keys jangling in her hands. Letting herself in, she was greeted by the smell of stale fags and she knew she was back home.

Shutting her eyes, she heard the memory of Stacey's voice in her head. *You ruined my life.* She pushed away the thoughts and reopened her eyes.

The place had been decorated since she had been there last. Gone was the pink and gold striped papered walls, replaced by a floral feature wall, and the rest was painted in a pale dusky pink. But some of the furniture was the same – the sideboard, and the dark shiny scratched dining table. There was a leather sofa and the beige carpet had gone, replaced with a wood effect laminate. Walking through the oblong lounge she reached the kitchen and stopped short, it was fitted out with modern cabinets and a shiny fibreglass aqua splash-back. Whilst the kitchen was modern, it was far from clean. The worktops were covered in packets and take-away cartons. The sink was full of plates and the tumble dryer was open, with clothes spilling onto the floor. Walking further into the room, she nearly tripped over an empty cat food bowl.

She's left the cat? she thought. Jaz opened the cupboard under the sink. The cat food was still there, where she used to keep the food for Binky. She knew cats could live for twenty years or more. *Is he still alive?* she asked herself. Binky or no Binky, the cat needed feeding. She pulled out a box of dried food.

'Where are you?' she called out. Listening and not receiving a response, she made her way back to the lounge, making kissing sounds with her lips, like she used to make years ago, when it was Binky's mealtime. She heard move-ment, from upstairs. *I'll have to go up there eventually,* she thought.

Jaz was excited at the prospect of seeing her cat. She had missed him so much when she'd left and had even consid-ered kidnapping him. Jaz felt herself morph back into her teenage self, the one with purple spiked hair, shaved around the edges. She touched the back of her head where underneath her dark hair, a small tattoo hid, of a purple fire-spitting dragon, which she'd had etched into her skin in a parlour in Weston-super-Mare, having convinced the artist that she was eighteen, using fake ID. These days she kept her hair its natural shade of darkest brown. She did not want that purple dragon showing through. It didn't match her new image one bit.

Grabbing the white painted bannister, the bottom stair creaked as she put a stilettoed foot on it. Again, she heard movement. 'Where are you?' Shaking the food box, she climbed the stairs. Binky would never recognise her after all these years, but she would easily recognise his black fur with a white patch across his left eye. A rush of warmth covered her, as she recalled how he purred when she stroked him, the affection a stark contrast to the lack of attention she had received from her mother.

Once on the landing, she headed for her mum's bedroom, remembering how Binky used to love it in there, curling up on the pillow most days. The door was already open and inside she took in the unmade bed and dirty clothes strewn on the floor. The room smelled of stale fags and stale human. Jaz shut her eyes, then snapped them open, hearing movement from under the bed.

'I can hear you,' she whispered. Bending down, she lifted the eiderdown and looked underneath.

Staring back at her were two brown eyes, which did not belong to a cat.

There followed a piercing scream and Jaz jumped back, holding her chest, while still on her knees.

The wardrobe door creaked from behind her and a pair

of hands grabbed her shoulders, pushing Jaz forward, until she was flat on the floor.

'I've got her. Get out the other side. Mikey, run. Now!' A high-pitched voice rang out.

Jaz didn't move, although she could quite easily have overpowered the child. She remained still, trying to make sense of what was happening. Mikey scrambled from under the bed as the hands left her shoulders. Pushing herself up from the floor to standing, she looked towards the door and saw two dark-haired children run out of the room.

'Oi,' she shouted as she put her hands on her hips.

The tallest child turned, then stopped still. Her big brown eyes blinked as her face widened into a grin. She rushed towards Jaz, nearly knocking her over until her warm arms encircled Jaz's torso.

The girl looked up. 'Jasmine, you came.' Glancing towards the door she called out. 'Mikey, it's okay it's Jasmine. Come back. Come see. She's here to rescue us.'

The little boy came in, staring at Jaz as if she was a pop star. His brown eyes were familiar to her, the same she saw in the mirror each day.

The girl's arms become tighter around her and Jaz could hear her crying. She knew they were Stacey's kids. Her heart thud and she felt dizzy again. Maybe their dad had brought them back here to live and she'd just waltzed in. *I probably scared the life out of them,* she thought.

She gently pushed the girl back so she could see her tear-stained face. If Jaz had not been wearing four-inch heels, the girl would probably be a similar height. 'What's your name?'

'Belle.' *That figures,* Jaz thought. Stacey was always obsessed with animated films.

'And your name is Mikey?' she asked the boy.

'He doesn't speak,' Belle said. She took her arms away and clutched her hands together. 'I knew you'd come. I wished and wished with all my heart that you'd save us.'

Jaz shook her head slowly not knowing how to react. 'How did you know it was me?'

'I've seen pictures.'

'And how old are you both?'

'I'm eleven and Mikey's nearly five.'

'And when's your dad getting home? I'm sorry I barged in like that. I must have scared you. The hospital gave me the keys.'

Belle stepped back and put her head down. 'Dad left ages ago. He went to France.'

'France?' Jaz looked around the room. 'Who's looking after you, then?'

Belle grabbed hold of her. 'Please don't tell them we're here. We don't want to go back.'

'Back where?'

'To the foster homes.'

'What? You've run away?'

Belle nodded. 'They took us to the dentist this morning, and we went to the park afterwards before I had to go back to school. We hid in the bushes when they weren't looking and they left.'

'They'll be worried sick.'

'We're staying here.'

'Your mum can't look after you right now. She's too sick.'

'I know, we saw her. She couldn't speak. Is she going to die?' She looked up, tears brimming, then falling from her long lashes.

'The doctors are doing all they can.' Jaz felt her voice falter, and a tear pricked the back of her eyes. It was as if she was talking to herself as a child. 'The foster family are there to look after you both and keep you safe. You can't live here on your own.'

Belle stepped back. 'We're not going back.' She took Mikey by the hand. 'They split us up. They said one family can't cope with us. I heard Donna say we have behaviour issues.'

That's no surprise, Jaz thought. 'Who's Donna?'

'The social worker.'

There was a high-pitched ring as the doorbell sounded. Belle shook her head and whispered. 'Don't answer it.'

Jaz hesitated, but as she looked at the kids, she knew they needed help, needed to be looked after properly and she certainly wasn't the person to do it. She shook her head. 'Look, I know what it's like. I had to go to foster parents for a while when I was your age.' Stacey had checked into rehab for two months. 'It might feel wrong now, but it's the right thing. They'll keep you safe.'

'No.' Belle shouted.

Jaz heard the creak of someone opening the letter box. A woman's voice called out. 'Belle? Are you in there? The Jacksons and Moores are really worried. Can you come down and talk to me please?'

Belle's chin quivered as tears streamed down her cheeks.

Jaz took a deep breath. 'I'm sorry, chick, but I could get into big trouble for hiding you. My car is outside, the neighbours will tell them I'm here, they saw me come in. I'll tell Donna that you want to be together and see if I can sort it out for you.'

Belle turned away, took Mikey by the hand and rushed down the stairs. Jaz followed as quickly as she could in her heels. As she reached the bottom stair, Belle was opening the front door.

On the doorstep was a woman with windswept hair, in a

green Parker coat with a lanyard around her neck bearing an ID badge with the emblem of the local council.

Belle put her free hand on her hip, the other still clutching Mikey's hand. 'We're not going back.'

Jaz noticed Donna visibly breathe out. 'Thank goodness, Mikey is with you too.' She shook her head. 'You gave us all a shock there, running off like that. Your families are upset and extremely worried.'

'They're not our families!' Belle shouted.

'No, but they're looking after you. And you might not think it, but they do care about you.' Donna looked up. 'Are you a neighbour?'

Jaz opened her mouth, but Belle spoke before she could get any words out.

'She's our sister, Jasmine, and she's come to look after us.'

Jaz sucked in her lips to stop herself from swearing out loud.

Donna lifted her eyebrows. 'Do you have proof of identity? You really should have contacted us. This is most irregular. It's certainly not helpful to allow the children to remain here without informing the authorities. We've been extremely worried for their safety.'

'I didn't –'

'I'm afraid I simply can't leave the children with you. We need to sort this out under the proper procedures.'

Well that's a blessing, Jaz thought, relieved.

'I'm not going. She *is* our sister.' Belle turned and ran into the house with Mikey at her heel.

Jaz licked her lips. 'I'm sorry about this. I've been up to Frenchay to see Stacey. It's been a shock. The hospital staff asked me to come to the house and pick up her belongings and when I arrived, I found the children hiding out.' She looked around then back and lowered her voice. 'They're upset about being split up. And I know how it is for them, I had to be placed in care for a while when I was a kid. If I'd had a brother or sister it would have been so much easier. You feel so isolated with people you don't know. Maybe you should ensure they're together? And what's wrong with Mikey he doesn't talk?'

'He can talk. He talks to Belle but no-one else.'

'Maybe that's another reason for them not to be split up.'

'It took a great deal of effort to set everything up for them at such short notice. And this is hopefully, only short-term. As soon as your mother is out of the woods, they can return. If it was long-term then yes of course we would look to place them together.'

'Surely there's something that can be done?' Jaz felt obliged to try, after all, she had promised Belle. She turned as she heard the children approaching. Belle had a purple box file with her. On the outside written in black marker-pen was 'Jasmine'.

'See?' Belle thrust the folder at Donna. 'Proof she's our sister and she can look after us.'

Jaz felt panic burn in her body. 'We haven't really discussed ...' *I can't look after them,* her inner voice screamed.

Donna opened the box and flicked through the papers. She nodded and looked at Jaz. 'I'm satisfied you are who you say you are. And on reflection, yes maybe it is best they are kept together, we certainly don't want them running off again.' She checked her watch. 'I can see the children are distressed and it is the end of the day. I'll log through an emergency recommendation. But on Monday morning at ten o'clock you all need to come into Wells Health Centre, so we can sort this out.' She passed the box to Jaz and gave her a business card. Turning away, she walked towards a green hatchback parked on the street.

'Wait.' Jaz remained on the doorstep, watching Donna drive away – she was clearly in a hurry. Jaz turned around.

Belle smiled. 'I can't believe it.'

Mikey looked at Belle then to Jaz and grinned.

Jaz stepped back inside the house closing the front door. She looked at the box. *What's in here?* she thought.

As if reading her mind Belle replied. 'It's Mum's memory box about you. She looks at it when she's sad. Which was a lot since dad went away.'

Jaz walked back into the lounge, placing the box on the old, battered dining table, which still had her name etched into it. Opening the folder she saw her birth certificate on the top – her original one with 'unknown' written in the section naming the father. Stacey said he had emigrated before she was born, so could not verify his paternity. Underneath that was a small envelope with 'Jasmine's hair' scribbled in faded pen. Her hand shook as she looked through the baby memorabilia. She swallowed as she came to newspaper cuttings. Photos of her in car sales adverts. Of her at the local car showroom when she won an award, a picture of her when she had helped organise the village fair and at the opening of Holly's arts hub. She snapped the box shut and took a deep breath.

Belle leaned against her. 'Mum always says, she's so proud of you.'

CHAPTER 6

*J*az sat at the dining table drinking a black coffee as she watched Belle and Mikey sprawled out on the sofa in front of the television, munching their way through a carrier bag full of snacks. She wondered how Belle had acquired such a large collection of sweets, hoping she hadn't stolen them.

Belle turned and smiled at her, lifting a chocolate bar. 'Want some?'

'No thanks,' Jaz said, especially not if they were hot goods. Her phone shrilled from her pocket, and she fished it out to see it was Holly calling.

She waved her phone at Belle. 'I'm just popping out the back, to take this call.'

The kids gave no response and continued to watch the cartoon, which Belle laughed at every now and again. Walking through to the kitchen, Jaz unlocked the back door and stepped into the garden. The grass was at least a foot high and the weeds even taller. She answered the call.

'How's it going? I've just noticed the time. I've a glass out for you and the wine is chilling in the fridge.'

'Holls, you're not gonna believe this. When I got to the house, I found Stacey's kids hiding out.'

'Oh, my goodness.'

'Yes, they've run away from their foster parents.'

'You need to call Social Services.'

Jaz stared up at the cloudless sky, taking deep breaths. 'I didn't have to. They turned up.' Jaz explained what had happened.

'She just left you with them?'

'Yes. It's unbelievable, hun. And I need to get back up north for Monday.' Glancing through the kitchen window, Jaz made sure the kids were out of earshot and lowered her voice. 'I'm no good with kids. How can I look after them? And the house is a pigging mess.' She put her hand to her forehead. 'I can't stay here. It should have a public safety order slapped on it. There's trodden in food, cat fluff and dirty washing strewn all over the place.'

'I'm coming over to help clean.'

'No. I'd be worried about you picking up germs.'

'Don't be silly – I'm pregnant, not sick.'

Jaz remained in the garden, after she had ended the call, taking deep breaths as she looked around the outside space. It had never been a pretty garden, with flowering plants, but she remembered spending many hours out there as a child. Especially when Stacey had had one of her men over. Her original swing was gone and in its place stood a wooden climbing frame with a slide and two swings attached. It looked like a good one, but needed a lick of wood treatment and because the grass was overgrown, the swing seats were partially hidden. She glanced at her phone to check the time. Holly would be there in about ten minutes.

Why didn't I run after the social worker and explain the situ-

ation? she thought. *What's wrong with me?* Why was she allowing the hospital to railroad her into coming here? And now the kids and the social worker? No-one ever told Jaz what to do. She felt as if coming back to see Stacey had sapped her energy.

She returned to the house to wait for Holly at the front door. Belle looked up and smiled as she walked past, as if this mad day was all quite normal. Mikey had followed her back in and sat with his sister.

Holly drew up outside, parking her transit behind Jaz's red Audi.

Jaz walked down the path to greet her. When she reached her, she hugged her. 'Holls, what am I going to do? Me and kids – it's a mare. I don't have a flippin' clue.'

'Well, let me inside and we'll have a think.'

As Holly came in, the kids looked up. Belle frowned. 'Who's this?' She grabbed Mikey. 'You're not taking us away, are you?'

Holly smiled and put an arm around Jaz. 'I'm Holly, Jaz's best friend. I own the nursery – you know, Lovelands?'

Belle's face relaxed. 'With the animals and play area?'

'Yes, that's right.' Holly had a small petting zoo with rabbits, guinea pigs, and a goat called Charlie.

Jaz looked at Belle. 'Have you been up there?'

'Dad took us sometimes.' Belle looked down, then back at the TV. Mikey turned back as well.

Holly smiled. 'She looks so much like you.'

Jaz nodded her head. 'Apparently so.'

Holly frowned as she looked around the lounge-diner.

'Total mess, isn't it? There's crap everywhere,' Jaz said.

'You're going to have to watch your language around the kids,' Holly said raising her eyebrows.

Jaz nodded towards the kitchen. 'Let's talk out there.'

Looking around the kitchen, Holly bit her lip. 'You can't stay here – it's unhygienic.'

'Tell me about it. And there's this.' Jaz pushed the purple box along the worktop. 'Apparently Stacey looks at it all the time. It's a load of stuff on me.'

Holly smiled. 'What like a dossier?'

Jaz laughed, feeling a sudden rush of warmth, pleased that her best friend was with her.

Holly opened the box and leafed through it. 'Stacey must have regrets,' she said picking up the newspaper cuttings.

'More like pretending she wasn't such a terrible mother. I bet she makes out I'm awful for not bothering with her. That file doesn't show all of my life. There are no pictures of me scratching my head as I forever had nits. No pictures of the bruises she gave me when she rolled in drunk and pushed me over. Or recordings of her screaming at me.' Jaz took in a deep breath.

'Darling. Come here.' Holly gave her a hug. 'Stacey was only young.'

Jaz swallowed. 'She was nearly our age when I left. I'd never do that to anyone.'

'Alcoholism can take over people's lives.'

'That's no excuse. The times she would blame the drink. Cry the next day, saying it wouldn't happen again.' Jaz stepped back. 'But it always did.'

'Sorry – it sounds like I'm defending her.' Holly pushed a blonde ringlet out of her eyes. 'I'm not. It's just looking through that box, it's clear to see she obviously hates what she's done. Maybe she's changed?'

Jaz shook her head. 'I've moved on. My life has been great ever since. So good, your parents, I saw as my own.

Stacey's a grown woman. She made a decision every time she lifted a glass, or bottle, to her lips.' Jaz stopped to breathe. She didn't want to cry. Crying was something she had sworn she would not do again, ever since she had left Eversley Burrows and cried for hours. She had not even wept when Holly's parents had died in a car accident, holding back the tears herself, so she could support her best friend.

Holly fished a pack of tissues out of her dungarees and wiped her eyes. 'Sorry, it's my hormones. I've been welling up all over the place.'

Seeing Holly cry made Jaz feel stronger. Her protective instinct cut in. 'Hey, don't worry about that. I'm so pleased you're here.' Jaz shook her head. 'Not only did that woman make my childhood a living nightmare, I'm the one left to clean up the mess she's left behind, due to drink, no doubt.'

'Have the hospital said that was the cause?'

'I haven't clarified the details. But I expect so.' Jaz sighed. 'I can't talk about this now, hun. I don't want to lose it. I need to be calm for the kids.'

'Do you want to show me upstairs and I'll help you get some things sorted to take to the hospital?'

As they climbed the stairs, Holly put her hand up to her face. 'Since I've been pregnant, my sense of smell has become acute.'

'Trust me, you don't need a super sense of smell to realise this place needs a good clean.'

Upstairs, Jaz showed Holly the bedrooms.

'You can't stay here,' Holly said. 'We're never going to get this placed cleaned today. But Mitch has a batch of students coming over to the farmhouse. Two have already arrived. I'm not sure how we can fit the kids in too.' She turned to Jaz. 'But you can stay in the –'

'Caravan?' Jaz interrupted.

Holly smiled. 'Yes.' Before Holly and Mitch got together, he had given Holly his Uncle's old caravan, which she had lived in on her land after the fire. 'I'll get back and give it an airing.'

*J*az was surprised at how excited the children appeared as they bundled into her Audi. She had texted Donna to let her know that she was relocating the children, and why.

'Buckle up,' she said, switching on the engine as Tina's front door opened. She'd done well to avoid the neighbour so far and gave her a quick wave before reversing away.

'What a cool car,' Belle said, on the bench seat in the back with Mikey at her side. Jaz didn't have the appropriate car seat, but it was a brief journey and the bench was child size, anyway. Holly had helped Jaz collect a few bits and pieces for Stacey, including lounge wear for the hospital, and she had taken the clothes back to the farmhouse for a good wash with a few outfits belonging to the children.

Jaz paused at the end of the close, waiting for a break in the traffic. 'When we get to the caravan, we need to clean you two up. There's a shower.'

'Urgh, no.'

'Urgh, Yes. When you're clean, we'll get food.' She turned the car right at the end of the close.

'Not some fancy food?' Belle said.

'You like pizza?'

'Yes,' Belle replied.

Jaz looked in the rear-view mirror and saw Mikey nodding.

'Pizza delivery it is then.'

'How long are we gonna stay in the caravan?'

'Just a couple of nights. We can't sleep at the house. It needs new bedding and probably new mattresses. The cat has peed all over the place.' Jaz reached the end of the estate and stopped at the junction and swung around in the seat. 'Is it Binky?'

'Binky?' Belle asked.

'The cat?'

'He's called Simbah.'

'Oh.' Jaz felt a sting in the back of her eye. *Stop being so stupid,* she thought. 'Where is Simbah?'

'Tina's looking after him.'

Jaz faced front and turned the car onto Eversley Road, towards the village.

'How long will it be until we can move back into our house and get Simbah?' Belle asked.

Jaz looked in the rear-view mirror as Belle grinned and took a deep breath. 'You know I live up north, right?'

Belle looked down at her hands. 'But you're our family.'

Jaz looked ahead. 'Yes, and it's nice to meet you.'

'Why haven't you visited before?'

Jaz sighed. 'Me and your mum haven't spoken for a while.'

'Mum told us you were too busy.'

I bet she did, Jaz thought. 'I have a big job. I'm supposed to be going back home on Sunday, but I can't now. We have to meet Donna on Monday.'

'But we don't want to go back,' Belle shouted.

'Look. I'll do everything I can to make sure they place you somewhere together.' She hoped Social Services could persuade one family to take both of the children. 'And I'll be coming down for an entire week at the end of the month for Holly's wedding. I'm sure she'll want you two to come along as well – now she's met you. I can get you a pretty dress to wear.'

'A pretty dress? Urgh.'

'Okay, not pretty – just a dress. Let's take one day at a time. I've got to go over to the hospital tomorrow as well.'

'Can we come?'

'I don't think so, Stacey, I mean Mum, must stay calm at the moment. But hopefully you can see her as soon as she gets better.'

'What are we going to do? When you're at the hospital?'

'You can sit in the nursery cafe and eat cake.'

'Yay.'

Jaz reached the village green, then turned towards the nursery. She wished she could see this as much of an adventure as the children clearly did. She drove along the short lane to Lovelands Nursery and Arts Hub. As soon as she arrived in the customer carpark, she saw the familiar green static caravan perched on the brow of the hill, which sloped towards the farm where Holly currently lived with Mitch. As she parked up, Joe approached the car. He had worked at the nursery for years, well before Jaz had moved in with the Loveland family.

He smiled and opened the door for her. 'Welcome home, pet.'

Jaz got out and accepted a hug from Joe. She leaned backwards and smiled at him. 'You look well – not thinking of retiring then?'

'I might be sixty-six, but the missus works from home and would hate me getting under her feet.'

Belle got out of the car, followed by Mikey.

'Who do we have here then?' Joe pushed his cap back so he could get a good look at the children.

'This is my sister, Belle and brother, Mikey.' Jaz didn't think that half-sister and half-brother sounded that nice.

'You can tell the family likeness.' He looked from Belle to Jaz, smiling.

Belle stared at the caravan. 'It's massive. I thought it was going to be little, like the one on Mrs Shaw's driveway. This is like a proper holiday caravan.'

Mikey beamed and followed Belle towards the static van.

'I'll get the bags in then, shall I?' Jaz said, shrugging as she watched the children run towards the caravan.

'I'll do that,' Joe said, laughing. 'You take the kids in. Holly's already brought your case over from the farmhouse. I've put it in the little room Holly used to paint in.'

'Thanks, Joe.'

'Oh, and Val's bursting to see you.'

Jaz felt a pang of guilt. She should have already popped over to see Val, who had been like a grandmother to both her and Holly when they were growing up. 'How is she?'

'You'd never know she had that stroke. She's definitely back to her old self,' he said with a chuckle. 'Let's get these bags in.' Joe lifted the boot.

Jaz followed Joe towards the van, wishing she had worn more appropriate footwear as her heels sunk into the tufty grass.

Joe handed Jaz the key. 'Welcome home.'

Once inside the caravan, the kids were hyper.

'It's so cool. The colours are mad in here,' Belle said, looking at the cerise and lime green colour scheme.

Jaz agreed. She had thought it looked amazing when Holly had upholstered it, two years ago, although now — it seemed loud. She usually went for a calmer colour scheme herself. A minimalistic look. Jaz watched the kids running around, bashing into the seats and doors, wondering if the reason the kids was so hyper, was the sweets they had eaten, or the emotions that they must be going through. Quiet one moment, loud and energetic the next. Although Mikey only squeaked. Whilst Donna had said he spoke to Belle, Jaz had not overheard him.

After an hour, Jaz's head pounded as she heard the familiar yaps of Trixy.

Belle ran to the window. 'Look at that cute dog.'

Jaz opened the door as Holly and Mitch approached. Holly had Trixy on a lead, and Mitch carried a large laundry bag over his shoulder.

Holly let Trixy off the lead, and she bounded in, running around the children and sniffing them.

Belle stroked the dog's head. 'What's its name?'

'Trixy,' Mitch said. 'Trixy by name and tricksy by nature. Watch out, she'll be in your bed.'

Mikey gingerly stuck out a hand, and Trixy licked it. He let out a little giggle.

Jaz gulped. He was, she admitted, a sweet lad.

'We won't stay,' Holly said. 'We just needed to drop off the clothes for the kids. And those for tomorrow.'

Jaz figured Holly didn't want to mention Stacey in front of the children, who were clearly happy.

'Have you got food?' Holly asked.

'I've ordered pizza.'

After a short chat, Jaz watched Mitch and Holly walk away from the caravan, hand in hand. She wished she could feel that blissfully happy.

As Jaz waited for the food delivery, her head pounded. Whilst the caravan was technically a six birth, it was not big enough for the Swift siblings. *If that's what they're called?* she thought. After all, Swift was her mum's name. They may be named after their father. Thinking of the father, Jaz took in a deep breath. How could he leave his two children to fend for themselves, while Stacey was on what could be her deathbed?

The caravan shook as her siblings jumped up and down and as nice as Holly had made it – the van itself was old and creaking and Jaz wasn't sure it would hold up under the strain. Hearing the delivery car pull up, she opened the door.

The driver pulled two large pizzas from his bag, followed by two smaller boxes with wedges and cookies, and passed over a carrier with a tub of ice cream and a large bottle of soft drink.

Jaz gave him a generous tip, as it had been a bit of a drive for him. Inside, the kids sat themselves on the soft seating area.

'Come on, you two, we'll be eating at the table,' Jaz said.

'Table?'

'Yes, that's what dining tables are for – eating at.'

'We always eat in front of the TV at home, or in our rooms.'

'Well, here in the caravan, we eat at the table.'

Jaz placed the boxes on the small dining area with soft seating one side and two stools the other. Opening the boxes, she did not feel that hungry but could have scoffed the whole tub of chocolate fudge brownie ice cream.

Both the kids were wearing the freshly laundered PJs, which Holly had dropped off and had wet hair from their showers, because there was no hairdryer. She had the heater on. Even though it was spring, she didn't want them to catch colds.

'Where's the TV?' Belle looked around.

'There isn't one.'

She heard Mikey take in a sharp breath as if she'd just announced a world shortage of chocolate.

Jaz laughed. 'I think you two should get an early night.'

Belle pulled a face. 'Mikey can't get to sleep without the TV. Can't you get our one from the house?'

'It won't work in here. There's no aerial.'

'What's an aerial?'

Jaz wasn't sure whether televisions still worked off an aerial. 'There's no Wi-Fi.' *That's language they can understand,* she thought.

'No way?'

Remembering she had her tablet with her, Jaz checked her phone, she had a signal and 5g. 'Come on, eat this pizza, otherwise it'll go cold.'

Mikey and Belle picked up a slice each.

'I've got my tablet with me. You can stream a film. You take the double bedroom and I'll be sleeping out here.'

After they had eaten, Jaz made up a bed in the lounge area of the caravan. She planned to read a book using the app on her mobile phone.

This is some flipping nightmare, she thought as she eased herself back on the pillow. She didn't know what she was going to do on Monday. She dreaded calling Giles to say she would not be back in Cheshire as planned. *He'll go ape*, she thought. He was constantly pushing her to close the three-car contract. And she needed that deal to go through, to wipe the smile off Preston's face. Would it take days to sort the kids out? 'Can I really take that much time off?' she mumbled to herself.

Settled under the duvet, Jaz tossed and turned, but as soon as she tried to sleep, she bolted awake again. She kept having visions of a younger Stacey, slurring, drunk, staggering around the house.

Jaz got up and poured herself a glass of water, in an effort to calm her mind. Tiptoeing through the caravan, she peeped around the bedroom door, which she had asked the children to leave half open. Both were asleep, and the tablet was facing the ceiling, glowing and flickering as it continued to play a film. She gently lifted it, glancing down at the peaceful-looking children. Staring at them, she could not help but feel a warmth. They had her eyebrows, a kink on the left-hand side where the hair did not grow. Hers no longer showed this, of course, due to some semi-permanent make-up magic from her favourite beautician in Cheshire. Even though they were half-sisters – it was true, Belle looked like her twin, if they'd been the same age. *Poor scraps,* she thought. She hoped Stacey had not given them the same treatment she'd had. Taking the tablet with her, she plugged it in on charge in the kitchen area.

Finally, in the early hours of the morning, tiredness won through and she fell into a deep sleep.

JAZ WOKE WITH A START.

'Give it back.'

Who's that? she thought, as she prised open her eyes. She saw a vision of her bedroom back in Cheshire, which soon faded to reveal the caravan. *Urgh,* she thought. It wasn't a bad dream – she really was in Eversley.

Mikey ran around with the tablet in his hands as Belle pulled at his pyjama top, trying to grab at it.

'Oi,' Jaz called.

'Mikey won't let me have the tablet.' Belle stopped and crossed her arms, cocked her head to one side, and pouted.

Mikey clutched the device to his chest.

'Guys, come on, you'll break it.'

Mikey's eyes darted around as he panted.

'Belle, leave him.'

'But —'

'No. Come here.'

Belle stomped over to Jaz.

Jaz sat up and patted the seat next to her, motioning Belle to sit down. 'Look at Mikey. Is he often like this?'

Mikey had slumped to the floor and was rocking backwards and forwards.

Belle shrugged.

'He doesn't look very happy.'

'I'm not happy either.' Belle's bottom lip quivered.

Jaz took a deep breath. *They're both so messed up*, she thought. 'I know, chick.' She patted Belle's hand. 'If you're both good for me, I'll buy you a tablet each.'

Belle snapped her head up. 'Really?' Her eyes were wide open.

Jaz may not have any parenting techniques, but she sure had plenty of money.

Belle wrapped her arms around her. 'You're the best sister ever.'

Jaz doubted that, considering she was bribing them and had made no effort over the years to contact her siblings. There was a sickness in her stomach. She knew ultimately she was going to let these kids down because she had to get back to Cheshire. She had to get that contract through. Her goals were within touching distance. Stacey had a lot to answer for.

Glancing at her phone, Jaz saw it was just after seven

and remembered she needed to drop Stacey's things up at the hospital. Holly had offered to mind the children at the nursery cafe. Jaz knew Holly would be great with the kids – she was used to having children over at the arts hub and had said she would find some craft activities for them.

Opening the curtains, Jaz studied the nursery buildings. They had been transformed after the fire, and were not as she remembered them as a child. Now, instead of two large barns made into a make-shift shop and showroom, the structure was a mixture of stone, wood, and glass. She had worked at the nursery from the age of fifteen, until she had started her first car sales job, after leaving college. When Holly had left to study art in London, Jaz had stayed on with Holly's parents, until she had saved up a deposit for her first flat. Holly's parents had rescued her from Stacey, and she would always be thankful for that. Sighing, she pictured their faces the day they collected her on her fifteenth birth-day. She had begged them not to tell Social Services about Stacey, scared that she would be placed again into foster care.

Jaz turned, the kids were stretched out on the rug. She was consumed by a large pang of guilt at the realisation that she intended to leave them with a foster family, and hotfoot it back up north.

Mikey had given up wanting the tablet to himself, real-ising he needed Belle's help to put something on to watch.

'I'm going to have a shower,' Jaz said to the children. 'I'll use the bedroom to get dressed, then when I'm done, you two can get changed.'

The children didn't reply, as they watched the tablet, chewing sweets.

'And sit on the sofa – you'll get cold sat down there,' Jaz said, but they didn't move.

CHAPTER 8

*J*ulian's alarm cut into the peace of the morning. Reaching for his phone, he squinted at the screen and turned it off. After putting the phone on his bedside table, he pulled back the sheets. Today he had organised a trial of the new bistro.

Once out of bed, he stretched as he would do before a rugby game. He needed to get in the zone. He had taken over the pub from his parents a few years before, as a going concern and this was his first ever solo project. The pressure was on. It needed to go well.

Once showered, he glanced around the room, remembering Jaz being there, laughing. Since he had seen her driving through the village, she kept popping into his thoughts. It had been the most carefree relationship he'd ever had. But he did not want to dwell on her.

The room used to be his parents and had old dark wooden beams mixed with white painted walls. Gone was the twee floral wallpaper his mum had used to decorate the walls with. His old room was now used by Noah and the remaining two bedrooms were let out every now and again to paying guests.

Noah was with his mother, Sophie, for the weekend, they were on good terms. She was not aware of the pregnancy until some months after she had split with Julian. Rather than forcing a relationship, they agreed it would be better for Noah if they brought him up separately, especially as Sophie had already fallen in love with someone new. Julian had to hand it to Ruben. He'd stood by her, even though she was carrying another man's child.

After dressing, Julian descended the creaky stairs to the bar. He made himself a coffee from the machine, as the smell of the beans brought him to life. Simon arrived and took over while Julian went to the bistro.

Julian rearranged tables in the bistro's dining area.

Adam entered via the kitchen. 'Are you ready for the big opening?'

'Yeah, the delivery will be here in half an hour,' Julian said, rubbing his hands together then scratched his head.

'You look nervous, mate.' Adam laughed.

'Does it show?' Julian said, grinning.

'Don't worry. In my experience, these trial runs are great fun. Who doesn't love free food?'

'But we're talking about villagers here. Eversley villagers who complain about everything.'

'How many of our neighbours make up the diners?'

'Good point. They're probably outnumbered by folks from Wells. Although I've invited a few of the parents from Noah's school. The monied incomers who are used to fine dining.'

'Good move. It'll be all over social media. Honestly, mate, you've nothing to worry about. I've cooked in some of the top spots in London and can assure you, well-cooked

British grub is the most popular.' Adam had prepared a menu to include all the old favourites – beer battered cod, sausages and mash, shepherd's pie and a sweet potato curry as the vegan option.

'I trust you, Adam, and love your food.'

'Thanks for giving me this chance.' Adam had done well in London and had a great career, but the stress led to a drug habit that eventually led to his demise. Adam was the son of Jim and Helen Kelly of the auction house. Julian had bumped into him at a corporate rugby game, just after Adam had left rehab. Adam's parents were oblivious to his problems. Their son had convinced them he'd left London due to stress, which was true to some extent.

Julian patted him on the back. Adam was a sound bloke. The chance of him getting hold of any hard drugs in Eversley was pretty remote, and he didn't even drink. He realised he was taking a chance but felt confident Adam had turned a corner, and he deserved a second chance.

The men chatted away and drank coffee until there was a knock at the door. Julian glanced at his watch. 'The first delivery.'

Julian directed the delivery guy to the back entrance of the restaurant and helped him take the boxes into the new professional kitchen.

Adam picked up the produce, sniffed it, and nodded. 'This is great stuff.'

'Thanks for sourcing it,' Julian said.

'No worries, you're paying me. And the rest is coming over from Booth farm in about half an hour.'

'I hope I don't let you down at front of house.'

Adam smiled. 'Opening nights are always nerve wracking, but this one seems special. It being our home, where we grew up as kids.'

Julian nodded. They had been friends since school and whilst Adam had got him into some scrapes over the years, he always made life an adventure.

AT SIX-THIRTY, the restaurant was filled with delicious aromas from Adam's prep and the tables had been set. It wasn't a huge seating area, but enough for thirty covers. Natalie, who Julian had employed as a waitress, was in her final year at college and busied herself making sure the cutlery was lined up.

'It looks perfect, Natalie.'

'I'm keeping myself busy. It helps me to calm down.'

'Hey, relax. You're making me nervous,' Julian said. 'I know everyone coming tonight and you won't have any rude customers.'

'I hope not.'

Julian turned at a familiar voice.

'Hi ya.' Kimberly wandered over to him. She popped a kiss on his cheek and squeezed his arm. She was attractive and sophisticated, and he didn't know what she saw in him. He knew he wasn't the typical tall, dark, and handsome. Okay, he was tall, but he was also broad, and not a pretty boy. He briefly thought of Jaz, she had called him her Viking.

Julian pulled his attention back to Kimberly, who had made it pretty obvious that she liked him, since the day he first saw her standing nervously at the school gates and introduced himself.

'I'm so proud of you, Jules,' she said in perfectly pronounced English, which stood out against the West Country lilt of the locals. 'You've done a superb job to get this far. When you think of what it used to look like in here. It's transformed.'

'True. I'm seating you with Adam's parents and his uncle, if that's okay?'

'That's super. I'll be cheering you on. It smells simply divine in here already and I'm famished.' She took his hand. 'If I drink too much, I could stay over.'

Julian swallowed. 'I'll be shattered tonight. Don't worry about not drinking, though, I'll ask Simon to drive you back.'

Kimberly pushed her sleek shoulder length hair behind her ears, 'Maybe another night then.'

Julian released her hand and gestured around the room.

'We've only one sitting this evening, but we'll expand to two sittings when things take off.' While he wasn't charging that evening's customers for food, he aimed to break even through drink sales, hoping that a few of the guests would have a pre-dinner drink in the pub. He had given Simon strict orders to promote cocktails, which had the biggest mark-up. 'Shall we go next door to greet any early customers in the bar?'

Walking into the pub with Kimberly, Julian was met with cheers. He stopped. *It's like a surprise party,* he thought. The pub was heaving. He turned to Kimberly. 'Just a few in for pre-dinner drinks then?' he said with a laugh and relaxed. At least the evening would not be a huge loss-making exercise.

Ethan, a friend and architect, slapped him on the back. 'Congratulations on the opening.'

Ethan's girlfriend Nina, a local councillor handed over an envelope.

'Thanks.' Ripping it open, Julian found a card inside with *Good Luck,* written on it.

'You've a fantastic turn out,' Nina said. 'Can we get you a drink?'

Julian laughed. 'I'm on the water before service, I need my wits about me.'

'I can't wait to try Adam's food. How on earth did you convince him to come back to Eversley?' Ethan said as he placed an arm around Nina's waist.

Julian smiled and tapped the side of his nose. 'I have the power of persuasion.'

Kimberly squeezed his arm.

He felt someone slap him on the back and turned. It was Jim. 'Good luck boy, we're proud of you and our lad.'

'Hey, save it for the end of the evening,' Julian laughed. 'And I need constructive criticism too – no saying it was great if you think we can improve things. That's what this evening's all about. A trial for us and market research.'

'I'm sure it's going to be amazing, Julian, you've both worked so hard,' Jim's wife, Helen said.

'I agree,' Ethan said, raising his pint.

Julian clapped his hands together. 'Check out the cocktails everyone. Simon has a few new recipes up his sleeve.'

Simon nodded at him from the bar as he rattled the cocktail shaker.

After milling around the pub, seven o'clock zoomed up and Julian slipped off to the restaurant. Inside, he turned the closed sign to open and unbolted the front door. 'This is it,' he called out to Adam and Natalie.

Julian texted Kimberly, asking her to announce that the restaurant was open. After a couple of minutes, the first customers appeared at the door. It was Holly and Mitch.

'Welcome to Eversley Bistro,' Julian said, stepping aside to let them in.

'Thanks, Julian,' Holly said. 'We're honoured to be invited.'

'As if I'd not invite you two, after all the extra interest and business you've drummed up for the village. We've all been benefiting from it.'

'Not everyone is pleased, though,' Mitch said.

'True, some of the old folk say we're overrun, but then they spend a lot of money out of the village,' Julian said. 'We wouldn't survive without the outsiders coming in.'

Holly nodded. 'The nursery would have closed years ago if we had to depend on the locals.'

'Come on you lot, stop gas-bagging and let us in,' Helen called.

Julian laughed and then showed Holly, Mitch, and Adam's parents to their tables.

After a busy service, quite frantic at times, Natalie was serving coffees. Julian called Adam into the restaurant from the kitchen, and everyone applauded. Julian glanced around the room, savouring the moment. It had been like a birthday party, having so many people in the room that he was friends with. And such a diverse mix, from villagers to local business people. One of whom was Councillor David Bunning, owner of a caravan and motorhome showroom, on the other side of Wells. He had brought what he described as his new 'lady friend'. Florrie was an attractive woman in her fifties, who, David was telling everyone, sung on cruise ships for a living as a Shirley Bassey tribute act. This was confirmed when she had stood up between the main course and dessert to give an a-capella version of 'Hey Big Spender'.

Standing at the door, Julian bade his diners farewell, thanking them as they filed out, complimenting him and the staff on a great evening. As Holly reached him, she kissed him on the cheek. 'It was amazing, Julian, and everyone loved it. Congratulations. When are you opening to the public?'

'Next weekend. I thought we'd give ourselves time to make any changes. And please give us any criticism you have.'

Mitch tapped his stomach. 'Nothing negative from me. It was a tasty meal. And I loved the entertainment from Florrie.'

Julian laughed. 'I know, maybe I need to have a singer in – I could make space in the corner.'

'Or a little piped music?' Holly said.

'Good point. It's things like that you don't think of. I hear Florrie sells CDs on her website.'

'Maybe she'll sing at our wedding,' Holly said. 'I'm not up on music – although Jaz always seems to know what's in and what's not.'

At the mention of Jaz's name, Julian shifted position and cleared his throat.

Holly smiled. 'Jaz is staying in the caravan. She's got a few family matters to attend to.'

Julian wondered what family matters they were, since he knew she was estranged from her blood relatives. But did not ask or respond.

'Personally, I don't think any more changes are needed,' Mitch said, as if desperate to fill the silence. 'It was spot on.'

'Thanks for your help,' Julian said. 'Adam was impressed with your produce saying it was as good as any he used up town.'

'I appreciate that,' Mitch said.

'We'll hopefully see you tomorrow,' Holly said. 'I was thinking of coming to the pub for our Sunday lunch with Jaz and the kids.'

'Kids?' Julian frowned. Then regretted it – he didn't want to instigate a conversation about Jaz.

'Oh, you haven't heard? Stacey's in hospital and Jaz is down looking after her brother and sister.'

Julian felt his eyes widen. *Well, that's a surprise,* he thought.

'It's a long story," Holly said. 'But I'll let her tell you herself.'

Julian watched as Mitch led Holly out, wondering how Jaz was coping with her siblings. After closing the front door to the restaurant, Natalie approached, grinning from ear to ear. She pushed her hand forward with a wodge of notes. 'Tips.'

'Wow, well done. You did an amazing job — I received lots of compliments about you.'

'And these are the takings.'

'What?' Julian frowned as she passed him what looked like hundreds of pounds.

'They left it on the tables. Most people left a twenty-pound note each and one couple left sixty.'

Julian shook his head and smiled. 'I don't know what to say.'

'You deserve it,' Adam said. 'Now I don't have to feel bad about accepting my wages.'

Julian laughed. 'Thanks for your hard work, both of you.' He turned to Natalie. 'I'll see you on Tuesday and we'll go over everything.'

Natalie waved as she fetched her coat and left via the back door.

Adam sat at a table, drinking a pint of water.

'So how did it go out there in the kitchen? Do you think you need an assistant?' Julian asked.

'No, mate. If we keep the menu small, then it's do-able.

We can, of course, change the menu weekly. After a time, favourites will emerge and if you're making a big profit – yeah, employ kitchen staff.'

'If you're sure? I don't want to pile any pressure on.'

Adam looked up. 'Honestly – this is not pressure. I'd tell you straight away if there was an issue. Ultimately yeah – we'll get someone in. But we want to get a good solid base first. I've seen a couple of restaurants crash and burn because they went too quick.'

'Thanks, Adam. I appreciate your advice.'

There was a tap at the back door. Adam stood up and opened it and Kimberly waltzed in then cosied up to Julian with a glass of red wine. She smiled at him. 'Well done - that exceeded my expectations. This place is going to be a gold mine.'

'I don't know about that, but we're hopeful of breaking even the first year, considering the renovations.'

Adam stood up. 'I told you it would go well. Let's go next door and get you a drink.'

AFTER AN HOUR'S LOCK-IN, the pub was quiet. Everyone had gone. Julian was alone, wondering about Jaz. The door creaked and Simon came in, having dropped Kimberly home. He walked behind the bar and poured himself a whisky, and sat at the table with Julian.

'Why are you looking so down? You've had a blinder of a night.'

Julian scratched his beard. 'Women.'

'You should count yourself lucky, bro. I get no action and you have them falling at your feet.'

'Hardly.'

'That Kimberly's well into you - didn't stop talking about you all the way back to her parents' place.'

'I'm not feeling it.'

Simon shook his head. 'I tell you, I'd be feeling it – she's a stunner. A real classy bird.'

Julian nodded his head. 'I feel bad keeping her at arm's length when she's giving me signals that she wants more.'

'You must be mad not seeing anyone since that Jaz Swift. Everyone knows she's a –'

'Simon,' Julian growled.

'I'm just saying, Kim's a beaut. Your kids are the same age, you get along. I think you're mad not giving her the time of day.'

'I do give her the time of day. Just nothing more. Anyway, if you're so interested, maybe you should let her know.'

Simon looked Julian up and down. 'By the looks of it, she doesn't go for good looks and charm.'

Julian laughed.

'I don't have your bulk, money, or anything in common with her. What's the deal with her ex?'

'He was freshly separated when they met, then married Kimberly too soon. She had Max and then her husband ended up going back to his first wife.'

'Brutal.'

'Which is why I won't string her along. She deserves better.'

'Those cakes she makes. She's the sort of woman a guy wants to hold on to.'

'I don't like the mothering kind, unlike you.'

'What do you mean by that?'

'Mummy's boy?'

'I moved out of my parents' place months ago.'

'Because they threw you out.' Julian laughed and took a

sip from his glass, feeling pleased that he had deflected the conversation and the spotlight was now on Simon.

'They didn't throw me out. They put the house on the market to downsize.'

'Haven't sold it yet though, have they?'

'These things take time.'

'Especially when you take the for-sale board down.' Julian chuckled.

Simon frowned and stared into his glass.

'Hey. No disrespect – there are plenty of women out there who want to mother a guy and a stock of men that want to be on the receiving end – but I'm not one of them. I prefer someone who's independent.'

'Like the Swift bird.'

Julian ignored Simon's comment, but he saw it plain and simple. It was what he loved about Jaz, and something which didn't go with being part of a small family with him and Noah. He sighed and glanced at the clock on the wall. 'I'm off to bed now.' He slapped Simon on the back. 'I was only winding you up, about being a mummy's boy. But seriously, if you like Kimberly – show some interest.'

$\mathcal{I}$t was a sunny Sunday morning, and Jaz opened the front door to the caravan and sat down on the metal steps. She could hear the kids laughing from inside. Looking up, she saw Holly's van chug into the customer carpark.

My saviour, she thought as she stood up and walked over to the green van and opened the door for her. 'Hi, hun, thanks so much for yesterday.'

'You sound as if I did you a massive favour. I only entertained the kids for a couple of hours while you went to the hospital.'

Jaz looked over her shoulder, then back at Holly. 'Trust me, that was a big favour. I've worked seven-day weeks back-to-back and never felt this shattered.'

Holly laughed, then reached out and rubbed Jaz's arm. 'You've a lot on your plate. What with Stacey and that big contract you have bubbling up north. Have you spoken to your boss yet?'

'I called him last night. He went ape when I said I won't be back tomorrow.'

'Oh dear.'

'Yeah – not happy. But once I explained about the kids and Social Services, he soon backed off. In fact, by the end of the call he seemed pretty impressed – said he'd seen another side of me.'

'So have I. You're doing really well under the pressure.'

'That's not how I feel inside. I don't want Giles thinking I'm going soft. If there's a directorship coming up – I want it offered to me, not Preston.'

'When we visited, I thought Preston seemed really nice and by the way he looked at you, I thought he had a bit of a crush.'

Jaz scrunched up her face as she took a bag from Holly and helped her down. 'Rubbish. He's a snake. He was just turning on the charm.'

Holly shut the van door. 'How was it left with Giles?'

'I convinced him I'm on top of the City deal. I told him I'd prepare the contracts here and that, come what may, I'll be there Wednesday, to seal the deal.' Jaz linked her arm in Holly's and led her to the caravan, carrying her bag for her. 'The kids said they loved the art they did with you yesterday.'

'I used them to trial a couple of activities that I'm planning for half-term. So that's positive feedback.'

'How did you get them to sit still for that long? I can't keep them quiet for more than a couple of minutes without the tablets I bought them.'

Holly laughed. 'I loved it and Belle, she's so like you, They really feel like family to me.'

Jaz stopped. 'They do?'

'Of course, and you must feel that way too?'

'I don't know how I feel, hun. My mind is flippin' scrambled at the moment.'

Holly pulled her towards the caravan. 'Make us a cuppa and tell me all about it.'

Jaz lifted the bag that Holly had brought. 'What's in here?'

'Cake and a bat and ball set for the kids to play with.'

'Good thinking. They're going to love you a lot more than me.'

'I doubt that very much. They adore you. Belle is always chattering away about you.'

They entered the caravan.

'Holly's here. She's got cake.'

Belle and Mikey ran into the main part of the caravan, which rocked from side to side.

Holly laughed. 'Don't get too excited. It's only lemon drizzle cake.' Holly took out a large white paper bag full of cake and placed it on the table. 'I hope you like it.'

JAZ AND HOLLY carried their drinks and sat on a bench near to the caravan, which looked out down the sloping land, where it met Mitch's farm with the Mendip hills rising in the distance.

'They don't do lemon drizzle this lush up north, hun,' Jaz said. 'Mind you they have other treats. The pies are amazing.'

'The food was de-lish at the restaurant last night.'

I wondered how long it would take her, Jaz thought, knowing that Holly had been to Julian's new restaurant. 'That's nice.'

'Adam's a brilliant chef and Julian was in his element. He seemed so confident. A great host and he's doing well for himself.'

'I'm pleased for him.'

'There was a woman there, though, gazing at him all night.'

'He's bound to have a girlfriend.'

'Hmm, I don't know if she was his girlfriend. He wasn't all over her, not like when he was with you.'

'He's not going to kiss her in front of the customers when he's working.'

'I remember him grabbing you and hoisting you over the bar for a kiss!'

Jaz blushed. 'I get you're a true romantic and all that but it would never have worked.'

'Sorry, I'm being a nuisance. I miss Julian and you being together – I miss the double dates.' Holly turned to her. 'Maybe I just miss you.'

Jaz smiled at Holly and touched her arm. 'I miss you too, hun. There's no way I'd have taken the Cheshire job if you'd not got together with Mitch. I know he looks after you.' Jaz felt a lump form in her throat and quickly swallowed it away.

Holly nodded and smiled. 'But who looks out for you, Jaz?'

Jaz felt like saying she didn't need anyone. *Do I need anyone?* she asked herself. Jaz and Holly had stuck together through thick and thin. She certainly felt like she needed help now – with the kids. Looking away, she took a deep breath and watched the kids playing. Chasing the ball down the hill every time they missed it. Getting lower and lower down the slope. *Now why didn't she think of that?* Jaz thought. She should have bought them some games. Holly was a natural with children and she knew she was not.

Holly turned to Jaz. 'So, how did it go at the hospital yesterday? You didn't tell me when you picked the kids up.'

Jaz groaned. 'I was trying to forget it. Truth is, I felt well guilty. Dr Raj was there and he was so nice. Much younger than I expected, he's still training and using Stacey's case for a thesis. And he was proper genuine.'

'What's his plan?'

'He's developing a new method of therapy and wants to observe how Stacey relates to me, and to our discussion of memories. He wanted me to sit and reminisce while he took notes.'

'Oh, my goodness. Did you tell him your history?'

'Not every detail, but I said I'd not spoken to her for years and that we didn't part on good terms.'

'How did he react?'

'He said that sometimes, when we are estranged from family, we forget all the good times and only focus on the negative bits, making out it was worse than it was.'

Holly put her hand on Jaz's arm. 'You didn't snap his head off, did you?'

Jaz shook her head. 'No, but I was short with him. I felt a bit patronised. I refused, and he said he'd have to observe Stacey looking through the memory box without me. But that it would be better if I was there so he could compare our recollection of events.'

'This sounds more like family therapy than rehabilitation.'

'Exactly. I said she won't remember anything because she was drunk for most of my childhood.'

Holly put a hand to her mouth. 'What did he say?'

'He backed off a bit. But he did point out that Stacey is my mother ... the woman that gave you life. And now I feel guilty.'

'How did you leave it?'

Jaz sighed. 'I said I've enough on my plate at the moment

looking after the kids. I told him I'd make contact once I'd sorted out their foster care.'

'You're considering it?'

Jaz shrugged. 'I couldn't give him a right-out no.' Jaz looked over at the children. They were laughing as they ran up the slope towards them. 'That's why,' she said. 'Whatever Stacey was to me, I know the kids have a different relationship with her. They love her and want their mum to get better.'

Jaz felt warm as Holly put an arm around her. 'I love you, Jaz.'

'You too,' Jaz said, yawning.

'Aren't you sleeping well?' Holly asked.

'It's not that – I think it's the feeling of responsibility. It's dragging me down.'

Holly smiled. 'I'm sure everything will work out in the end.'

Belle reached them, and Mikey was not far behind. 'What are we doing today?' Belle beamed and Holly put her arms out for a hug. Jaz marvelled at the natural way Holly was with the children. It seemed so effortless for her best friend, whereas Jaz always felt a touch awkward when Belle embraced her.

Holly released Belle. 'I thought we'd go out for lunch – a big roast dinner.'

'Will there be Yorkshire puddings?'

'Oh yes, the very best in Eversley.'

'No,' Jaz said, knowing there was only one place that served up a roast in the village — The Eversley Arms.

'Yes.' Holly looked at Jaz sideways and bit her lip.

'Have fun then,' Jaz said.

'You're coming too,' Holly said.

Belle grabbed Jaz's hand and pulled it. 'Of course you're coming, we're not going to leave you here,' she said.

Jaz felt the warmth of Belle's hand.

Holly stood up. 'You may as well break the ice with Julian because our wedding reception is going to be over there. I don't want it to be awkward on the day.'

'He might not want me there,' Jaz said.

'I told him last night that you and the kids were coming. Anyway, I need help planning the layout of the bistro next door for the wedding breakfast and I want your input.'

Jaz drooped her shoulders.

'I'm off now,' Holly said. 'I'll call for you at twelve thirty and we'll walk over together.'

*J*az walked across the green with Holly, the kids and Trixy who bounded around their legs. She wore tight jeans with heeled ankle boots and a fluffy off-the-shoulder jumper. It was a sunny day, so no coat was needed. The kids looked so different, with neat hair and new clothes. She had to admit that shopping with them the previous afternoon after her hospital trip had been a great tonic. The kids were made up with the tablets she had bought them. Clothes shopping had been fun, she likened it to buying dolls' clothes. Mikey had not objected to any of the clothes she had chosen and Belle looked cute in an outfit, not dissimilar to her own, but with flat boots.

As they walked over the village green, Jaz felt her stomach burn. She didn't even feel like herself anymore. In life, even though she had had a difficult background, she had always had the upper hand. Confidence was what she was about. Confident to seal the deal, confident when out on the town. Now? No confidence. She was out of her depth looking after the kids, worried she was doing the wrong thing being involved in their lives, worrying that she was losing her focus on work – was she going to get the deal over the line? And on top of that, she could not dampen the feelings that were rising to the top — the feelings for Julian she had brushed aside.

As they reached the other side of the green, she spotted Julian standing in the Eversley Arms doorway. She swallowed. His broad body looked so strong, his brushed back sandy hair, matched his beard. She blushed, remembering how it had felt to be in his arms.

Holly linked her arm in Jaz's. 'Be nice.'

'Of course, I'll be nice.'

'Hi Julian,' Holly called as they approached. 'I had such a fab time last night. I was telling Jaz how well it went.'

Jaz caught his eye and her body reacted, feeling her pulse increase, she flicked her hair. 'Hi,' she said in Julian's direction and instantly missed him. She took a deep breath and reminded herself that they were not an ideal match – no matter what had gone on between them. No matter the physical attraction.

'You're looking great, Jaz,' Julian said. His blue eyes were open wide so she could see the flecks of grey in them.

She gave the sort of smile she usually reserved for clients. 'This is my sister Belle and my brother Michael.'

'Mikey,' Belle said. She frowned at Jaz. 'Are you feeling hot?'

Jaz pulled at her jumper. 'I should have worn something lighter – summer's coming.'

Julian smiled at Belle. 'You look so much like your big sister.'

'That's what everyone says.' Belle beamed at Jaz.

Jaz smiled back, glad the kids were with her, there would

be no chance for any awkward chat with Julian about their past relationship.

Julian stepped aside. 'We've beef and turkey today. Adam's taken over the roasts on a Sunday. They're amazing.'

'I thought you and Simon did a great job yourselves,' Holly said holding tightly onto Trixy's lead.

'Thanks,' Julian said. 'But we're glad to have passed that job on.'

'Have you got Yorkshire puddings?' Belle asked.

'Of course.' He gestured across the room. 'I've saved you the window table.'

Jaz caught his eye. He'd always saved that seat for her and Holly over the many years they had been to the pub. Since before they were old enough to drink in there, when the strongest thing his dad would serve them was a lemonade shandy.

Once seated, Holly settled Trixy under the table and then smiled at Jaz. 'See, it's all nice and civil. Better to face it now than at the wedding.'

'Are you having the reception in the pub or the restaurant?' Jaz asked.

'Both. After lunch, I'll book a time for us all to go over it together. It'll be great to have your input.'

They enjoyed a sumptuous meal of roast beef, turkey and huge crispy Yorkshire puddings, followed by berry crumble and custard.

Julian collected the plates.

'That was amazing,' Holly said to him, rubbing her bump. 'I see what you mean by Adam's cooking. Are you free tomorrow to show Jaz the bistro? I want her to see the room so we can do a seating plan.'

'Yeah, sure, what time are you free, Jaz?'

She looked up at him, noticing the natural blonde

streaks glint in his hair as the sun came in through the window.

'I have a meeting tomorrow morning with the kids. I'm not sure what time I'll be back.'

'Text me,' Julian said. 'Assuming you still have my number?'

'I do,' she said. 'And yes, I'll text.'

Julian walked away.

'Do you fancy that man?' Belle asked Jaz in a loud voice.

'No,' she replied.

Holly raised her eyebrows. 'Your sister used to go out with Julian.'

'Holly.' Jaz narrowed her eyes.

'Ooh.' Bell dug her in the ribs.

'No point keeping that secret from the kids. Belle clearly sees what is obvious to everyone on the planet.' Holly gestured towards the bar. 'That you and Julian were made for each other.'

Belle laughed.

Jaz stood up. 'Time to go.'

Mikey drained his glass of squash before they gathered their things. Jaz noticed a young woman walk in with a boy. She'd not seen her before. She was tall and elegant, oozing an air of sophistication which she herself did not possess. The woman waved at Julian who flashed a quick glance over to Jaz. *Hmm, it's like that, is it?* Jaz thought.

Holly touched her arm. 'That's Kimberly, the woman from last night, so you need to get in there quick, if you want him back.'

Jaz folded her arms. 'It's over.' But as she swung around, she felt a sickly feeling deep inside as she witnessed Kimberly kiss Julian on the cheek.

❀

'I DON'T WANT TO GO,' Belle said, on Monday morning as she crossed her arms.

'If we don't meet Donna, she'll come looking for us. And I'll get into trouble. Come on, Belle,' Jaz pleaded.

'But we're really happy here.' Bell's bottom lip trembled.

'We can't live in this caravan for much longer – it's way too small.'

'But I love it here.'

'I know, so do I. But I have a job and you have school and I can't commute hundreds of miles every day to look after you. You know this and we've already talked about it.'

'But we don't want to go to foster homes,' Belle cried out with a sob.

Jaz softened her voice. 'I promise you, chick, I'll make sure you two get placed together and hopefully your mum will be out of hospital in a few months.'

'She's your mum too,' Belle said.

'Sure. And you can go back to live with her when she's better.' Jaz hoped Stacey would get better. Really better, although part of her wondered whether the kids were better off with a foster home, if Stacey continued to be the sort of mother she grew up with. 'Come on, otherwise we'll be late. You already agreed to this.'

Belle stormed out of the caravan with Mikey trailing behind her. Jaz grabbed her handbag and followed, sighing as she locked the caravan.

Twenty minutes later, she reached Wells Health Centre, where Donna had agreed to meet them, saving Jaz a drive out to Taunton, where the main Social Services offices were situated. Getting out of the car, she smoothed down her work suit, hoping the clothes would help her feel confident in this unfamiliar territory. The kids were also looking a lot smarter in new outfits.

The three of them soon sat in the office with a very flustered looking Donna.

'So, as I understand it, Jasmine, you're due back to Cheshire tomorrow?'

'I was due back today, so I really need to get this matter resolved.'

'Placing children takes time. We have emergency care, but we're not able to put Mikey and Belle together.'

'But Jaz, you said,' Belle cried.

'Right, kids,' Donna said. 'I need to go through some paperwork with your sister, so could the two of you go with Jane? We've got somewhere you can wait.'

The children followed Donna's assistant after reassurance from Jaz that they were not being whisked away.

'Right, as I said, this is a bit irregular.' Donna played with her lanyard. 'When I found the kids with you, I didn't follow the correct procedure. So I would also like to get this finalised as smoothly and quickly as possible.'

'That's fine, Donna. I'm not about to stitch you up and create a scene. I just need them placed together. Because although you say it can't be done – I promised the children I'd arrange that. They've been let down so much, I'll lose their trust if you can't come through for me.' Jaz felt her natural negotiation skills rise to the top.

Donna put her hand to her temple. 'It's very hard considering what has occurred over the past few weeks. You know the kids.'

Jaz cleared her throat. 'Actually, I don't. Friday was the first time I'd ever met them.'

Donna sat up straight. 'You're joking?'

'No, I'm not. Has Stacey neglected them?'

Donna shook her head. 'Not at all. Sometimes kids, of course, don't tell you everything, but there's no evidence to suggest she has been anything other than a loving parent.'

Jaz puffed out. At least Stacey would seem to have improved as a mother. 'What are the odds on getting them placed together?'

'Mikey might be better off without Belle. He relies too heavily on her.'

'Why is he not speaking?'

'It's often a form of withdrawal from the world, when a child does not like what is happening. It's a way of them taking control. He's deciding when to speak and when not to speak. I'm sure that once he feels he's in a secure environment, the words will flow.' Donna shuffled the papers on her desk. 'How's your mother?'

'The doctor is hoping for a full recovery, but her rehabilitation could take months. She misses the children.' Jaz swallowed. She hoped she was saying the right thing here. Remembering her own childhood with Stacey. She felt sick to the core, and the responsibility sat heavily on her chest. But all she could do was think short-term – the kids needed to be together. Social Services would not put them back with Stacey unless she was in the right state of mind. She was sure of that.

'I'll speak to the Jacksons and the Moores and ask if either can accommodate both children in the short-term and then we'll assess your mother's progress to see if we need a long-term solution.'

'Thanks, Donna.'

'I can't make any promises. But leave it with me. You can either wait in the offices or I'll call you.'

'I'll take the kids out.' Jaz stood up and outstretched her hand. 'Thanks again, Donna.'

Donna shook Jaz's hand. 'And thank you. I must say the children look notably better than when I saw them last. They're well-mannered and happy with you. They seem like a totally different pair of kids.'

'I doubt that's down to me.'

'Nonsense. It's a real shame you live out of the area.'

JAZ WALKED up the High Street with the children. Whilst it was deemed to be a city because of the existence of the cathedral, Wells was a small town. They reached the cobbled square, which often hosted stalls with various wares on offer. It wasn't market day that day, but there were still a few people milling around, a lot of them day trippers. She headed for a café, just to the left of the cathedral.

Once inside and having been served, Jaz watched Mikey stuff chocolate cake into his mouth and wondered whether he understood what was going on. It was difficult, with him not communicating. Belle picked at her oversized cookie. Jaz didn't feel hungry either and sipped her coffee, chewing on a small piece of croissant. It was only half an hour after they left the health centre, when her mobile phone rang.

Jaz took a deep breath and answered it. 'Jaz Swift.'

'Hi, it's Donna. Good news, the Jacksons said they can accommodate Mikey, as well as Belle, on a short-term basis. They have a small office, which they can clear out and make into a bedroom for him.'

'Thank goodness.'

'This is temporary though and it's also going to be difficult, as Mikey has to start school, because they can't look after him during the day. I'm not sure if you're aware, but

Stacey has not yet registered him for primary. Children are expected to start at four these days, although it's not the law until they are five.'

'No, I didn't know that.'

'We've already set the ball rolling and Eversley Primary confirmed Mikey has a place. Children in care shoot to the top of the list. But he can't start until after half-term.'

'I see.'

'It will be quite a handful for the Jacksons.'

'I'm very grateful to them.'

Belle put her head in her arms, clearly overhearing the conversation.

Jaz glanced out of the window. 'So what's next?'

'There's a further complication, in that the Jackson's have a holiday planned for next week. Which is half-term. They were going to take Belle with them but they can't take Mikey too.'

'Right.'

'So unless you're able to stay here for the next two weeks, Mikey will have to remain with the Moores.'

Jaz looked up to the ceiling. 'I see.' She felt sick – how was she going to seal the City deal and care for the kids at the same time?

'Is there any way you can have the children for the next two weeks?'

Jaz glanced at Belle with her head in her hands and then to Mikey, who was oblivious and had chocolate cake all around his lips. *I can't tell them they'll be split up,* she thought. 'I'll arrange something.'

'So, you agree to be their temporary guardian for the next fortnight?'

'Yes.' *How am I going to sort this out?* she thought.

'Excellent. I'll confirm it with the Jacksons now. Come back to the centre and I'll process the paperwork.'

Jaz put the phone on the table. 'The Jacksons can take you both,' she said to the children.

Belle began to sob.

Jaz reached across the table.

Belle pulled her hand away. 'I don't want to go back there.'

'But you and Mikey can be together.'

'He won't like it.'

Mikey looked from Belle to Jaz, his eyes widening.

'It's only short-term.' Jaz smiled at Mikey. 'And it's not going to happen for over two weeks.'

Belle blinked a tear from her long brown lashes. 'So, we'll be split up for two weeks?'

'No. You'll be with me,' she said, feeling her career crumble around her. She didn't want the children to sense her disappointment, so smiled. It wasn't their fault. 'Come on, let's get back to the health centre and sort this out.'

TWO HOURS LATER, Jaz watched the kids from the caravan window, as they played tag outside. Turning away from the window she opened the caravan fridge, wondering if it was possible to make a meal out of its limited contents. Her phoned dinged with a text – it was from Julian.

Are you still coming over to discuss Holly's wedding?

Jaz took a deep breath. She did not want to face Julian, especially when she was in a mess. But she did have to support Holly.

Sorry, been with the kid's social worker. I can come later.

Her phoned dinged shortly afterwards.

OK - I have rugby training late afternoon. See you at six?

Jaz confirmed to Julian that she would be there and texted Holly to let her know the time she needed to arrive at the bistro. She decided to be as helpful as possible, because she needed to ask Holly a massive favour – to have the children on Wednesday and overnight, so she could get back to Cheshire and finalise the City deal.

CHAPTER 11

As Julian arrived at The Eversley Arms with Noah, after training, he noticed Jaz immediately. She was sitting with her brother and sister, eating dinner at the window table.

Simon shouted out to Noah from behind the bar. 'Did you win?'

'It was training. We didn't play anyone,' Noah replied.

Julian noticed Jaz look up. She nodded at him and smiled. His mind flashed to a time when they were together. He returned her smile then looked away quickly, not wanting his mind filled with that sort of memory.

By the time he and Noah had showered and dressed, it was approaching six.

'Are you going to be okay up here on your own?' Julian asked his son.

'Why? Where are you going?'

'I've got a meeting with Holly and Jaz.'

Noah's eyes widened. 'Jaz? Can I come?'

Julian scratched his head. Normally he would have said no. He knew how upset Noah was when Jaz had left, but he would see her at the wedding, so better that Noah was upset today than then. And Jaz had her brother and sister with her. 'Okay, she's downstairs. We're going next door to the restaurant to plan Holly and Mitch's wedding meal.'

Both dressed in jeans and t-shirt, Julian led Noah down the stairs to the bar.

Jaz approached them.

Noah rushed up to her. 'I haven't seen you for ages.'

Jaz smiled at Noah. 'That's because I live two hundred miles away. I'm down for a while, looking after my brother and sister.' She pointed behind her.

'I didn't know you had a brother and sister?' Noah said, staring at the kids. He frowned. 'Is that Belle?'

Jaz nodded. 'Do you recognise her from school?'

Noah nodded. Julian thought Noah looked uneasy. If Belle was anything like her big sister, she was probably the sort to scare the life out of his mild-mannered son. Belle looked a few years older than Noah.

Julian placed a hand on Noah's back. 'Why don't you go over and say hello?'

'Don't mind Mikey,' Jaz said. 'He doesn't speak much. But Belle makes up for it.' She laughed.

Noah approached the table.

'Noah's got much taller since I saw him last,' Jaz said.

Julian smiled. 'Kids grow up so fast. If you blink, you miss it.'

Jaz shifted her feet and looked away.

'Noah lives with me most of the time now.'

Jaz turned, raising her eyebrows. 'He does?'

'Yes, Sophie's got herself a new job, working longer hours. It made the school run tricky for her. It was easier all round if he stayed here. She has him every other weekend.'

'How are you finding that?'

'I think Noah and I are still in the honeymoon period. No doubt that will wear off.' He laughed. 'Talking of honeymoons, where's Holly?'

Jaz played with her necklace. 'She just called. She can't make it.'

'Do you want to rearrange?'

Jaz lowered her gaze, then looked back up at him.

His body reacted as it always did when he looked into her big brown eyes.

'She said the main reason for the meeting was for me to see the restaurant, so asked us to carry on without her.' Jaz flicked her hair.

'Is she okay?'

'Just tired I think – what with carrying twins.'

'Twins?'

'Oh, flip.' Jaz slapped her hand over her mouth, and he saw her skin colour up.

Julian laughed and lowered his voice. 'I take it you've been told to keep that a secret?'

Jaz looked around, then back at him. 'You won't tell anyone, will you?'

Shaking his head, Julian felt his apprehension melt away. 'Not the best at keeping secrets, are you?'

Jaz placed a hand on her chest. 'I don't do it on purpose, Ju.'

Julian's chest burned at her familiarity. No-one but Jaz called him Ju.

'I hate people telling me secrets. I can never remember that it's only me that's supposed to know.'

'Don't worry about it, It'll be common knowledge soon enough.' Julian felt an overwhelming urge to scoop Jaz into his arms. Jaz had always been fiery, but there was a vulnerability about her, something that called out to him – not that other people seemed to notice it. Most of the guys he knew appeared terrified of her. One thing he was sure of, Jaz gave as good as she got. 'Don't worry, no-one heard. Do you want to go through?' He gestured towards the bistro.

Jaz nodded and smiled up at him.

Looking over to the kids, Julian noted Mikey was staring out of the window. Belle tapped away at a tablet and Noah fidgeted, staring at his hands.

'Come on, kids,' he called out.

Belle frowned at him.

She even has the same mannerisms as Jaz, he thought. 'How old is Belle?'

'Eleven going on sixteen,' Jaz replied with a sigh.

'I thought she was much older. She's nearly as tall as you.'

'I was this tall at eleven, as well. I just haven't grown since.'

Julian felt a surge of energy. *Just get on with it, man,* he told himself. 'Let's go out the front way.'

Julian led Jaz and the kids out of the pub, to the restaurant and unlocked the door. 'Welcome to The Eversley Bistro.'

'Wow, Ju, this is amazing. I can't believe this was the old dusty skittle alley and pool room.'

Julian was taken aback. Jaz appeared genuinely impressed.

'I can't blinking believe it.' She swung around, looking at the room. 'It's decorated lovely too.'

'Holly helped with that.'

'I should have guessed. It's classy and contemporary, yet still has personality, with the beams exposed. It has bags of character.' She ran a hand over one of the oak tables. 'Nice furniture. So what nights will you be open?'

'We had the trial run last Saturday and we'll open for real this Friday evening. I'm starting with Friday and Saturday evenings. A reporter from the Gazette is coming in this week and I'm fully booked. Adam's a fantastic chef.'

'So I heard. How did you get him back to Eversley?'

'I bumped into him at a game.' Whilst Jaz was rubbish at keeping secrets – Julian excelled and did not elaborate.

Jaz looked up at him. 'I'm so proud of you, Ju. Well done.'

The children sped around the room. 'Hey kids, cool it,' Julian said.

Noah stopped and pointed at Mikey. 'He hit me!'

Belle shook her head, crossed her arms, and leaned to one side. 'He's playing tag you muppet.'

'Belle,' Jaz said. 'Be nice, please. Noah doesn't know Mikey.'

Mikey hid under a table.

It surprised Julian how the atmosphere could change so rapidly. He watched Jaz approach Noah. 'Hey, sorry, Noah, Mikey loves playing tag. I guess you thought he was hitting you.'

'What's wrong with him?' Noah asked.

Julian saw concern flash across Jaz's face.

'He's sad, our mum isn't well and is in hospital,' Jaz said.

Noah raised his eyebrows. 'Is she going to die?'

Julian heard Belle breathe in sharply.

'No. No – she's just poorly, and it's going to take a while for her to get better,' Jaz said.

Mikey's feet stuck out from under the table.

Julian realised that Jaz clearly had a lot to deal with at the moment. *Funny how things turn out,* he thought. Even though they'd had a relationship, which had spanned nearly a year, she had never spoken to him about her blood relatives. It seemed that whilst Jaz found it hard to keep secrets relating to other people, she was pretty good at keeping her own. He wondered how she was coping with the kids, when she had dismissed any type of family life with him and Noah. Remembering the way Jaz had dumped him, he came back to the present. Jaz was crouched in front of the table, trying to coax Mikey out.

Noah tapped Julian's arm. 'Sorry, Dad. Is it my fault?'

He ruffled Noah's hair. 'Of course not, son. It's a misunderstanding.' Julian clapped his hands and rubbed them together. 'Right, guys. Do you want to go upstairs and watch Netflix? I'll get some crisps from behind the bar and then me and Jaz can chat about Holly's wedding.'

Mikey appeared immediately from under the table. Jaz stood up, her mouth agape, as the kids followed Julian like ducklings waddling after their mother.

Julian smiled back at her. 'I'll take them up. You have a think about room layout. I'll be back shortly.'

After finding something for the boys to watch, Julian smiled at Belle. 'I take it you'll keep them in check?'

Belle nodded, reaching for a packet of prawn cocktail crisps.

Back in the restaurant, Julian found Jaz carrying a chair. 'I thought it would be easier to move the tables around and get a sense of what it would look like on the day.'

'Holly's invited about thirty-five for dinner,' Julian said as he lifted a table.

'Yes, we've added Belle and Mikey.'

'You're great with the kids, Jaz.'

Jaz appeared to ignore his comment. 'Holly seems to have invited the whole village to the party in the evening. I don't know how she's going to manage. The pub won't be big enough, will it?'

'We're hiring a marquee, which will go out front.'

'What on the village green?'

'Didn't Holly tell you?'

Jaz slumped in a chair. 'To be honest, Ju, I've had so much going on with the kids and their mother. We haven't discussed it at length.'

'How is your mum?' It felt odd to Julian to be talking about Jaz's mother, when she had never wanted to discuss her before.

'She's in a right state in Frenchay Hospital. That's why the kids are with me. They're getting placed together with foster parents – but that's not happening for another two weeks.'

Julian swallowed. This overtly vulnerable side of Jaz was having an effect on him. He sat down also, fearful he would rush over and pull her close.

'I'm a rubbish friend, aren't I?' she said.

'Of course not. You've done so much for Holly over the years. Sometimes life bites you in the butt.' And didn't he know it – like when she walked out of his life.

'I feel like it's chomping at me constantly now.' She paused, then stood up and brushed herself down. 'So how did you swing the marquee on the green?'

'The village committee have been impressed with how Holly's arts hub has brought money into the village – so she's got them eating out of her hand.'

Jaz scanned the room. 'Maybe we should have a long table – with Holly, Mitch and his parents on the top table here?' She pointed to the back wall.

'I'm sure she'll want you up there with her, too. With you being Maid of Honour.'

Jaz frowned. 'Maid of Honour sounds so old. She's not doing the whole bridesmaids thing. I'm a witness though.'

Julian nodded his head. 'I'm a witness too. Well that's how Mitch described it, but I think I've been roped in to being Best Man, as he has asked me to do a small speech before we serve the meal.'

Jaz laughed. 'We've both been had.'

Their eyes met and Julian felt a closeness to her – something he had missed. Her small smile slowly grew and her eyes widened. And while a loud voice in his head, told him not to, he rose from his seat and approached her. He felt the need to tell her, that his feelings had not faded. But he stopped in his tracks as the bistro door opened.

It was Kimberly.

'Jules, there you are,' she said, not taking her eyes off him. 'You left your hoodie.' Kimberly handed the blue top to him. 'I've laundered it for you.'

'Cheers.' *Why am I acting guilty?* he thought as he glanced over at Jaz, who caught his eye and then turned away.

Kimberly touched his hand. 'Simon told me you were wedding planning? How exciting! I love a good wedding. And Holly is so adorable. I can't wait to celebrate with her.' She kissed him on the cheek. Then turned around and walked over to Jaz. She was much taller than Jaz who Julian thought looked like a cute puppy, being approached by an elegant Afghan hound. 'Are you the wedding planner?' Kimberly asked.

Jaz took a step back and crossed her arms, losing the puppy and taking on more of the pit bull.

Julian rubbed his bearded cheek. It's not like he'd even left the hoodie at Kimberly's. He'd left it on the rugby pitch.

Jaz's face relaxed. 'Yes, I'm planning Holly's wedding. But I'm her best friend. And you are?'

'Kimberly. Julian's ...' She looked across at him and smiled, '... friend.'

Julian moved his gaze from Kimberly to Jaz, whose smile widened into what looked like a fake grin. Her eyes were certainly not smiling. 'I see. Well, it's going to be a great wedding and I'm sure you'll love the party in the marquee.'

Kimberly looked around at Julian and raised her eyebrows. He had not invited her as his plus-one. 'Thanks for the hoodie. I'll call you.' He smiled at Kimberly, but she frowned back.

'See you, later,' Kimberly said as she left.

Julian heard the tick of the clock on the wall.

'I think I've seen enough,' Jaz said. 'I better get the kids.' She passed him on her way to the door.

'Jaz ...' he called after her.

She turned. 'Yes?'

Julian had so much he wanted to say – but his mind went blank, not knowing where to begin. 'Thanks for your help.'

Jaz walked out of the door without comment.

Julian remained where he was. He had felt elated when Jaz said she liked the place. When Jaz had accepted the job in Cheshire, they'd had an almighty row. He had told her there was more to life than money and she had ripped him to shreds. 'It's alright for you with your flipping silver spoon sticking out your mouth,' she had screamed. 'Having this place left to you by your parents. Private education – holidays abroad. Some of us are not that privileged.'

Her words had stung him. The split had prompted him to set up the restaurant. To prove he could create wealth himself. To be fair, his parents had not given him the pub – he was buying the business from them, not inheriting it. Even so, he wanted to prove that he had what it took to start a business from scratch. With Jaz complimenting him, seemingly genuinely impressed, it had meant a lot.

Locking the bistro door, he wanted to find Jaz and the kids to say goodbye, but when he reached the bar, Kimberly was perched on a stool, chatting away to Simon. She turned, her blond hair sitting on her shoulders. 'There you are. I just called Mum. She's minding Max, so I can spend some time with you.'

Jaz ushered her siblings through the bar – she nodded at Julian as she passed.

'So who was that?' Kimberly smiled, running a finger around the rim of her glass.

Julian guessed Kimberly was well aware of who Jaz was, but still replied. 'Jaz.'

'Your ex?' Kimberly frowned.

'She needed to see the restaurant as part of the wedding planning.'

'So should I be worried, Jules?' She placed a hand on his chest.

Julian looked up and saw Simon smirk before turning to serve a customer.

'Jaz works and lives up north and it's been nearly a year since we split.'

Kimberly smiled. 'In that case, I take it you need a plus-one for the wedding breakfast?' She took a sip of her drink.

CHAPTER 12

*I*t was Wednesday morning. Jaz wore her work clothes.

'Come on, kids,' she called out.

Belle and Mikey were slumped on the sofa, next to the designer sports brand backpacks she had purchased for them.

I've spent a small fortune this week, she thought. But considering she had missed all of their birthdays, she felt this justified spoiling them a little.

'I don't want you to go,' Belle said.

'I thought you loved spending time with Holly?'

'I do, but I'm itching.'

'Where?'

'Here.' Belle lifted her top to reveal an angry-looking rash.

'What's that from?'

'Do you think I've caught a disease?'

Jaz moved forward, looking at the small pin prick spots.

'Is it catching?' Belle blinked.

I can't leave her with Holly, Jaz thought, remembering

that pregnant women had to be careful, especially with German Measles, and this looked a lot like that. She checked her phone. 'I wonder what time the doctor's surgery opens.' Although she did not have time, she would have to leave in half an hour, at the very latest. Pacing around the caravan, she clutched her forehead. *I'll have to take her with me. And Mikey,* she thought, then plugged Holly's number into her mobile.

'Hi Jaz, all set?'

'No – there's an issue.'

'Oh no. Has the deal fallen through?'

'No. Belle has a rash. I can't leave her with you. It could be measles or something.'

'Does she seem unwell?'

Jaz looked at Belle. 'Do you have a temperature? Or a sore throat?'

'I feel a bit hot.'

Jaz put the phone back to her ear. 'I can't risk it, hun. Not with you being pregnant.'

'You're not going to take them with you, are you?'

'I've no choice.'

JAZ FELT sweaty as she crawled along the M5 in the Audi. 'No, no, no,' she said, slapping the steering wheel. Then looked beside her at Mikey — his eyes were wide open.

'Sorry, matey. There's lots of traffic.'

'How come he gets to sit in the front all the way? It must be my turn now?' Bell said.

'I've already told you. His child seat won't fit in the back. This isn't a family car.'

'Are we nearly there yet?'

'No.' Jaz looked at the dash clock as her nerves bubbled to the surface. She couldn't be late.

'Shall we play I-spy?' Belle asked.

'There's not much to see other than cars. What about a memory game?'

'They're boring. We play them at school.'

'Do you miss school? You haven't been for a week. You should be there this week, too.'

'I hate it. I don't miss it at all.'

'Not even your friends?'

'They don't like me.'

'I'm sure that's not true. It's only one more term and then you're leaving.'

'Exactly. There's no point in going. I've done my SATS, there's nothing to do except practice for the leavers' assembly. They're just singing and acting all day and I don't want to be in that stupid show.'

'I bet you're a brilliant actress. And I've heard you singing in the shower. You've an amazing voice.'

'They didn't give me a good part.'

'If you'd been there more often, maybe they would have. Donna told me you've had lots of time off this year.'

'I'm not going back.'

'You'll have to go when you're with the Jacksons after the holidays, chick, because they'll be at work. Mrs Jackson is a librarian at Appleton Academy. She won't be there during the day.'

'Mikey isn't going to school.'

Jaz did not want to get into conversation about Mikey. She knew from Donna that Mikey would start at Eversley Primary, soon after half term, come what may. That was the condition of the Jackson's taking him on. But she had not explained that to him yet.

Jaz sighed. They were still one hundred miles away and looking at the clock, she was going to be cutting it fine. She did not want to phone the showroom unless she knew she would definitely be late. The news on the radio informed the listeners that there was a seven-mile tail back after the police stopped the entire northbound lane because of an accident.

Why is everything going to rot? Jaz thought, as she took deep breaths, trying to remain calm and send out positive vibes, like Holly did, to the Universe. Even though she did not believe in that sort of thing herself.

Finally, they were through the traffic and Jaz pushed her foot down, cursing the speed restrictions she had to adhere to. And with the kids on board, she could not afford to take any risks.

With ten minutes to go, she had reached the road holding the showroom. She had no time to freshen up.

'Belle?' Jaz looked in her rear view mirror. Belle had earphones in. She put her hand behind her and tapped Belle's knee. 'Belle?'

'Yes?'

'We're running late, so I won't be able to drop you at my apartment. Are you going to be okay to wait in the car?'

'How long for?'

'Just a little while, then I'll bring you in, to sit in my office once the paperwork has been done. I'll make it up to you afterwards.'

Jaz parked down the street from the showroom and got out. Smoothing her skirt down, she sprayed a little Chanel. Then got back into the car and reapplied her lipstick.

'Let's do this,' she said, slowly cruising down the street before pulling up at four on the dot. 'Now, sit tight until I collect you. I'll leave the windows open. Help yourselves to the snacks and drinks.'

She grabbed her file, inside which she had placed the contracts she had prepared using Holly's office equipment. Walking into the showroom, she put her sunglasses on top of her head. *Go get them,* she said to herself as she walked in. But stopped short. Preston was sitting at the table in her office with the door wide open. Three members of the City team were each taking it in turn to shake his hand, as he passed over car keys, as if awarding them medals.

Jaz saw red. 'What the ...'

The men turned to her.

Preston smiled as she reached them. 'Jaz, you're here.'

'Of course, I'm here. We said four o'clock?'

'The guys arrived early, so I've signed off. I saw from the GPS earlier that you were stuck in the tailback. Then the signal disappeared.'

'GPS?'

'Yes, your company phone? All our phones have tracking devices on. Didn't you know?'

The snake – he must have known I was nearly here, she thought.

'I had the paperwork ready just in case you were a no-show. I told the guys you've had family issues.'

I bet you did, she thought. 'I've never missed an appointment in my entire career.' Jaz stared at him, transported in her mind back to her younger self – the one who no-one messed with. *I can't believe he's done this,* she thought. Just because he knew she would be the top sales exec. Giles would get to hear about this – how dare he steal her clients and show her up. It was so unprofessional. Noticing the clients exchanging glances, she took a deep breath and smiled. She didn't want them to witness her anger.

She moved forward, broadening her smile. 'I hope Preston has looked after you?'

'We were really early, so he took care of the paperwork. Thanks for your help, Jaz. It wouldn't have happened without you.'

Jaz smirked at Preston. That was all the confirmation she needed. 'I'll take you over.'

The three luxury cars were lined up. A collective total of four hundred and fifty thousand pounds. She walked the men to their new purchases and talked about their cars like the pro she was. She was aware of Preston observing her as he leaned against the door frame of her office. Boy, was she going to shoot a rocket up his backside when she was done.

She heard a familiar voice.

'Jaz?' It was Belle.

The kids, she thought as she swung around.

Belle was holding Mikey's hand. He was crying.

'Mikey's wet himself. I've brought his bag with his spare clothes in.'

Preston approached the children. 'I'll show you where to go.'

'Erm, yes thank you, Preston.' Jaz nodded at Belle that it was okay to go with him, and Preston showed them to the customer toilets. *How could I have forgotten them?* she thought.

Once the cars had growled away, Jaz located Preston and saw that the kids were sitting in her office.

She turned to Preston. 'Thanks for sorting the kids. But what's the big idea? That was my sale, and you can make sure the records reflect that.'

Preston laughed. 'We're on the same team. Giles doesn't care so long as the cars sell.'

'Since when? You're jealous, you always have been, ever since I set foot in here.'

Jaz was aware of the other staff dispersing as her voice echoed around the showroom. The shutters came down, signifying closing time. She took a pace closer to him.

Preston put his hands up as if he thought she was going to hit him. 'Jaz, there's no competition between us. I'm not pinching your deal. The whole competition element was a wind-up. Giles said you were competitive and asked me to pile it on.'

'What do you mean?'

'He knows you work best in a high-pressure environment. You're the only one on individual commission.'

'That's total rubbish.'

Preston shook his head. 'It's not. I was told I'd get a bigger team bonus if you beat the historic sales figures.'

Is this for real? Jaz thought. 'Take your lies elsewhere, Preston. Just admit it. I'm better than you.'

Preston laughed. 'We all know you're better than us – with all your awards. It's why they headhunted the super-woman of the car sales industry — that's how they described you to the staff. And we're glad about that because your work benefits all of us. We've all been paid more this year, thanks to you.' He softened his voice. 'Giles sees us as the future.'

'Us?'

'Me and you. They want us to run this branch as they're opening a showroom down south. That's where they are now.'

Jaz took a step backwards, wondering whether Preston was winding her up.

'I've seen the draft contracts. It's nothing like I've been

offered before. Directorships and shares in the company, if we pull it off.'

'Why have I been kept out of the loop?'

'I've been here since I left school. I started here washing cars. Giles is a close friend and my boss. And thanks, Jaz, I mean it, I really do. You've shaken this place up.' He gestured at her. 'I've got to hand it to you. I was sceptical when I saw you turn up, but you lived up to your reputation. Me and the lads are well impressed. The hours you work, the way you get clients on side. You're ace.'

'Are you done now?' Belle said as she walked towards them. 'Preston said we're going for tea?'

Mikey followed, wearing a fresh pair of trousers.

'He did?' Jaz touched her forehead. Her mind was swimming.

'Come on,' Preston said. 'We'll go to Funky Fred's. They have a play area. I take my kid brothers there all the time.'

Jaz didn't know if she trusted Preston, but a directorship? She wanted to know more.

CHAPTER 13

'How's your rash?' Jaz asked Belle when they were in the car.

Belle lifted her top. 'Gone. I sometimes get a rash when I wear new clothes.'

Jaz shook her head. 'And you didn't bother to tell me that before we left?'

'I just remembered,' Belle said in a small voice. "I haven't had any new clothes for ages.'

Preston hooted her and Jaz turned to see that he had taken the Bentley, which he borrowed from the showroom and had made his unofficial company car. She started her engine and followed him towards the pub. She felt the need to clear her head, to feel herself again. Jaz the executive, not Jaz, the stressed-out big sister. Having the responsibility of the showroom and the staff did not phase her at all – it excited her. Having responsibility for her younger siblings scared her to bits.

As they arrived at Funky Fred's, she felt Preston was being uncharacteristically friendly. He was great with the children and signed them in to the play area, which they could view from their table through a huge glass partition. She had been worried that Belle would have turned her nose up at it, but she was all smiles as she helped Mikey into a ball pit.

When Preston returned, he sat opposite Jaz and leaned forward. 'I'm glad this year's nearly up. Don't get me wrong, I like a bit of banter, but I've been feeling bad of late winding you up.'

Jaz crossed her arms. 'You're a natural at it.'

He laughed. 'To be honest, I've missed you this week. I mean, really missed you.'

What's his game? she thought. 'Now you really are winding me up.'

'I'm not. It's been dull. We work well together. I've not been able to say anything because I had to keep up the competition thing. But I like you and have done for ages.'

'Like me?'

'Yeah, as in – I think you're amazing.'

'Come off it,' Jaz said shaking her head.

Preston looked sincere. His brown eyes, not dissimilar to her own, gazed into hers. He was a good-looking guy, and she imagined he had wooed a lot of women with his chat.

'I'm sure you've plenty of girlfriends, Preston. A lot hotter than me.'

'I've never met anyone like you, Jaz. You're beautiful, you've got the banter and the brains. I thought of you all the time you were away. I've got used to seeing you every day. To be honest, I rarely worked a seven day week before you rocked up.'

Jaz took a gulp of cola. Had Preston been taken over by an alien? She hardly recognised him.

'Now I've said too much.' He leaned back in his chair. 'What the heck.' He leaned forward again. 'I'll put it out there. I want us to be exclusive.'

Jaz laughed. 'You're joking? We haven't even been on a date.'

Preston's face fell. 'I thought that's what this is?'

'I know nothing about you, and you know nothing about me.'

He stuck his hand out. 'Preston Walker.'

She shook his hand and a smile formed on her face. 'Jasmine Swift.'

JAZ WOKE in her little apartment, on the sofa. The morning sun streamed in. It felt good to be back in Cheshire, and she felt a lot calmer than she had in a long while. The curtain billowed in the morning breeze. She stood up and stretched, thinking of Preston. He lived in the opposite apartment block. They were modern and low-rise with metal and glass balconies. Carefully tended gardens separated the two buildings. She smiled, remembering the evening they'd had, although she couldn't tell how she felt about it emotionally.

She realised the calm would not last for long with the children around. The square footage of her apartment was no bigger than the caravan. Her mobile phone dinged with a text, it was from Preston asking if she had time to meet.

A picture of Julian flashed in her mind. It annoyed her that even after a year, she still thought about Julian every day. But now he had someone new in his life – that was plain to see when Kimberly returned his perfectly laundered top. And why wouldn't Julian move on? It had been a whole year since they had split up. She cringed at the memories of their break-up, at how harsh she had been when they argued about the job in Cheshire and how she had sloped off, without even saying goodbye to Noah. No — she had well and truly burned that bridge.

She texted Preston to say she would call him once she had freshened up.

When Jaz was showered and dressed, she took a few slices of bread from the freezer and made toast for the kids.

'Belle, Mikey,' she called out. 'Breakfast's ready.'

They tumbled out of the bedroom, scruffy haired, in their PJs.

'Right, you two. I've put the TV on. Eat while I get changed.'

Once in the bedroom, she called Preston using her mobile.

He answered immediately. 'Hi, beautiful.'

'I don't know about that,' she said. Not used to this new guy who looked and sounded like Preston but did not act like him.

'When are you leaving? Any chance of a catch up?'

'Sorry, no. I can't do anything with the kids here and I've told Holly I'll help organise the wedding.'

'Have you got a plus-one?'

'What for?'

'The wedding, of course.'

Jaz laughed. 'You want to gate crash? Or are you being nosey about my love life?'

'You told me last night – you've not had a bloke for a year.'

Jaz groaned, *did I?* she thought, wishing she had not over-shared the previous evening.

'I want to go down south and meet your family and friends.'

'Easy, tiger. I haven't even agreed to a second date yet.'

Preston laughed. 'We get on great. I want to get to know you more.'

'What about inter-work relationships? Isn't there something about that in our contracts?'

'Not likely. Giles met Faye at the firm.'

She knew Giles' wife worked at the showroom, but didn't realise they'd met there. Her attempts to fob Preston off seemed fruitless. But, she realised, the new Preston was right up her street. He had a great sense of humour, and the conversation had flowed between them all night. And they wanted the same things, he also had the goal of being a millionaire in his thirties. They were definitely on the same page. Not like Julian. She felt a rush of sadness as his name echoed in her head.

'Are you still there?' Preston asked.

'Yeah. Sorry.'

'Were you thinking about your mam?'

'Er, yes,' she lied. 'I doubt she'll be out of the hospital for some time.' She had not told Preston the details of her relationship with Stacey. It was not something she had discussed with anyone, other than Holly and brief conversations with the hospital staff.

'What time are you leaving?'

'As soon as the kids have eaten breakfast and I'm packed.'

'You've got such a big heart. I can't imagine having kids myself.'

'Me neither. I never want to have my own.'

'See, something else we have in common. We're made for each other.'

Jaz laughed.

'Will you invite me to the wedding or not?'

Jaz thought it was a bit too soon to introduce Preston to Eversley, considering they had not even had a proper date. Although the idea of turning up to the wedding without a date when Julian would be there with the tall and glamorous, Kimberly allowed her to ponder on the idea. She didn't like the thought of watching Julian with his posh girlfriend.

'It'll be great. You can take the Bentley down today. It must have been a squeeze anyway, with the kids in your car. I'll knock off early at the end of next week and get the train down after work. Then we can travel back together in the Bentley after the wedding.'

'Are you sure?' Jaz knew Preston loved the Bentley. 'It's a nightmare getting to Wells on public transport.'

'It'll be worth it. Can I stay with you?'

'I'll be with the kids and there isn't enough room.' She did not want to tell him that she was living in a caravan because her mother's house was a health hazard.

'Is there a bed and breakfast in the village?'

She flushed hot and cold. There was yes, at the pub, but there was no way she'd want Preston staying at Julian's. 'It's all booked up because of the wedding.' *That's probably true,* she thought. 'There's a decent chain hotel though, a couple of miles away.'

'So, that's a yes, then?'

Jaz laughed. 'I haven't asked Holly yet, but I'm sure she won't mind. I'll just have to see if we can squeeze you in for the meal – if not, you'll definitely be invited to the party later in the day. In fact she's invited pretty much the whole village and we've no idea how many will turn up.'

While Jaz packed for the trip back to Eversley, Giles

called to congratulate her on sealing the City deal and said he wanted to discuss a proposition with her. It seemed Preston was right – an offer was forthcoming. Giles also agreed to her taking leave until after Holly's wedding. Things were turning around.

CHAPTER 14

The drive back to Somerset was much better than the journey up. Partly due to the luxury car, but mainly because of the lack of traffic and deadline stress. The sun shone, and Jaz was grateful for the excellent air-con, far superior to the one in her red Audi, which she knew she would have to give up at some point. Giles had moaned at her for ages about driving a car which they would not sell and one that was also over ten years old. Audis did not feature on the forecourt of Hodges and Carter.

Jaz pulled up at Lovelands. There was a coach in the car park with a group of pensioners disembarking. Holly attracted the mid-week holidaymakers, and was popular with the coach firms, which stopped by with their clients enjoying refreshments at the café, before having a mooch around the nursery and arts hub. One firm even offered a craft workshop as part of their Somerset tour.

After cutting the engine, she exited the car. The kids followed in silence, lethargic from the drive. After making a cup of tea in the caravan, she settled down. Picking her phone up she saw she had a few texts from Preston, she smiled, but she would not be striking up a romance unless she was completely sure it would work, it would be a career disaster if it went bad. But they could still be friends, and he was the perfect plus one for the wedding. She bet he had a great family, parents still together, living in a pleasant house in a pleasant area, beef for Sunday lunch and after dinner walks. She wished she hadn't told him that her mother's house was a cottage.

The children were in the bedroom. Jaz picked up her mobile and called Holly.

'Jaz, are you back?'

'Yeah, Belle's fine. The rash has gone – it was an allergy to clothes dye or something, which she failed to warn me about.'

Holly laughed. 'She probably wanted an excuse to be with you. She must feel ever so insecure about the future. Poor scrap. Do you speak about it?'

'I don't know what to say that I've not already said.'

'Kids need reassurance, that's all. Let them know that, whilst they have to go to the foster home, you'll always be there for them, even if it is just on the phone.'

'I'm rubbish at this stuff.'

'No, you're not. I should know, you're my best friend. You've always been there for me – my rock for as long as I can remember. Maybe don't think of them as kids. See them as little adults.'

Jaz laughed. 'As you think I'm such a great friend – I'd like to ask a favour?'

'Fire away.'

'Can I add someone to the wedding meal?'

'Sure, who?'

'Preston.'

'Hang on, Preston from Cheshire? The one you called a snake?'

'It's a long story, but we spent some time together out of work, and he really wanted to come. Absolutely nothing has happened. I'm just inviting him as a friend and nothing more. Although, we have so much in common and he likes that I don't want kids.' Jaz looked up. Mikey stared at her from the door. 'Can I get you anything?'

He shook his head and returned to the bedroom.

'So, can we add him?'

'I would have been hesitant, because of Julian. He's not charging us for the room hire at all and parading your new man in front of him would have been mean. Considering you left him heartbroken.'

'So you think I should put Preston off?'

'No, because I've added Kimberly, after bumping into her and Julian yesterday at the nursery. I'll pop over for a cuppa.'

Jaz ended the call feeling relieved that Preston was going to be her wedding date. As she waited for Holly, she realised how much she missed her. She knew part of the reason she had not been back to Eversley was because she was jealous of Mitch. Even though he was the best guy on the planet and they were made for each other. She had always been Holly's protector, and now she wasn't.

Jaz stood up. She would try to get the children out of the bedroom before Holly arrived. 'Kids. Holly's coming over. Do you want to help me make tea?'

Belle appeared at the door with Mikey peering around her. 'Mikey told me you said you didn't want us.'

'What?' Jaz frowned. 'I never ... Oh. No, I said I didn't want to have kids. You know.' She put a hand on her belly. 'To give birth.'

Mikey frowned.

Belle laughed. 'Oh, I see. Yuck me neither, anyway, you don't need a baby because you've got us now.' She rushed over and gave her a hug. 'What are we doing this week?'

Jaz stroked Belle's hair as she hugged her, feeling herself relax into the warmth of sisterhood. 'I'm sorry about the situation – about me living away. But let's have a fun week together. We're in this caravan, it's half term next week. In between the wedding planning, we can have a few days of fun.'

'Like what?'

'Days out. You know, farms, zoo, theme park type of thing.'

Mikey jumped up and down.

Jaz laughed. 'Where do you want to go, Mikey?'

He put his head down and looked at his hands.

Jaz felt bad for pushing it. 'Sorry, don't worry. Tell Belle later.'

Belle released Jaz. 'He loves Digger World.'

Jaz smiled. 'I've never been there. So yes, why not?' There was a rap at the door and Jaz opened it. 'Val!' She blinked at the familiar face, maybe a little more lined than the last time she had seen her, but Val was well into her eighties. Jaz practically jumped down the steps and grabbed hold of her, in not a dissimilar fashion to the way Belle had embraced her.

'Oh love, I've missed you so much. You're very naughty, not coming down to see us.'

'Leave her be,' Len, Val's husband, said. 'You know our Jaz has her career. She hasn't got time to come down here to see the likes of us.'

Jaz leaned back. 'Val's right, Len. I should have booked some time off sooner.'

'Well, I'm glad you're here.' Val looked over Jaz's shoulder. 'Now let me see the little ones.' She put her hand up to her face as she stared at Belle. 'And what's your name, beautiful?'

'I'm Belle.'

'It's like looking at you,' Val said to Jaz.

'And this is my brother, Mikey,' Belle added.

'Let's get in,' Val said. 'I've got a Victoria sponge.'

Holly soon joined them and Jaz felt warm as they shared cake. Val told a few stories detailing the naughty things Jaz and Holly got up to as kids and the children loved it. Even Mikey laughed. Jaz felt they were going to have a lovely time together.

JULIAN STOOD behind the bar opposite Kimberly, who was having a drink with him. Noah and Max were upstairs in the living accommodation, watching television. They often had a meal with the kids on a Thursday after the school run. Every time Julian looked at Kimberly, he wondered why on earth she was interested in him. Especially as her ex was a stockbroker in the City. Julian was hardly her type.

Kimberly smiled at him. 'Would you like to spend a day with me and the boys? Seeing as rugby training isn't running during half term?'

'From Wednesday I'll be busy preparing for the wedding.'

'In that case, let's do something Monday. Also, Mum and Dad want to know if you'd like to come for a meal one evening?'

Julian hesitated. He wasn't sure if he was ready to officially meet her parents, although they were already customers of his. He had not had a clear discussion with Kimberly about their relationship going forward, and he felt he was casually slipping into something which looked like a serious relationship. The last thing he wanted to happen, was to find himself in a situation that was awkward to extract himself from, especially with the boys involved.

'Come on, they don't bite.'

'I might not be the usual type of guy you take home to your mum and dad.'

Kimberly smiled. 'My parents have lived here for a couple of years, they know exactly who you are. I know you keep referring to yourself as a barman, Jules, but you're a local businessman. A restauranteur no less. Why do you put yourself down? I think you're a fine man.'

Julian laughed. 'I'll have to employ you as my promotions agent.'

'I'll do anything for you, Jules,' she said, looking over the rim of her glass.

The pub door opened and Holly and Mitch approached the bar.

'Hi, guys.' Julian waved, relieved at the interruption.

Kimberly turned around. 'Thank you both for inviting me to your wedding.'

Holly smiled. 'I'm glad you can come.'

Mitch shook hands with Julian over the bar.

'What can I get you?'

'A pint of Thistle and a Florida orange.'

'On the house.'

Mitch pulled a note from his wallet. 'No it's not. You'll go out of business with the freebies you throw our way. Not forgetting the free room hire for the wedding.'

Julian laughed as he pulled the pint. 'Are you eating?'

Holly nodded. 'Although I wanted to know if we could squeeze another body in for the wedding reception meal?'

'Yes, of course,' Julian said. 'Who else has got a ticket for your glittering event?'

Holly stared him in the eye. 'Jaz's plus one. Preston.'

The pint of beer Julian was pouring spilled over. He lifted the pump and shook the beer off his hand and poured a little off the top and placed it on the bar, wiping down the glass with a beer towel. He looked up, noticing Kimberly staring at him with her eyebrows raised.

'I've been having problems with this pump,' he lied. 'It needs a service.'

'Preston is from Cheshire,' Holly added.

Julian poured lemonade onto the top of orange juice with a dash of lime and placed Holly's drink on the bar. 'I'll be over to collect your food order. Adam has baked a beef and ale pie.'

'I'll have that, please,' Holly said.

'Make that two,' Mitch added.

Julian went back to the kitchen, where Simon was preparing a steak sandwich.

'Two orders of pie. Holly and Mitch are in, so make them decent portions.'

Simon stopped what he was doing. 'What's up with you?'

'Nothing,' Julian growled.

'Boss, your neck is red, and you look like a cage fighter.'

Julian laughed and relaxed. 'Okay. Jaz is bringing a bloke to the wedding.'

'You need to consider getting back with your ex or get over it.'

Julian felt odd, taking advice from Simon. But if Simon could see it, so could the entire village. Kimberly was lovely, and he needed to move on, especially as Jaz was involved with someone new.

He returned to the bar to find Kimberly staring into her drink. She smiled as he approached. 'So, are you coming to my parents' for dinner? Maybe Tuesday night?'

He smiled. 'Of course.' It was time to move on.

CHAPTER 15

*J*az had googled *what to take on a day trip with kids* and spread the items on the caravan dining table before placing them in Belle's backpack. Plasters, wet wipes, water, emergency snacks, rain macs and sunblock. The list had seemed endless for just one day out. She was looking forward to the trip, having often passed the small theme park, when driving down to Devon for meetings in Exeter. She had wondered what it was like and never had an excuse to visit. But now, on this sunny Monday morning, with two kids to entertain, Digger World was on her radar.

The kids were hyper, even though they loved being at the nursery. Before they left, Belle had run up to the petting zoo to tell Charlie the goat she was going out for the day.

'Are we having a picnic?' Belle asked as she arrived back, panting.

'I've checked their website and they sell food.' Jaz didn't have enough room in the bag for that, or a picnic blanket.

'What sort of food?'

'Kid food – nuggets, pizza, burger, chips.'

'Yay,' Belle called out and Mikey jumped up and down. Jaz wished he would open up and speak to her. She guessed it would take a bit more time. Until then, she still had to use Belle to ask him questions out of earshot and report back.

They piled into the car and Jaz felt a little guilty taking the Bentley out, considering it was on loan. The roads were busy with holiday traffic but the traffic was moving freely. She pulled into the attraction's car park and drove to the far side of the gravelled expanse, not wanting the Bentley to get dented by a child opening a car door onto it. *Maybe I should have borrowed Holly's van?* she thought.

Out of the car, they followed the signs to the entrance. They all wore Hunter wellies. Jaz realised she should really drop her love of designer when shopping with the children. It was eating away at her savings.

Once inside the park, Mikey's eyes were wide open. There were diggers of all shapes and sizes ready to jump in and shift earth. Mikey pointed to some in action.

'I need to go on with you, Mikey,' Jaz said, taking him by the hand. They lined up and were soon shown to a digger, and Belle climbed in the one next to them. Jaz lifted Mikey up and then sat beside him as the assistant showed her how to work the controls.

Once strapped in, Mikey moved the lever forward towards a mound of earth. She watched as he laughed, digging up the earth and tipping it out again. He seemed to really come out of himself. Soon, their turn ended.

Mikey turned to her and opened his mouth. 'I ...' He looked away and clammed up.

Jaz rubbed his shoulder. 'Come on, monster, let's jump out and go on something else.'

After a good hour travelling around the rides and taking trips on various machines, the kids ran over to the play area.

Jaz sat down on a bench, watching them. Today was a good day. It was the type of scene she did not recall from her childhood. Did Stacey ever take her out for the day? Why could she not remember any good times? There must have been some. She hoped the Jacksons would take the kids out when they stayed with them. She would be sure to give the Jacksons money for fun activities.

Two boys ran past her in a race towards the wooden fort, which was the focus of the play area. Recognising the sandy hair, her heart burned. Noah. Looking behind her, she saw Julian in jeans and a smart blue short-sleeved shirt, and with him Kimberly, in tailored shorts and a floral sleeveless blouse. Jaz knew if she wore that outfit, she would look frumpy, but Kimberly carried it well. Like royalty, it looked timelessly fashionable on her.

Julian carried a huge wicker picnic hamper smiling, and Jaz thought that they looked like a happy couple from a holiday company advert. She glanced down at her phone, hoping they would not notice her, although realising it was inevitable. With Belle and Mikey in the playground, she would soon be discovered.

Jaz looked up as she heard a scream. Without thinking, she ran across the grass to the play area and up the stairs of the small wooden fort.

'You stink, everyone says it,' she heard a boy say.

'Go away, Max. You total muppet.' Belle had Mikey hiding behind her and her eyes were narrowed.

'What's going on here?' Jaz asked.

Noah spun around and his eyes widened, then he looked down.

'Who are you?' the boy, who she assumed was Kimberly's son, asked.

'I'm their sister and I don't like the way you're speaking

to them.' Jaz felt as if she was transported back to her days at school.

'Do you stink too?' Max laughed and gave a sideways look to Noah, who did not look up.

'Shut it,' Jaz said through gritted teeth.

'Excuse me?'

Jaz swung around to find Kimberly pulling herself into the fort, which was difficult considering her height.

'Your son needs to learn some manners. He's being rude to my brother and sister.'

'Max doesn't lash out unless he's provoked.' She looked down her nose at Belle.

Belle crossed her arms. 'I didn't say nothing.'

'Quite.' Kimberly shook her head and sighed.

Jaz felt her heartbeat quicken. She wanted to lash out, but not in front of the children. 'Come on, kids,' she said through gritted teeth. 'Let's get food. Excuse me,' she said to Kimberly, who adjusted her position to let them pass.

At the foot of the steps, she found Julian. Jaz looked into his eyes, not deep brown, like Preston's. They were blue. And neither was he dark with chiselled looks, but he made her feel warm inside. His red tinged beard was neatly trimmed, and she instantly remembered how it felt against her skin.

'Is everything alright in there?' he asked.

'Kimberly's son was being obnoxious to Belle. But it takes more than a bit of name calling to upset a Swift.' She turned to the kids. 'Isn't that right, gang?'

Belle put her hands on her hips. 'Yeah.'

Julian laughed.

'What's so funny?' Jaz asked,

'Belle is so much like you.'

Jaz looked back at Belle and felt her heartbeat slow and

smiled. She noticed Kimberly was having trouble getting down the steps of the fort. 'I think your girlfriend needs help.' Then she walked away, smiling.

ORDERING herself a large burger and chips and the kids chicken nugget meal deals, she carried the full tray to the table they were sitting at.

'So, did you provoke that boy?' Jaz asked Belle once she was half way through her burger.

'Max Edwards? No. He just started calling me names. Like all the kids at school do.'

'They pick on you?'

'Yeah, call me nit head, the stink, that sort of thing.'

Poor mite, Jaz thought. 'Well. You don't smell. You're wearing new clothes, very expensive clothes. So don't take any notice of them.' Jaz ate another mouthful, acknowledging that part of the reason she loved designer clothes and a smart image, was because of the names she had been called at school because of her shabby uniform. 'Is that why you don't enjoy going to school?'

'I guess so.'

Jaz made a mental note to speak to the Jacksons about it and ask them to mention it to the teachers, so they could keep an eye on things when Belle returned to her classes.

CHAPTER 16

'*I* hate being the centre of attention,' Holly said. 'What on earth was I thinking, getting married when I'm this pregnant?'

Jaz smiled as Holly had her final dress fitting, two days before the wedding.

'You look beautiful,' Nina, the owner of the bridal boutique, said as the seamstress worked on the hem of the dress. The shop was situated on the edge of the market square in Wells.

'You know how important it was to you,' Jaz said. 'To be married before the babies ... the baby's been born,' Jaz corrected, nearly giving away Holly's secret.

'And you said no-one cares about that sort of thing these days,' Holly replied. 'I'm an idiot.'

'No-one thinks you're stupid, Holly,' Nina said. 'You're all people talk about these days. It seems everyone I speak to is going to your wedding.'

'That's another thing, we've no idea how many are coming,' Holly's voice broke. 'And I look like a barrage balloon.'

'Of course you don't, hun,' Jaz said. 'And bump or no bump, you're beautiful and once the flowers are in your hair, you'll look like a Greek goddess.'

'Really?'

'Yes really. And you're so slim anyway — with the dress waistline under your bust like that, you can't really tell you're pregnant.'

Holly turned sideways on and glanced at her reflection in the mirror. The top part of the dress was closely fitted, then swathes of ivory material flowed over her bump to the floor. 'I find that hard to believe.'

The seamstress smoothed down the long skirt. 'You look amazing, Holly, just as your friends say.'

'And I've so much to do – when my body is feeling worn out from lugging the extra weight around.'

'Like what?' Jaz asked.

'I have a long list. Unless everything is ticked off, I won't sleep tonight.'

'Let's get you out of the dress, Holly,' the seamstress said.

'I'll make sure it has a final press and is put safely in the bag for Saturday,' Nina added.

Jaz picked the to do list from Holly's bag as she was helped out of the dress. 'Wow, there's tonnes of stuff on here.'

'Tell me about it,' Holly said.

Jaz shook her head. 'You know what? Relax for the rest of today and put your feet up. I'll see to it.'

'If there's anything I can do, just let me know,' Nina said.

Jaz nodded. 'There are a couple of things you could help with.' She turned back to Holly. 'I'll need to borrow your van by the looks of it.'

'No ... I ... ' Holly protested.

'You're going to have to accept our help otherwise you'll

be so tired, you'll sleep through the whole wedding,' Nina said.

SITTING IN THE BENTLEY, Jaz checked her emails, she'd had a manic couple of days clearing everything off Holly's to do list. Looking up, she heard the bus arrive. She waited until she saw Preston enter the car park and honked the horn. He waved as he carried a holdall and a suit bag. Watching him stride towards her, he was, she thought, exceptionally attractive. And she was pleased that he was her wedding date, likening it to having a designer handbag.

'That's one hell of a journey,' he said as he opened the door of the Bentley. 'The bus took ages.'

'I did offer to pick you up from Bristol, but you wouldn't have it.'

'You were right – as per usual.'

Jaz laughed, and he leaned over and gave her a kiss on the cheek.

'So where are we off to? The hotel?' He raised his eyebrows.

'Down, tiger.' Jaz laughed and sped away as Preston quickly attached his seatbelt.

'The Bentley's looking smart.'

'Yes, of course,' Jaz said, having had it valeted. The back seat had been full of crisp crumbs and muddy footprints. She hoped he didn't notice the dent in the leather from Mikey's child seat, which, fingers-crossed, would pop back into its usual shape.

Once they reached his hotel, Preston opened the passenger door.

'I'm dropping the car in Eversley and getting a lift back.

I'll be about twenty minutes,' Jaz said. 'I'll meet you at the bar.'

'I'll get us a bottle of wine, then. Any requests?'

'Surprise me.' She knew Preston loved his wine, although his taste was probably a lot more sophisticated than the wines on offer.

When Jaz arrived back at the caravan it was quiet. *Anne must have taken the kids out,* she thought. It was a mild evening and the sky was tinged orange, as the sun set.

Jaz waited outside the caravan for Joe, who had offered to give her a lift. He rolled up in his Volvo estate.

'How are you, love?' he asked.

'Great, thanks,' Jaz said as she got in the car.

'You're doing a good job with them kids. It suits you, Jaz. I've seen a new side to you.'

'I don't know about that,' she said as she buckled up. 'I spoil them rotten just to cheer them up. Hats off to the parents of this world. I'd make an awful mother.'

Joe drew away. 'Nonsense. They're fond of you. And great kids.'

'You see them on their best behaviour. Behind closed doors, it's a different story.'

Joe laughed. 'That's the way with all kids, love. But some are naughty at home and in public.' He swung onto the main road. 'So, you will not be staying permanently, then?'

'No.'

'Not now, you have a new young man.'

'It's early days, Joe. We've not even had a proper date.'

'You must like him to bring him to the wedding?'

Jaz nodded. 'I think we're suited. We want the same things.'

'Sounds like a business deal to me, rather than a romance.'

Jaz laughed. 'Maybe if I approached my love life like business, it would be a lot more successful.'

Joe soon turned into the drive leading up to the hotel, which was built in the grounds of a large Victorian house. 'How are you getting back?'

'Taxi. Anne has the kids, so I won't be late. And I want to be fresh for the wedding tomorrow.'

'It's going to be a special day, seeing our Holly so happy.'

As Jaz entered the hotel, she saw Preston leaning against the bar, smiling at her. She approached him and he took her in his arms. He felt warm and natural.

'Missed you, half pint.'

She stepped back and grinned. 'Call me that tomorrow and I'll kill you.'

He laughed and so did she. She enjoyed laughing with Preston. He didn't make her feel hot and bothered.

'Shall we go to the restaurant? I'm starving,' he said.

'Don't expect too much,' Jaz said.

'This place suits me – you know what you're getting. Nothing too fancy.'

'You surprise me. I had you down as the sort of guy who'd be into a tasting menu.'

He sat down in a booth. 'Plain food suits me fine.'

Once he had ordered their food at the bar, he returned to the table with a bottle of wine and poured them a glass each. 'So, tell me all about your childhood home. Am I going to see this cottage of your mam's?'

She groaned. How was she to know that this was going to happen? 'About that,' she said.

'What?'

'Look. You were winding me up and I'm really private about my personal life. I didn't want to say at the time – but the truth is, I wasn't brought up in the village. I lived on the not-so-pretty housing estate about a ten-minute walk away from the green.' Jaz looked down into her drink.

Preston laughed.

Jaz looked up, frowning. 'Alright, you don't have to act like an idiot about it.'

'I'm not laughing *at* you. I was also brought up on an estate. And I'm sure it was a lot rougher than an estate around these parts. This isn't the old days, you know, when people cared where you came from. No – it's something to be proud of.'

'It mattered at school. There were the kids from the village that thought they were a cut above everyone else – compared to us lot from the estate.'

'But that's what drives us, eh? We want more.'

Jaz smiled and clinked her glass with his. 'Too right.' She took a sip of her wine, which was a dry white.

'It's stupid to put down your past. I did it myself for years and all that happens is that we become the snobs. Because no-one else cares.'

Jaz laughed. 'I've never viewed it like that before. That I'm a snob.'

'Still – I don't broadcast my background either.' Preston smiled.

Jaz sipped her wine. 'I moved in with Holly and her parents at their garden nursery when I was fifteen.'

'Did your mam throw you out?'

'She went on a drinking binge and told me to never come back.'

'Booze kills families.'

'I hadn't spoken to her since, not until I saw her in the hospital two weeks ago.'

Preston gave a low whistle. 'You've had some grief to deal with.'

Jaz nodded. 'And I'd never met the kids before, either.'

'Hats off to you. Let's drink to us,' he said, lifting his glass. 'Here's to a successful future.'

'To the millionaires club,' Jaz said as they clinked glasses. It felt good talking to Preston. She didn't feel as if she had to impress him. Maybe she could open up to him – like she hadn't done with any man before.

CHAPTER 17

'*I* hope I'm doing the right thing,' Holly said after the hairdresser left.

'What?' Jaz said as she admired the simple ring of fresh flowers on Holly's head as they sat in her bedroom in front of the dressing table.

'I'm joking. I feel so nervous, I'm trying to lighten my mood.'

'Loosen up, hun. The day is going to be amazing.' Jaz smiled at Holly's reflection, also seeing herself in the mirror. She wore a lilac dress, in the same style as Holly's.

Holly looked down at her small bouquet and lifted it to her nose. 'It's because Mum and Dad are missing.' Holly caught Jaz's gaze in the reflection. 'Dad would have been giving me away.'

Jaz squeezed Holly's shoulder. 'Who is walking you down the aisle? Joe or Len?' Jaz knew Holly had been torn about who to ask.

'Neither, I've chosen you.'

'Me?'

'Yes, Jaz. We've been through so much. Only you could

give me away.' She squeezed the hand that Jaz had placed on her shoulder.

'Don't, hun you'll make me cry for the first time since I was a kid.'

They heard loud honking and wild yapping.

'What's that?' Holly asked, while Jaz knew exactly what to expect.

Looking out of the window, they both laughed. Outside was a red tractor with a trailer covered in white and lilac flowers. The herdsman, Greg sat in the cab wearing a suit. Trixy was tied to a seat on the trailer.

'That's what you get for leaving it to Mitch to sort the wedding transport,' Jaz said.

'I absolutely love it,' Holly said.

'Come on.' Jaz took Holly's hand. 'Let's do this.'

Once Holly and Jaz had been helped onto the bench, which had been nailed to the trailer, they began the short and extremely slow journey to the church. Mitch had clearly given Greg orders to go carefully due to Holly being pregnant, and Jaz felt they would never get there.

Once out of the farm, the road to the Church was lined with villagers. And Holly received waves the entire way as Trixy yapped.

'I feel like we're on the beauty-queen float at the carnival,' Holly said.

The tractor shuddered to a halt ten minutes later and the photographer took a few shots before they clambered down, helped by a few people as they began the walk along the villager lined path to the church.

Entering the small stone-built building, the guests hushed, giving them a collection of smiles. There were complimentary whispers as they walked along the aisle to *Annies Song*. Jaz saw the look on Mitch's face as they approached. She knew he was the perfect match for her best friend.

Reaching the altar, she was aware of Julian, but did not look in his direction. She kept her eyes focused on the vicar as the service began.

'Do you Holly, Ivy, Loveland take Mitchell, Sidney, Booth to be your lawful wedded husband?'

Jaz felt her bottom lip quiver as Holly replied. 'I will.'

There was rapturous applause as soon as the vicar pronounced them husband and wife.

As the couple kissed, Jaz thought how beautiful they looked. Holly in her ivory chiffon with fresh flowers in her hair. And Mitch looking dashing with his dark hair neatly tamed, wearing a darkest blue suit and a lilac tie. They really were the most beautiful couple, and she imagined their babies were going to be gorgeous, whoever they took after.

Looking past them, Jaz was aware of Julian, staring at her. Her heart skipped a beat. He had brushed up well. His beard was trimmed so short, it was a dusting of stubble. She'd guessed he must have been to the barber that morning. As strong and imposing as his physique was, his eyes were soft as they stared deep into hers. She couldn't drag her gaze away, so smiled and nodded at him. He was obviously as touched by Holly and Mitch's relationship as she was. It was more than two people coming together. The Loveland and Booth families had fought for four generations, and this symbolised something special, making the village a stronger unit. At that thought, Jaz felt a tear sting the back of her eye and took a deep breath. *Get a grip*, she told herself.

Mitch held Holly's hand and approached Jaz and hugged her. 'Don't get emotional. I haven't taken her away from you. She's still your best friend.'

Jaz laughed. 'I wasn't getting choked up about that. I was just thinking about the Booth-Loveland feud ending and it was like watching a tearjerker of a film.'

Holly laughed. 'Don't – you'll make me cry and I don't want to ruin this make-up. I have pictures to pose for.'

'It's still intact and you look so beautiful.' Jaz looked around at everyone watching, some wiping tears, others with hand to heart. 'Come on then, get that register signed so we can start the celebrations.'

After the four of them had signed the register, Mitch and Holly turned towards the congregation of the small Eversley Church, filled with Mitch's family from Essex and Holly's friends. As Holly's parents had died, her only blood relatives in the room, were an old aunt from Oldham and a cousin she had never met before, Holly's staff were taking up her family seats. Belle and Mikey sat in the front row with Val and Len and were very excited to be considered family. Mikey looked cute in trousers and a white shirt with a blue bow tie and Jaz had convinced Belle to wear a lovely Ted Baker fifties style dress in black and white, which they had bought in the nearby designer outlet. She'd had her hair styled by the same hairdresser who had styled Jaz and Holly's.

A tingle went down Jaz's back as she heard Julian's deep voice behind her and she turned around to face him.

He nodded towards Belle. 'She looks like your mini-me.'

Jaz felt flustered at the way he was making her feel. She looked away, scanning the church for Preston. Catching his eye, she waved.

Holly and Mitch walked back down the aisle, kissing

cheeks, hugging and shaking hands with guests as they went. She followed them with Mikey and Belle until she reached Preston.

'You look absolutely beautiful, Jaz,' he said. 'Hello, you two,' he said over her shoulder to Belle and Mikey.

Belle pursed her lips, then walked away.

'Don't worry, she'll warm up,' Jaz said. 'I think she blames you for me going back to Cheshire.'

'No worries, I'd probably be the same.'

Jaz rubbed his arm, acknowledging how understanding Preston was.

Although the church was small and only accommodated about forty people, it seemed as if the entire village had turned up outside to watch them come out of the church as the bells peeled. It really was like a royal wedding.

Once outside, the photographer got to work. Holly wanted a few pictures with just herself, Mitch, Jaz, and Julian. Jaz felt warm as the photographer asked them to squeeze in close together. She looked out for Preston, but he was chatting away, seemingly easy in unfamiliar company.

'Make an arch everyone,' the photographer called out. 'Kids, get ready with the confetti.'

Julian turned to Jaz, outstretching his hands. She took them and lifted them up as high as she could. Julian did not take his eyes off her. Jaz wished he did not look so sexy dressed up. And why was she even finding him sexy when Mr Chiselled and Perfect was standing a few feet away? She felt her hands become hot against Julian's palms.

'Come along, you two,' she called to Mitch and Holly.

After turning his camera to video mode, the photographer filmed as he walked backwards down the tunnel of arms as Holly and Mitch travelled through, to cheers from the crowd. As soon as they passed, Jaz let go of Julian's hands.

He stepped forward. 'Jaz, I just wanted to say how beautiful –'

'Jules, you look positively dapper.' Kimberly moved in front of Jaz. She wore an elegant, body-hugging teal satin dress, which complimented her tall figure and long legs. She kissed Julian full on the lips. 'Weddings make me so romantic.' She put her arms around his waist.

Julian smiled sheepishly over her shoulder at Jaz.

As if I care, Jaz thought, then turned and flounced off without acknowledging Kimberly. *Where's Preston?*

CHAPTER 18

*J*ulian watched Natalie serve the desserts in the Bistro. She was assisted by Koby, who usually worked at the nursery. The toasts had been held before dinner was served, and he was pleased to get his speech out of the way. It had gone down well with the guests. The meal had been amazing, as expected, Adam had done him proud with a perfect beef Wellington.

Julian's gaze rested on Kimberly beside him. He had placed himself at the opposite end of the top table to Jaz. Kimberly was in her element and getting along well with everyone. He had seen a few heads turn her way and a couple of guys outside the church had slapped him on the back and called him a lucky git. So why did he keep staring at Jaz and that model she had brought with her? Maybe this Preston was an escort Jaz had hired. He certainly looked as if he had stepped out of an aftershave advert. And the guy never left her side, pulling out her chair, pouring her drinks, staring into her eyes. But Julian knew deep down that Preston was someone Jaz knew well, as she seemed so at ease with the guy.

Shaking his head, Julian took a deep breath and turned to Kimberly. 'I'm off to check on the marquee and make sure everything is set up.'

'I'll come with you.' Kimberly smiled at him as she stood up and slipped her arm in his.

They left via the back. He had kept the front doors shut, with the blinds closed, to protect the privacy of the wedding party. They entered the pub from behind the bar. It was packed.

'A good day's business for you, Jules.' Kimberly squeezed his arm.

'Way hey, look at the happy couple,' shouted one local, pointing at Julian and Kimberly. 'You'll be next.'

Julian laughed. Hoping that he didn't sound too nervous as Kimberly smiled at him.

'Let us pass, otherwise the marquee won't be ready for you all,' he said.

Once outside, the warmth hit him as the sun beat down, Julian wore a waistcoat and shirt, having left his jacket in the bistro.

'It's glorious weather,' Kimberly said, stopping and looking up into Julian's eyes. 'What a super day. I'm having such a lovely time. I just love spending time with you, Jules.' She stroked his bicep, through his shirt and smiled sweetly.

They carried on towards the marquee.

Inside, Simon approached them. 'Alright boss? We're all set with the booze and the food is arriving at about six.'

'More food?' Kimberly asked.

'Yes, a buffet of cheddar and biscuits, and pies and pasties. They were supposed to be bite-sized, but that's only if you have a mouth the size of a shark's,' Simon said. 'Julian got a great deal.'

'You're such an amazing businessman,' Kimberly said.

Julian wasn't sure anyone would have said that to him a couple of years ago. 'Are we ready to go?' he asked Simon.

'Yep, I'll give a nod to the band.' Simon walked over to the musicians to make sure they were ready and then turned back and gave Julian the thumbs up.

BACK INSIDE THE BISTRO, Julian called to the guests. 'Would everyone, except the bride and groom, please make their way outside.'

Julian asked the guests to assemble on the green, in front of the huge white marquee, which was decorated with floral garlands, interwoven with fairy lights. There were well over three hundred people there. With Trixy yapping at the font as Belle held onto her lead. Julian beckoned Holly and Mitch to exit the bistro.

'Oh My,' Holly said, putting a hand up to her face as they came outside. 'They'll never fit in the Marquee.'

'It takes two hundred and fifty. There are plenty of benches on the green and it's going to be a balmy evening,' Julian said.

As Mitch led Holly to the opening in the marquee, the band struck up the song which Holly and Mitch had chosen for their first dance. Holly wiped her eyes. 'I didn't know there was going to be a band as well as a DJ?'

'Just one of my rugby mate's skiffle group,' Julian said.

'I love it,' Holly said.

Julian guided Holly and Mitch in, as the rest of the wedding party followed. Everyone watched as the newly-weds swayed on the dance floor. Julian expected a massive queue at the bar, so he loosened his tie. Turning to Kimberly, he said, 'I'd better get to work then.'

She smiled at him, 'My parents have their eyes on the

boys.' She removed her heeled shoes. 'I'll join you.' She slipped her arm in his and accompanied him towards the bar.

JAZ FELT a little dizzy from the drink and hugged Holly. 'What a blinking wonderful day, hun.'

'I know and thanks so much for helping.'

'I've not done half as much as I should have.'

'Nonsense. And you've had the children.' Holly nodded at Belle and Mikey who were with Noah, stuffing their faces with sweets at the candy cart. She laughed. 'You'll have fun getting them off to sleep later.'

'You have all this to come.' Jaz put a hand on Holly's bump.

'They've been moving all day.'

Jaz scrunched up her petite nose. 'That must be off-putting.'

'Not at all. It's comforting. I know they're okay.' She scanned the room. 'Now, where is that totally gorgeous man of yours?'

'He's chatting to Helen from the auction house.'

'Oh yes.' Holly cocked her head to one side. 'I must say I was sceptical, and hell bent on getting you back with Julian, but I see what you mean about Preston. He's such a lovely guy.'

'He's an ideal match.'

'An ideal match? It sounds like you're choosing a pair of curtains.'

Jaz laughed. 'I think we go well together – that's all.'

'What about Julian?'

Jaz shook her head, looking at Kimberly gazing up at

him at the bar. 'We didn't want the same things. We had different interests. We looked odd together. He's laid back and I'm ambitious.'

'Well, I agree maybe on the earlier points – not that any of that really matters, they aren't a reason not to be with someone. But as far as ambition is concerned, Julian seems to have come into his own.'

'True. I wonder what got into him?'

'Indeed,' Holly laughed. 'Oh, here's your man now.'

Preston approached them and took Jaz's hand. 'What have you two been talking about?'

'You,' Holly said.

Preston laughed. 'All good, I hope?'

'Yes, and may I say you two look gorgeous together.'

'And you, Holly, are a most beautiful bride.'

Holly glanced down at her bump and laughed. 'I'll probably regret not waiting when I look back at the wedding album.'

They were interrupted by David Bunning and Florrie who engaged Holly in conversation.

Preston turned to Jaz. 'And now the final test.'

'Test?'

'Yes, to see if you really are girlfriend material.' He smiled.

'Cheeky. So what is this test?' Jaz asked.

'You're perfect so far, but I can't accept your begs for me to be your man, until I see your moves on the dance floor.'

Jaz laughed. 'As if I would beg anyone.' She put her hands on her hips. 'And I can dance the socks off you, mister.' She strutted towards the dance area.

Once there, the music changed to a slow one and Preston took her in his arms. She felt slightly giddy with the wine and the romance of the day, as she swayed to the music. Compared to the stress and drama of her life, this moment seemed simple. She lifted her head and Preston kissed her for the first time.

❀

JULIAN LOOKED AWAY as his heart banged against his chest, having witnessed Preston and Jaz in an embrace. He finished serving Ethan and Nina then put up a sign saying, 'cash bar'. Holly and Mitch's generous bar tab had ended, which was no surprise considering the entire population of Eversley village had turned up to the wedding.

Looking up, he saw Jaz approaching with Preston. He slapped a smile on his face. 'What can I get you?'

'What would you like, darling?' Preston said to Jaz.

Julian noted the tender way Preston touched Jaz's shoulder.

Jaz smiled at Julian. 'A diet cola for me.'

'And you?' He turned to Preston.

'Same for me,' Preston said. 'We have a long old drive tomorrow.' He turned to Jaz. 'I'm taking this beautiful lady back home.' He turned back to Julian. 'I take it you two probably know each other quite well – with this being a village?'

'Sure do.' Julian put the drinks on the bar, slightly sloshing them. 'That'll be two pounds.'

Jaz looked away.

Preston passed over a two-pound coin then turned to Jaz. 'Come on lass, let's have a couple more dances.'

Julian watched them move away in a kind of dance-walk. *He even dances,* he thought. Julian didn't hit the dance floor unless he was drunk — very drunk. Drunk enough not to remember the experience the following day.

Kimberly approached the bar. 'Can you have a break and have some fun?'

'I'm no dancer. I'll just watch you.'

He noticed her blushing. Kimberly had been so much help today. He had to admit, Simon had a point. She was a real catch and as Julian looked out at Jaz, caught up in Preston's arms. He yet again told himself – it was time to move on.

CHAPTER 19

The following morning, Jaz rinsed her mug at the caravan sink. She heard the crunch of footsteps outside. Turning, she saw Preston at the foot of the steps of the caravan.

'I wasn't expecting you until later,' she said.

'I thought you might want some moral support.'

'How did you get here?' She approached the door.

'I walked.'

'It must be two miles.'

'I wanted to clear my head before the drive. Although, I thought you might be a little more pleased to see me?'

Jaz breathed out. 'Sorry. I'm a bit uptight.' She leaned forward and planted a kiss on his cheek. With her being on the steps and him on the ground, they were at eye level.

Preston smiled at her. 'I left my bags at the hotel reception. I'll pick them up later.'

He looked sincere. If they were going to have a relationship, she guessed he should be involved in all aspects of her life. She nodded. 'Thanks. I'm not used to anyone making a fuss of me like this.' That wasn't quite true and she knew it.

Julian flashed into her mind – he'd treated her like a princess. But she'd pushed him away. *What was I so afraid of?* she thought before expelling the vision of him from her mind. 'Come in. I'm trying to get the kids sorted.'

Stepping aside, she allowed Preston to pass.

'Hello, Belle,' he said.

Belle flicked her hair as she sat at the table and crossed her arms. 'What's *he* doing here?'

'Preston knows today is going to be sad for all of us – because I have to go away.'

'You don't have to. That's a lie – you want to.'

'Look Belle, I've got a job – a responsibility and a contract. Sometimes in life you make a promise to someone – you sign a piece of paper to say you will work for them and you're not allowed to just up and leave. Life as an adult can be complicated.'

'You made a promise to me. You said you'd look after us.'

'Until I found you somewhere, you could both live together, Belle, you know that.'

'I don't like the Jacksons.'

'Well, they like you – they've rearranged their lives. Moved a load of furniture out and bought a new bed so you and Mikey can each have your own space. That's a big change for them.'

'They're rich. What do they care?'

Mikey picked up a cushion, laid on the soft seating, and put it over his head.

Jaz lowered her voice. 'Belle, you're upsetting Mikey. Please don't.'

'I'm upsetting him? That's crap – you're the one that's upsetting him.'

'Hey,' Preston said. 'Mind the language, lass, your big sis has really put herself out for you. She's got feelings too.'

'What do you know? You know nothing.'

'I know Jaz loves you and it won't be forever, kiddo.'

Belle screamed. 'Everyone leaves us.' She ran into the bedroom and Mikey ran after her. The door slammed behind them and the caravan shuddered.

Jaz's throat contracted, and she looked at Preston. 'Thanks for your input. I know you mean well, but I'm not sure it's making things better.'

'Sorry, I've got kid brothers, not a sister. I think you need to get it over with.' He put a hand on her shoulder. 'Let's drop them off first and then come back here and collect your things afterwards. You've done so much – many of your friends said to me at the wedding how good you've been and how you've surprised them. What a natural you are with the kids.'

Jaz blinked rapidly. 'Did they?'

He nodded. 'We can come down and visit once a month and spoil them. Maybe we can book a holiday and get some winter sun abroad later in the year.'

'I doubt they'll have passports, but they've already said they'd like to go to Butlins.'

Preston pulled a face. 'A holiday camp?'

'They have some great accommodation these days – not just the old-style chalet type thing.' She sighed. 'But they might not even speak to me again after this.'

'They won't thank you now, but once they're settled in, they'll be fine. They'll look forward to seeing you.'

'I'm not so sure.'

Jaz heard Belle crying as she entered the bedroom and felt again, as if she was staring at her younger self. She went to the bedside and put her arms around her while Belle sobbed.

'I'm so sorry for letting you down,' Jaz said. 'I just need to do this. Once I'm set, I promise I'll make it up to you.' She stroked her sister's hair. 'I love you Belle.'

Belle cried louder, and she held her for a good five minutes.

No-one spoke as they pulled into the road on which the Jacksons lived.

Jaz turned to Preston. 'It's probably better if you stay in the car.'

As they got out of the Bentley, Jaz took out two large gift bags. 'Presents for you two to open once you're settled in.'

The children took them from her in silence. The front door opened as they skulked up the drive with Jaz carrying their bags behind them. Belle walked in, passing Pauline Jackson without a word.

Pauline walked towards Mikey and bent down to his level, putting a hand on his shoulder. 'Don't be worried, Mikey. We're going to make your stay here as fun as possible. And it doesn't have to be forever. Hopefully Mummy will be better soon. I have arranged for us to visit her next week. Would you like that?'

Mikey nodded his head as he wiped his eyes.

Jaz was pleased that Pauline was in contact with Stacey, it would mean she would not have to phone the hospital herself. She could see how motherly Pauline was – Jaz felt she had a naturally soft maternal aura that she did not possess herself.

Pauline looked up and smiled, holding Mikey's hand. 'Don't worry, we've had a lot of kids through here. Most of them settle in fine after a few weeks. I'm sure, when you come to visit, everything will be much better and they'll come to understand why you've had to go back.'

Jaz nodded and took a deep breath. 'I've given Belle a mobile phone, so she can text or call me. It's on a monthly unlimited contract, so at no cost to you. And it's insured, so if she loses it – just let me know.' She looked down to Mikey. 'And I got Mikey some presents, but won't say what they are, so he can unwrap them with you when I've gone.'

Mikey's bottom lip quivered.

'See you little one, I'll be back in a few weeks to visit.'

She bent down to kiss him, but he looked away.

Jaz gulped and stood up. 'I'll be off then.'

As she reached the end of the path, she heard her name being called.

'Jasmine.'

Turning, she expected to see Belle, but it was Mikey crying out her name as Pauline gently moved him towards the house.

'Jaz, Jaz,' he shouted as he outstretched his hand to her.

Jaz took one step forward, then stopped, knowing she would only make it worse. She watched as Pauline took a sobbing Mikey over the threshold.

Preston got out of the car and came around and put an arm around her shoulders.

'He spoke,' Jaz said in a hoarse voice. 'Mikey spoke to me.' She swallowed hard as the Jacksons' front door closed.

As Preston drove her away, Jaz looked back at the house, seeing Belle's face at a top window, her hand on the glass, watching them leave.

JULIAN GROANED. His head creaked when he moved his neck from side to side. Opening his eyes, he saw an empty bottle of wine by the bed. When the wedding party had finished, some of the guests had moved over to the pub for a lock in. He felt movement beside him. Snapping his head to the right, he saw blonde ruffled hair.

As Kimberly lifted her head, her hair stuck to her face as she looked at him, bleary-eyed. 'Hi ,handsome.'

He was taken aback.

'Hey, you fell asleep last night – there was no chance of getting a cab and I didn't fancy walking alone in the dark, so I took the liberty of staying. I hope you don't mind?' Kimberly wore one of his t-shirts.

'Of course not. Yeah, I was beat. I'll go down and make us coffee. What would you like Latte? Americano? Cappuccino?'

'I'd love a cappuccino.' She leaned up on her elbow and smiled at him.

'I won't be long,' he said as he left the room.

When he re-entered with the drinks, Kimberly had clearly been to the bathroom to freshen up, and the smell of toothpaste lingered in the air. He didn't feel wholly comfortable with this situation.

'Here you are.' He placed her frothy coffee on the bedside table.

Kimberly took a sip. 'This tastes amazing.' She smiled at him. 'Unfortunately, I need to get to my parents' house soon, as they have to go out today. Are you coming to pick Noah up?' Kimberly's parents had taken both boys back to their house after the wedding party.

An hour later, both showered and dressed, they walked across the green. Kimberly put her arm in his. She was in the dress she had worn the night before. They waved at the team dismantling the marquee. And one of the guys gave them a thumbs up.

'The grass isn't that bad, considering the footfall yesterday,' Kimberly said.

'The beauty of good weather. Maybe the Village Committee will change their mind about holding the annual fair on the green.'

The village fair, which had run annually for decades, had been stopped after the rains of 2009 had ruined the grass. Whilst Holly had taken to hosting the fair on her land, Julian wished it would return to the centre of the village, and guessed Holly would too.

They reached the street and were just about to cross when a sleek charcoal Bentley slowed. Julian saw that Preston was driving and Jaz was by his side. Preston stopped and Julian nodded at him as they crossed the road. Jaz looked up – her eyes had a troubled expression. He hesitated until Kimberly tugged at his arm, and once they reached the pavement, the car sped away.

Approaching Kimberly's parents' house, he took a deep breath. This was a new phase for him. He had the restaurant, he had gained respect from the village, Noah was with him full-time and he was starting a relationship with Kimberly. Kimberly's Mother gave him a warm welcome. She was an attractive woman in her fifties.

'Would you like to stay for elevenses? The children are out the back playing.'

'That would be nice,' Julian said, as he stepped into the extended family environment.

CHAPTER 20

*J*az looked over to the empty side of Preston's bed. Preston had been understanding. They had only hugged the night before. He knew her mind was not in the right place and said he wanted their first time to be special. She was so surprised that the guy she had spent a year hating was actually one of the nicest she had ever met.

His apartment reminded her of her place in Wells, lots of white, shiny cabinets and glass – a single person's pad. It had been updated from the original kitchen supplied by the builders. It was a look she loved, but now, having spent a week in Holly's caravan, it appeared sterile. And quiet – so quiet. No voices in the background, no Netflix or music playing – or kids fighting. Just the distant sound of traffic and the coffee machine. Heaving herself out of bed, she went to the bathroom to freshen up.

In the open-plan living area she found Preston was busy making breakfast. He looked up as she walked in. 'I'm doing scrambled eggs on toast. – hope you like that?'

Jaz nodded.

'You look gorgeous,' he said. 'I've dreamed of having you here so many times.'

Jaz smiled. 'It's certainly not something I used to dream of.'

'Great. You're sounding a lot more like your old self,' he said with a laugh.

'I'm sure I'll be back to normal soon and you'll regret getting to know me better.'

'I think you're great, whichever Jaz you are. I loved the old one as well as the new one.'

Jaz smoothed her hair, ignoring the 'L' word. Since they had shared a kiss, their relationship seemed to be moving at warp speed and she had been going with the flow but felt like she needed time to reflect. 'I'm sorry about this, Preston. You must wonder what you've got yourself into.'

Preston shook his head. 'Me and you – we're so similar. The stresses my family have had. You would not believe. Family is to be visited, but to live our best life, maybe we need to distance ourselves from them.' He walked over and put his arms around her. 'We're perfect together, me and you. We're going places. Then when we've made it, we can really live our lives.'

Jaz felt him kiss the top of her head. But something inside had changed. She felt as if there was a piece of elastic attached to her, with the children at the other end. Hopefully, after a couple of days, this feeling would pass. She ran a hand through her hair, then looked up and let Preston kiss her.

Pulling away, he smiled at her. She guessed he was right, and they were perfect for each other. She would definitely give it a go.

'Have you told anyone at work that we're together?' she asked.

'I told them I was going to your best mate's wedding. They were surprised.'

Jaz laughed. 'I can imagine. I guess they'll be winding us up today then?'

'Me yeah. But I think they'll be too scared to wind you up,' Preston said.

'I'm not that bad.'

'Maybe not. But they're still frightened of you.'

THE NEXT WEEK, was productive for Jaz. She had gone through the contract Giles had given her and emailed it to her solicitor to scrutinise. Giles wanted Jaz and Preston to buy shares in the company. This not only gave the company funds towards the opening of the new southern showroom, but it tied the new directors in, giving them an incentive to push the company forward. After five years, Jaz had the option to sell her shares if she wanted out. Jaz had originally planned to work for the next three years – taking her to thirty-five and then to have time off, assess where she was, as that's when she had planned to reach her million. However, the deal looked too good to refuse and if the company grew at even half the rate it had been – she would exceed her original goal by a long way.

It took over a week for Belle to text. Jaz had been checking her phone regularly, even through the night. She had decided that if Belle did not contact her by the end of the second week, she would call the Jacksons to make sure everything was okay. Then, finally, whilst drinking coffee at her desk, her phone dinged with a text.

Belle wrote, *I love you*, followed by a heart and a crying emoji.

Jaz pressed the phone to her chest – looking out of her office, to see if anyone was close. Her eyes smarted so much that she could not focus on the screen.

She texted back.

Love you too and miss you every moment. I'm sorry. Can't wait to see you again xxx

No reply came. She replaced the phone on the desk. She knew, as sisters do, that Belle was crying. Where was she? At school? Bunking off? At the Jacksons? She would phone Pauline at the weekend. For now, she had to focus on the plans for the showroom.

She looked up, hearing footsteps. It was Giles.

'Have you had a chance to look at the contract yet?'

Jaz nodded. 'My solicitor is happy, it's now with my accountant. It's a really generous offer.'

'You'll be expected to work for it, lass. You won't have much of a life outside of this place.'

'What's new?'

Giles nodded. 'That's what I like about you, dedicated. Prepared to throw everything at it. Just the sort of person we need to drive the business forward – while we try to break into the southern market.'

'How's it going with the showroom purchase?' she asked.

'We're completing next week, so I need you to sign on the dotted line as soon as possible, so we know we've got this place covered.'

'Right.' Jaz swallowed. She didn't know what had stopped her so far. her accountant had already told her it was lucrative and her financial advisor was preparing the release of funds. As long as the showroom didn't go backwards, after five years she and Preston would have enough to retire on, if they invested it wisely.

'I take it you'll have the signed contract with me by Friday?'

Jaz nodded. Her mouth felt dry. 'I'll chase my advisers.' Her phoned dinged with another text.

'I'll leave it with you.' Giles left the room.

Jaz picked up her phone and opened the text. It was from Belle.

We miss you. When can we see you?

Jaz decided to reply later, when she was not in the office. She brought the contract up on her computer screen to give it one last read through, before printing it out to sign. Looking at the terms, long weekends away to Somerset would be a no-no. If she was lucky, she'd be able to get away for one Sunday a month. Not only would she oversee sales, but there would be a mountain of paperwork to do.

She looked out at Preston chatting to a customer on the forecourt. She could hear him laughing, appearing so happy. *Focus,* she told herself. *This is an amazing opportunity.*

THURSDAY EVENING AT HOME, her intercom buzzed. Preston was bringing Chinese food. As he walked in, she could smell the fresh pine scented shower gel he had used. Preston always smelled great and looked impeccable.

Smiling at him, she let him pass with the bag of food, which wafted a sweet and savoury scent. Her stomach rumbled. She had not eaten all day. Whilst she had lost her appetite, her body still craved food.

'Do you have that bottle of Dom Pérignon on chill?' Preston asked.

Jaz nodded. 'Yes.'

'Sign that contract now and we can relax, eat and drink.'

Jaz's palms felt clammy as she walked to the table where she had left the contract with a pen on top.

Sitting down, she stared at the page. The financial adviser had called earlier that day, advising that she was ready to transfer over the six-figure sum required to seal the deal.

'I can't do this,' Jaz said.

'What?' Preston frowned.

She put her head in her hands. 'I can't sign the contract. I can't commit for that long.'

'I'm sure Giles can change some of the terms if you're worried about it.'

She lifted her head. 'It's five years.' She felt a tightening in her chest, so strong it restricted her breathing. Something had changed since her trip to Eversley. She had tried to get her mojo back, to drag it back and had even made a couple of extra sales in an effort to ignite the old Jaz within. But all she could think of were the children. If she stayed for five years, Belle would be sixteen before she extracted herself from Hodges and Carter. Her childhood would be over and Jaz would not have been a part of it.

Preston lowered his voice and put a hand on her shoulder. 'It's only natural to get cold feet. What's holding you back?'

She looked up at Preston, noticing a sadness behind his eyes. Such beautiful eyes, but the fogginess she had experienced this past week was clearing. She had grown up without family. No siblings – just her and a drunk Stacey and a few would-be stepdads that never hung around for long. Having met her family, a real family who looked like her, who acted like her, who loved her regardless of the fact that she had left for Cheshire — she did not want to give them up. And she loved them back, without condition.

She took a deep breath. 'What if the kids came up here and started a new life in Cheshire? They could come for the six weeks' holiday and then decide themselves whether to go back to Somerset, depending on how Stacey is.'

'Here?' Preston gestured around the room. 'This place is way too small.'

'Or even if we move down to Somerset. I've loads of contacts. We could open our own car sales business.'

Preston shook his head. 'Jaz, it's all planned out. It's only five years. Branching out on our own would be madness at the moment. And me and you – as much as I want it to work out. We've not even …'

'Of course, yes, sorry – I was just thinking aloud.' Jaz pointed to the papers. 'I'd feel I was having my wings clipped if I signed that.' She had always felt a sense of freedom. 'As if it limits my options.'

Preston paced the room. 'Do you think you've commitment issues? Is that why you're single?'

'No. It's because I feel committed to Belle and Mikey.'

Preston stopped and placed his hands together. 'This isn't what we discussed.' He shook his head. 'It's not for me. It's not what I want. We said no kids.'

'I know.' Jaz put her head in her hands. 'I don't want kids either – no way. But Belle and Mikey are my family.'

'They're fine with the couple they're living with – it's a great house in a brilliant area, much better than where I was brought up in concrete city. You're over dramatising it Jaz – they're well looked after.'

Jaz shook her head. 'They need their family, blood family. You had that growing up – it means more than rolling hills and country living.'

'They've got each other. And your mam. How would she feel if you took them away?'

'Trust me – she's not up to the job.'

'I thought you said you weren't up to the job either? You said you were useless with kids.'

'It's nice to be around people who look like you. Where you know what they're feeling without them saying. I can feel how they feel and it's ... it's different.'

Preston placed his hands on her shoulders. 'I get it – you miss them. But don't do this Jaz. We'll make far more as directors of Hodges and Carter. And we get a share of the business in London, too. Do you want to go back to selling second-hand hatchbacks in Somerset?'

As lovely as Preston was, Jaz knew there was something missing between them and missing in the life he painted. And that something she'd had a few weeks of.

Jaz stood up. 'I'm sorry, Preston. It's not that they need me. The truth is they probably are better off with the Jacksons. But I'm not better off without them. I'm a better person with them. I need them. I can't live without them.' Saying it out loud, Jaz felt everything slot into place.

Preston shook his head and sighed. 'Please don't do this. Take a few weeks – give it a month. I'll ask Giles to give you more time. You're just missing them.'

'I don't need more time. And honestly, we may have known each other for a year but our relationship is too new.'

He stepped backwards and ran a hand through his hair. 'It sounds like you've made your mind up. You have to go with your gut, I guess. But I can't do the family thing. Maybe we can see each other for dates but ...'

'No, Preston, as you said, Somerset is ideal for kids growing up. I'm leaving.'

'But your contract ...'

'Will have to remain unsigned. I'll do the right thing and let Giles know.'

Preston scratched his forehead. 'You're a determined woman. That's what I like about you, but I doubt you'll ever have a man in your life. Relationships are about give and take.' He walked towards the door.

'Maybe I won't ever have a man, but I'll have my family. And having felt alone throughout my entire childhood. I don't feel alone with them. I can't throw that away.'

Preston opened the door.

'Don't you want to eat?' she asked.

'I'm not hungry. Goodbye Jazmine Swift.' He closed the door behind him.

CHAPTER 21

*J*az drove south in her Audi, which was packed full of her worldly possessions. She was on her way home. *Home.* The word echoed in her head and she smiled. She'd never have imagined in a million years that she would voluntarily move back to Eversley Burrows.

Her case was belted into the passenger seat. *Goodbye Cheshire,* she thought as she drove down the motorway slip road. The very fact that she could fit everything she owned into the compact car made her feel as if she had very little in her life up north. Looking in the rear-view mirror, she could just about see over the duvet and pillows she had piled on the back seat. She was sure some would think she was running away again, pressing self-destruct on what seemed like another perfect relationship she had failed to commit to. Holly would hope she was running back to a relationship she'd missed with Julian. She was probably too late to resurrect that one and, anyway, she didn't want to dwell on that. The fact was, she was coming back to focus on her family. She had not yet told Holly, not wishing to interrupt her honeymoon with Mitch. They had rented a cottage in Corn-wall and were not due back for a couple of days.

Jaz was slightly nervous about what the future held, not having a job to go to. But she was great at sales and hoped she could get a new position as soon as possible. And she would have to sort the house out. She guessed Stacey would be in no fit state to look after the kids for some months.

Coming off the M5, Jaz decided to go straight to Stacey's house. She would have to move there in the short-term, so there was no point in going to the caravan, no need to delay the inevitable. She had to get on with this new phase in her life.

As Jaz approached Eversley Burrows, her stomach lurched. She stopped the car at the entrance to the close and looked at Stacey's place at the far end. *Is this such a good idea?* she thought staring at her childhood home. Tina from next door, was in her front garden chatting to another neighbour. *I'll wait for them to finish,* Jaz thought. Eventually Tina went back inside and Jaz started up the engine and slowly drew up to the house and onto the drive.

Once outside the car, she walked up to the front door, fishing the keys from her handbag. She opened the door. 'Here goes.'

Standing in Stacey's front room, Jaz looked around and groaned. *I forgot how bad it was,* she thought. She knew it had been dirty but now noticed other things wrong, a damp patch and fungus growing in the corner behind the television. Sighing, Jaz looked at her phone. It was one hour until the Council closing time, she needed to call Donna, before the weekend, to let her know she was going to be picking the children up. She wanted to settle them in, before she looked for work. There were enough car showrooms around, she didn't think it would take long to get a job, although she was not going to go back to her old showroom, fearing it would scream 'tail between legs'.

She dialled Donna's number.

'Donna Wall.'

Great, Jaz thought. *She's still there.* 'It's Jaz. Jasmine Swift.'

'Belle and Michael are getting on well with the Jacksons. I visited this morning. There's been a slight hold up with Mikey starting school but we are hopeful he can start at some point next week. There's nothing to worry about and they are interested in extending it as long-term foster care. I understand your mother is unlikely to be fit to take on parental responsibility for at least six months.'

'I'm actually calling to let you know that I'm back in Eversley.'

'I thought you were going to leave it a month. It might be too soon for a visit.'

'I've moved back permanently.'

'But what about your career and life in Cheshire?' Donna was not making this easy for her.

'I wanted to pick the kids up this weekend?'

'Pick up?'

'I want to look after them as their guardian until Stacey gets back.'

'I'm afraid it's not that simple. We'd need to evaluate your suitability. Not forgetting the hoops I had to jump through to get them with the Jacksons at short notice. They seem really settled there. We have to consider what's best for the children.'

Jaz looked at the ceiling and swallowed hard. *Nothing is straightforward, is it?* she thought.

'Is this a long-term arrangement you want with the children?'

'I'll have them until Stacey comes home, then I'll move out.'

'So, you will stay at her house in Eversley Burrows?'

'Yes, that's where I'm calling from. Once Stacey is better, I'll buy another place locally, so the children can stay with me whenever they want.'

'I see.'

The line went quiet.

Jaz broke the silence. 'So, could you make the arrangements?'

'I'll come and visit you next week.'

'I'd like to go over and see them now.'

'Under the circumstances, I don't think that's a good idea. You haven't told them, have you? That you're back?'

'No.'

'Good. Keep it that way because I don't want to get their hopes up if the decision goes against you.'

'What do you mean decision?'

'They may have to remain in care. Michael, for one, has started to talk to the Jacksons and has come out of his shell. This is a turning point for him. This has been a total upheaval for both children.'

'Exactly and I want to make it better – to make us a family. So we're together as we're supposed to be.'

'I need to ensure they're not let down. Stability is key. I'm sure with your history, you can appreciate that. And the house needs to be safe and in good order before I can even consider allowing them to live there. And the last time I saw the inside of the house, it was far from suitable.'

Jaz slumped on the sofa after ending the call. She had returned to Eversley, feeling like some sort of saviour and now felt as if she was irresponsible and messing everyone around. She knew she would need to overhaul the house if she was going to be assessed. She needed to make it a welcoming home. She lifted her phone and scrolled the internet looking for skip hire. There was no way she could make large tip runs, in her Audi.

This place has got to be gleaming, she thought as she looked around at the mess.

CHAPTER 22

*J*ulian opened the pub. The morning sunshine beamed in, telling him that summer had arrived. Life was good. The bistro was proving more popular than he could have hoped for and they were booked solid for three weeks. The Gazette had given them a great write up. Adam was interviewing staff and looking at expanding the menu so they could open six days a week, later in the summer. He planned to ask Holly to include the bistro in the Eversley Village flyer, which she sent out quarterly to promote the arts hub and farmers' market, which she ran with Mitch over the summer months. It was circulated as an insert with the Gazette and distributed around hotels within a ten-mile radius. Having looked at the numbers, Julian expected to make a decent profit in year one.

It was soon noon, and he had arranged to spend the afternoon with Kimberly and the boys.

'Are you okay with holding the fort today?' he asked Simon.

'Of course, boss. You can't be here twenty-four seven. You've promoted me to manager and given me a pay rise.'

'If you're sure?'

'You've already put in two hours and you'll be in the bistro tonight.'

'True.' Julian lifted the bar flap and walked out the back, hollering up the stairs. 'Noah, are you ready?'

As Noah reached the bottom stair, Julian ruffled his son's unruly sandy hair. 'Have you put a comb through this?'

'Don't need it.'

'Kimberly will get her clippers out.'

'If you two get married, I don't want hair like Max's.'

Julian laughed. 'It'll be a number two crop all over.' He ruffled his hair again.

'No way, Dad. I'm growing it.'

'Your hair – your choice, son. We'd better get going.'

As they walked across the green, Julian had an urge to hold Noah's hand and he felt a pang of sadness as he realised his son was growing up. Soon to be eight and already looking a lot older and tall for his age.

Kimberly's parents lived on one of the five cul-de-sacs which surrounded the village green. Entering Ashbury Gardens, the most affluent close, he eyed the large cottages with long front gardens and even larger gardens at the rear, which backed onto Holly's land. Kimberly's parents' cottage was the largest and had an annex, where Kimberly and Max were currently living. Julian approached and the door of the main cottage swung open.

Kimberly's mum, Patricia, waved at them. 'Come in.'

As they entered the house, Patricia gave them both a warm welcome. 'The kettle's on and I've warm scones. Go out the back, Noah and find Max.'

Noah went through the house, and Julian followed Patricia to the kitchen.

Patricia filled the kettle. 'I'm so pleased that you and Kim have got together. You've brought some light back into her life after Craig.'

'She's a lovely person. You must be very proud of her,' he said.

'I am. We are. She was in a dark place. We were pleased it was over, quite frankly. And it's lovely to have her back with us.'

Julian turned at the sound of footsteps.

'Hey. Are you stopping for elevenses?' Kimberly's father, Graham, asked.

Julian nodded. 'Yes, and I can't wait – the scones look amazing.'

Patricia laughed. 'I doubt my culinary efforts are competition for the meals you're serving at the bistro. We were very impressed, weren't we, Graham?'

'Yes, we'll be back soon.'

Kimberly breezed in, grinning. 'Hi Julian.' She turned to her mother. 'Shall we take it in the garden? The kids are climbing the cherry tree, so we'd better keep an eye on them.' She walked over to Julian and smiled at him. 'Nice to see you.'

Out in the garden, Julian felt warm and ate a delicious scone with jam and clotted cream. He had a weekly video call with his parents, who were currently residing in Portugal. He missed having family around. It was easy to slip in with Kimberley's family and the children appeared to love each other's company. He felt himself relax into what proved to be a pleasant family afternoon.

They bade farewell to Kimberly's parents, and the boys jumped into the back of Julian's BMW, which he had bought from Jaz, two years before. As she popped into his mind, he had a slight feeling of wistfulness – but brushed it aside. That chapter of his life was over. This was his new world – and from the signals he had been receiving from Kimberly, she was serious about him and he knew he would be mad to push her away.

'Where are we going?' Noah called from the back seat.

'Chalmer's Park, for a walk through the woods. You'll have more trees to climb. Then we'll stop at Wells later, for some tea.'

Kimberly smiled at him. 'I want to look in on the estate agents – I've been looking on-line at prospective homes for when the settlement comes through.'

LATER, after a walk and a game of hide-and-seek in the woods, the boys climbed into the back of the car. Julian's back seats were used to the odd splatter of mud from when he took the boys to rugby. He wondered whether it was time to let the car go. To get something a bit more robust than the sporty cabriolet.

Swinging into the carpark at Wells, Julian found a space and paid for the parking. Returning to the car with the ticket, he found the boys had changed into clean shorts and trainers.

'Good idea of yours to bring clean clothes after the mess they got into.'

Noah frowned as Kimberly wiped the back of his calves with a wet wipe.

'Come on then,' Julian said. 'I'm starving. Hopefully, we can find somewhere with space to eat.'

They wandered along the High Street making their way towards the cathedral. The boys wanted pizza and there was a nice Italian nearby with a large dining area. Kimberly put her arm in his and squeezed it. She stopped to look in an estate agent window.

'I'm hoping the sale of the Surrey house will go through within four weeks. I've a healthy budget for around here. I'd love to get a place with a paddock. Do you think that would be possible?'

'Once in the country, the prices are reasonable. It depends how far out of Eversley you want to be and if you worry about being isolated or having a much longer school run.'

Kimberly looked up at him. 'Maybe I should wait, to see how things go.' She smiled.

He knew she was referring to their relationship – rather than the housing market. Would he want to move in with her and out of Eversley? He'd lived there his entire life. It was too early in their relationship, and they were taking things slow – really slow. The last thing he wanted to do was mess her around.

Kimberly looked back at the window display. 'I'd like to do something with my life, to be something. Maybe start a new career.'

Julian smiled at her. 'You're a talented woman. I'm sure anyone would be lucky to have you on their team.'

Kimberly laughed. 'Thanks Jules. I like being on your team.'

'Seeing her eyes, full of hope, he leaned over and kissed her full on the lips

'Urgh,' Max said.

Noah blushed.

'Sorry, lads. Let's get some food.' Julian chuckled as he put his arm around Kimberly's shoulders and walked in the direction of the restaurant.

CHAPTER 23

*J*az heard the voice of her managing agent, Laila — but was not listening. She was staring over Laila's shoulder at a family group looking at the house adverts displayed in the window. Her mouth had become dry as she saw Julian gaze down at Kimberly before initiating a kiss. It was final confirmation that Julian was off limits. Jaz would never steal a man away from another woman. It wasn't her style.

'Jaz.'

She moved her gaze to Laila's face. 'Yes? Sorry.' She looked back at the window to see Julian leading Kimberly and the boys away.

'I was saying the contract for your tenants is up in two months. Do you want to give them notice now?'

'No. I don't know what will happen to the children. It won't be big enough for them to stay with me there. I'll probably get somewhere larger, and I don't know where I'll be working.'

'Okay. They're decent tenants. Whenever I've inspected, the place has been spotless. I have quite a few larger apartments and small houses on the sales market, if you want the details?'

'I won't be able to get a mortgage until I'm working. Although I do have enough invested to buy one outright, I'd rather not do that.' Jaz had her finances mapped out and hoped to keep on track with her goal.

'I've an investment landlord refurbishing a three-bedroom cottage which will be lovely when it's finished. You could stay there for six months, or a year, until you know where you're at.'

'That's the thing. Everything is so up in the air at the moment.'

'I'll wait to hear from you then.' Laila handed over a sheet of paper. 'Here are the numbers of our cleaning services and maintenance team that you requested.'

Jaz collected the details and rose from the chair. 'Thanks for your time and the recommendations. I'll be in touch as soon as I know what my situation is.'

JAZ WOKE on Stacey's sofa. She had slept in the lounge with her own bedding brought from Cheshire. She had ordered a takeaway meal and watched television, trying her best to blot out the vision of Julian kissing Kimberly, which kept flashing into her mind. He was off limits — she didn't want to think of him.

Glancing up from the sofa she looked around the room realising she had much work to do. The only cleaning she had done so far was to scrape the fungus from the wall behind the television. She put a hand up to her face, remembering the experience.

Jaz heard the skip hire truck rumble into the close and

quickly pulled on her jeans and a sweatshirt over her night-dress. She stood at the lounge window and watched as the huge skip was lowered onto the driveway, pleased that they had agreed to deliver it on a Sunday.

After signing a receipt, she stared at the large metal container – there was so much to do.

'Jasmine.'

Jaz looked to her left to see Tina from next door, wearing a purple dressing gown with matching slippers. *Oh no,* she thought. 'Hi,' she said.

'How's your mother?'

Jaz walked closer. 'They're hopeful for a full recovery.'

'Poor Stace, she must be beside herself worrying about the kids. How are they?'

'With a lovely foster family, I've met them myself. They're really kind. But hopefully the kids will be coming here, to stay with me until Stacey comes out.'

'Really? I thought you'd be too posh to move back here. We'll have to arrange a welcome home party.'

Jaz gave a silent groan.

Tina gestured at the skip. 'Anyway, love. You're gonna need some help.' She shouted into her house. 'Brian, get dressed. You gotta help Jasmine.' She turned back to Jaz. 'I'll just get myself sorted.'

TWO HOURS later the huge yellow skip was full, including four mattresses, a double, and three singles. It had worked out well, as Tina and Brian had drummed up a team of six. Jaz was grateful for the help, realising it would have taken her all day to fill the skip if she had done it on her own.

'Come to our place, love, for elevenses,' Tina said.

Tina's home was a lot different from how Jaz had

remembered it. They had bought the house from the council and extended it at the back, making a large kitchen diner with bi-fold doors through to the garden.

'Wow, Tina, this is amazing,' Jaz said. 'I love the kitchen.'

'Darren put it in for us.'

'Darren?'

'Yes. Your ... I mean ... the kid's dad,' Tina stuttered.

'Oh,' Jaz said.

Tina reached for the kettle. 'That was before he got laid off when Tinktons went out of business.'

Jaz had heard of the kitchen retailer. They'd had national showrooms and had gone into administration the previous year.

'It's a shame he had to go away. He did what he thought was best, I suppose.'

'It's more than a shame,' Jaz said, folding her arms. 'A man leaving his sick wife and abandoning his kids.'

'We've not been able to get in touch with him.'

'So he doesn't know?'

'No, he was going on a three-month contract to the French Alps. He said it was enough money to get back on his feet and then set himself up as a self-employed fitter over here.'

'I thought he'd left her?'

'No. But Stacey was dead against it and blocked his number from her mobile. Then she got sick and when I tried to call him, I got a message saying his phone was no longer in service and he's been gone now for nearly six months.'

'Who's he working for?'

'No idea, love. Trust me, we've tried to find him. Before he went he said he was working on some massive house for a rich geezer. Not a regular company. So we've just got to wait for him to come back.'

'If he comes back,' Brian said as he entered the room.

'Of course, he will,' Tina scolded as Brian opened the back door, lighting a cigarette as he went.

'He still shouldn't have gone, leaving the kids alone with Stacey, knowing she has drinking problems,' Jaz said, sitting down.

'What?' Tina said. 'Stace hasn't touched a drop in years.'

'Oh, I assumed the aneurysm was because of alcohol.'

'Is that what the hospital said?' Tina frowned.

Jaz realised she had not even asked them what had caused it, and had jumped to a conclusion. 'No.' She shook her head.

Tina came over to the table and passed Jaz a mug of tea. 'Stace has had her mental health problems, and yes, she used to use alcohol to deal with them, but she hasn't touched the stuff since the day you left. It really shook her up. She went into rehab for the last time and came back determined to make a go of life again.'

Jaz remained silent and sipped her tea, absorbing the information.

'She's always said the worst thing that ever happened to her was losing you. She'd loved to have reached out, but said if she ever went to Eversley, you would cross the street if you saw her. She was waiting, she said, to see if you came back.'

A meow cut the silence. Jaz looked in the direction of the noise, to see a light-coloured ginger cat. He sauntered over to her.

'Is this Simbah?' she asked.

'Yes. We can hang on to him until you get sorted.'

'You have a lot to answer for,' she said to the cat as she stroked his back.

'He's using the litter tray now, so won't be as much bother. And we're getting him spayed next week.'

'I'll pay for the vet bills, of course.' Jaz finished her tea. 'Thanks for your help. You've been totally amazing.'

'LOVE, COME IN,' Val said as she ushered Jaz into her house which was situated in one of the cul-de-sacs that branched out from the village green. 'Why didn't you say you were back? You know you could have been staying with us.'

'Honestly, Val, my mind has been frazzled.'

'Well, at least you're staying here for a few nights. I've got your favourite chicken stew in the slow cooker.'

Jaz gave Val a hug. It was a good job she was staying, as she had been bitten by fleas and had arranged for the house to be fumigated.

'And I can't say how proud of you we are, for what you are doing for them kids after what happened to you. I hope that mother of yours appreciates it.'

Jaz sighed and let go of Val as they walked to the kitchen. 'She doesn't know, but I'm getting the impression she regrets how she treated me.'

'How do you feel about that?'

'I haven't enough head-space to even think about it. But I don't feel like rushing over and forgiving the woman. I guess I feel numb.'

'So what happened to her?'

'I thought she was ill because of her alcoholism, but her next-door neighbour has told me she stopped drinking when I left.'

'She was only young, mind, when she threw you out.'

'The kids miss her. I think she's been a much better mum the second time around.'

'Help me lay the table and I'll call Len.'

After a delicious meal of chicken casserole with herb dumplings, Jaz sat back in her seat. 'I think I'm ready for bed already.'

Len laughed. 'My Val makes comfort food.'

'And how are you feeling these days?' Jaz asked Val.

'I have to watch what I eat and get my daily exercise to keep my blood pressure down. I take so many blooming tablets.'

'You look well,' Jaz said as she looked into Val's bright eyes.

'She's a strong old bird,' Len said. 'It makes me grateful for every day we have together, since I nearly lost her.'

'Oh, get away with you, you sentimental old goat,' Val said.

They laughed and Jaz felt pleased she was back in Eversley. As Jaz laid back in the comfy bed in the guest room, a text came through. It was from Holly.

We're back home - how's life in Cheshire?

She laughed but was too sleepy to send a detailed reply so sent a simple text back, to say she would call her in the morning, then drifted off to sleep.

CHAPTER 24

Two days later, Holly burst into Jaz's childhood home and threw her arms around her and promptly broke down in tears. 'I miss you so much. I can't believe you're back here for good. I've hated you being away. I didn't like to say.'

Trixy jumped up at their legs, yapping wildly.

'Hey, hun, those hormones, you need to keep them in check.'

Holly laughed as Trixy yanked at the lead.

Jaz turned and shut the door so Holly could let go of the excited dog.

'It's not my hormones. I just love having you close by. Wow,' Holly said as she stepped back and scanned the room. 'You've done an amazing job.'

'I can't take all the credit. The neighbours helped fill a skip. I've had cleaning contractors who also fumigated the place. And an odd-job guy has sorted a few issues.'

'It looks like a different place,' Holly said as she composed herself and wiped her eyes.

'I think the throws soften the room and brighten the place up a bit.'

'They certainly do.' Holly pointed to the mantelpiece. 'And the family photos are a nice touch.'

'All from your wedding.'

Holly picked one up of herself and Jaz. 'I've chosen this one as well, for the cottage.'

'When are you moving in?'

'Just under two weeks. We're having a warming party, in advance and now you're here, you can come too.' She returned to Jaz and held her hand. 'I can't express how excited I am that you're back.'

'Come and look in here.' Jaz pulled her by the hand towards the kitchen.

'Oh, my goodness, it's so modern I didn't notice it last time.'

'I'm guessing Darren, the kid's dad, put it in. He's a kitchen fitter, apparently.' She filled Holly in on what she had learned from Tina.

'So, this Darren could turn up at any moment?'

Jaz nodded. 'Tina thinks so, although she said Stacey reckons he's gone for good.'

Holly sighed. 'Stacey never had much luck with men. What about upstairs?'

We pulled up the carpets and put in new and I've got fresh mattresses. The cat had got to them. I nearly broke my back making all the beds up.'

Holly looked around. 'What happened to the cat?'

Trixy growled as if recognising the feline term.

'Simbah is with Tina. She's getting him spayed, hopefully that will stop him from spreading his scent everywhere. But I'd prefer it if Simbah stayed where he is, after the mess he created.'

'I don't blame you. It's a real treat having you back, Jaz. I know it's tough for you, but from my selfish point of view. I just love it that you're here.'

Jaz gave Holly a hug.

'And you never know. You and Julian ...'

'Hun.'

Holly shook her head. 'It's never too late.'

'From what I've seen, things have got serious between him and that Kimberly.'

'Like what?'

'I saw them walking back from his place the morning after your wedding. She was still wearing the dress from the night before.'

'That doesn't mean anything happened.'

'And I saw them house-hunting in Wells. They looked really loved up and he kissed her.'

Holly put her head to one side. 'Oh.'

'Exactly.'

'I guess I should lay off with the matchmaking.'

Jaz nodded. 'I'd never steal another woman's man.' She cleared her throat. 'Anyway, I wondered if you would mind being here for the assessment. You're so great with kids and have a local presence. It'll look good if I show Social Services that I've a wider support network, because I have no family.'

'We might not share blood, but we are family. You're my sister, as far as I'm concerned. When's she coming?'

'In half an hour.'

It was early evening and Jaz was leaving the house and closing the front door when Tina had arrived back in her car with Brian.

'How did it go with Social Services?' she asked Jaz.

'They were impressed. The kid's social worker said she would push the move through as soon as possible, as it's better for Mikey to be with me, before his first day at school.'

'So when do they move in?' Brian asked.

'Assuming all goes well, within the next couple of days. But Donna asked me not to mention it to the children, until it is officially signed off, just in case it doesn't happen.'

'We'll keep it quiet from everyone else then, because you know what people around here are like, for spreading news.'

Jaz thanked her neighbours before getting into her car. Checking the time on her phone, she wished she could back out of dinner at The Eversley Arms with Holly and Mitch. She had initially refused, but Holly had pointed out that she could not avoid the village like Stacey had, and the sooner she announced her return, the better. She started the engine and backed off the drive.

Arriving at the pub, Jaz remained in her car. Neither Mitch's pickup truck nor Holly's van were there. She assumed they had not yet arrived. Holly was becoming larger by the day, and Jaz did not imagine she would be walking there from the farmhouse, which was quite a bit further away than the nursery on foot.

As Jaz waited, she saw the pub door open and Kimberly appeared, wearing tailored shorts and a floral top. Kimberly waved at someone standing in the doorway, then walked across the green. Jaz watched the doorway and saw Julian step out, looking after Kimberly. Julian's head snapped towards Jaz.

There was no disguising her red car. *He's seen me,* she thought and considered driving away, but instead checked her lipstick was in place and got out of the car. *Just act like you're not bothered,* she told herself.

Smiling, Jaz walked towards the pub as Julian watched her from the doorway. As she reached him, she noticed his beard had already grown back since the wedding.

'I didn't expect to see you so soon in the village. Is Holly okay?' he asked from the doorway.

'Yes, I'm meeting her and Mitch for tea.'

'Are you visiting Belle and Mikey?' he asked.

'Sort of. I've come back to be their guardian until my mother is well. But don't tell anyone, as I'm waiting for the final approval from Social Services and the kids don't know yet.'

Julian's mouth opened and he blinked. 'Well, you'd better come in.'

Jaz passed him. 'I missed the kids, Ju. It was awful. I've never felt anything like it.' She looked around the pub which was relatively quiet.

Julian followed her. 'I'm pleased for you, Jaz. And how is it going with Preston?'

Jaz stopped as she reached the bar and Julian stood beside her. She looked into his eyes. 'It was early days for me and Preston. He can't give up his career for a relationship which may have never gone anywhere. We were only seeing each other for a week or so.'

'A week?' he rubbed his beard.

'Yes, we've known each other for a year but only got together recently.' Jaz laughed. 'The wedding was one of our first dates.'

'You aren't going to try it long distance then?'

Jaz shook her head. 'He's not into kids.'

Julian remained silent and she could hear her last words lingering in the air, realising how ironic the situation was.

'What can I get you?' he asked, going behind the bar.

'Just a diet cola for me, thanks.' *This seems very civilised,* Jaz thought, although her palms were sweating, and she felt a little warm. She would have to be friends with Julian. The village was too small for awkwardness. And she did not want to stick to the Eversley Burrows. Yes, they had a pub and a community, but the village was her home.

Julian carried her drink to a table, and she followed, nodding at people she recognised, then sat down and Julian sat opposite.

'So, where are you living? At the caravan?' he asked.

'I've just been through my mother's house, cleared out the junk and had it professionally cleaned. I'll stay there with the kids until my mother is well enough to move back in, if she ever gets strong enough. If she's unable to take care of the children, then I'll either rent or buy somewhere else – depending on my personal position.'

'Have you got your old job back at the showroom?'

Jaz shook her head. 'I couldn't, Ju. Not after ditching them like that. I'll have to look for something fresh.'

'I need a new car.'

Jaz looked up from her drink. 'Fed up with the BMW, are you?'

'I love it. But it's not really practical. The cream leather is taking a hit.'

'You want more of a family car then?' Her face blushed hard. *Don't show you care,* she told herself. Julian didn't answer, so she continued. 'Kimberly. She seems like a lovely person.'

Julian nodded. 'She is. I don't know what she sees in me.'

'You're a great guy and a successful businessman. Any woman would be lucky to have you.' *Why did I say that?* Jaz took a gulp of her drink.

Julian remained silent, staring at her.

'I'll keep an eye out for a family car,' she added quickly.

Julian smiled. 'That's great. I guess you have a guaranteed customer for your first day at the new job.'

She laughed, hoping there would indeed be a new job. She had run off a list of showrooms within ten miles. Jaz had never applied for a job before, having worked at the Wells showroom after being introduced by Val's son and then was headhunted by Giles.

'Make sure you add some decent commission when you charge me,' Julian said.

'No way. You're a friend.'

'Am I?' He looked into her eyes.

She felt that connection, the one that was different with him. The one she only had with him. She swallowed. 'Of course. We've known each other for years, not just ...'

'Jaz.'

She turned her head to the sound of Holly's voice.

'Hi, you two,' Mitch said, grinning.

Julian stood up. 'What can I get you?' He took their orders, then went to the bar to make drinks.

Mitch followed.

Holly eased herself into the chair opposite Jaz. 'What were you two cosying up for?' she asked.

'We were not cosy,' Jaz replied.

Holly raised her eyebrows. 'It looked that way from where we were standing?'

Jaz shook her head. 'We were discussing me sourcing him a car. A family car for him and Kimberly.'

'Are you sure?' Holly asked.

'Yes. Positive.'

Mitch sat down and gave Holly her drink, then turned to Jaz. 'Were you and Julian having a heart to heart?'

'What makes you think that?'

'We were standing at the door watching for ages,' Mitch said.

'Oh nice, you were spying,' Jaz said with a laugh. 'It was business. He needs a bigger car, as he is now a family of four.'

Mitch raised his eyebrows. 'It's serious between him and Kimberly, is it?'

'Seems so.'

Holly touched Jaz's hand. 'You don't have to source him a car. Tell him to go to the showroom himself. You've enough to do.'

'It's not urgent. I'll be using it to find a new job.'

'Ever the sales queen,' Mitch said.

'Too right.' Jaz watched Julian as he served at the bar, realising it was going to be more difficult than she thought, living around Julian. Especially if it was obvious to the whole world that she still had feelings for him.

CHAPTER 25

*J*az arrived at the Jackson family home. After cutting the car's engine, she saw Mikey pressing his nose up against the glass of the front room window. The door soon flung open and he and Belle appeared, with huge grins on their faces. As she got out of the car, the children pelted down the drive and bashed into her, wrapping their arms around her waist, both calling her name.

Pauline Jackson walked down the drive, carrying a collection of bags and smiled when she reached Jaz. 'This is an amazing thing you're doing for them. It's such a responsibility to take on as well.'

Belle moved away from Jaz. 'You got your cool car back?'

Jaz noted she wasn't the only one that preferred the Audi to the Bentley. Mikey was still hugging her. She plied him away and bent down to his level.

'Pleased to see me, matey?'

He nodded and whispered. 'Yes.'

She ruffled his hair and blinked away some moisture in her eye. Standing up she smiled at Pauline.

'Bless his cottons,' Pauline said. 'He's the sweetest thing. So, what happened with your job?'

Jaz shrugged her shoulders. 'It didn't seem as important. Onwards and upwards, eh? I'm sorry I messed you around, with you having to clear out your office for Mikey.'

'Don't worry about that. We needed a good clear out. And we borrowed the bed from my sister.'

'Can we go now?' Belle asked, standing at the car door.

'I hope you've said thank you to Pauline?'

'Oh yes, they have. They made us a lovely card.'

'It's open,' Jaz said to Belle. 'But be careful, the door's heavy. And get in the back, remember? Mikey in the front.'

Jaz watched as the kids struggled. *It's not just Julian who needs a different motor*, she thought. She loved her red sporty car, but it was not family friendly. But there was no way she was changing it.

After helping the kids in, she opened the boot, and with Pauline's help, bundled the bags inside.

'Say goodbye to Pauline.'

'Thanks for having us,' Belle called.

'Thank you,' Mikey whispered.

Pauline handed Jaz a printed sheet of paper. 'I prepared some details for you. School times for Eversley Primary.' She lowered her voice. 'Mikey starts tomorrow. I've packed his new uniform.'

'Okay.' Jaz nodded.

'This is a list of teachers, clubs, dentist appointments. Belle has been invited to two parties and you have tickets for her leaver's assembly. I made a note of foods and meals they liked, while they were here.'

'That's handy.' Jaz looked down at the extensive list. *Flipping heck,* she thought

'And good luck. You really are a Godsend to them.'

. . .

ARRIVING AT THE HOUSE, Jaz stood on the doorstep, keys in hand. 'There's a surprise indoors.'

'Really?' Belle asked.

Jaz opened the door and the aroma of cleaning products mixed with a new carpet smell hit her. 'Ta dah, I've given the place a make-over.'

Bell frowned and looked her in the eye. 'You haven't touched my stuff, have you?'

'Er. Well, yes, I had to. The cat had peed over everything and the place had to be fumigated. There were fleas everywhere, and I got bitten to pieces. I couldn't get Social Services to agree to having you here, unless everywhere was cleared out.'

Belle ran in.

'Oi, shoes off first. We've new carpets,' Jaz called after her.

Belle ignored her, while Mikey sat down and pulled off his trainers, flinging them on the floor nowhere near the new shoe rack, then followed his sister up the stairs.

Jaz removed her stilettos, placing them on the shoe rack and put her new slippers on, smiling. *They're gonna love their rooms,* she thought as she followed them up the stairs. Upon reaching the landing, Mikey was jumping up and down on his bed like it was a trampoline.

She poked her head around Belle's door.

'Where's all my stuff?' Belle had her hands on her hips.

'Most of the things lying around were ruined,' Jaz said.

Belle opened the drawers, lifting out Jaz's new purchases. 'These aren't my clothes?'

'The clothes you left must have been way too small, hun.'

Belle's bottom lip quivered. 'But they were *my* things.'

Jaz moved forward. 'I'm sorry, chick. I thought you'd like the new clothes. I did it to cheer you up. I didn't realise ...'

Belle crossed her arms. 'You would have if you'd bothered to ask.'

'I wanted it to be a surprise.'

Belle's eyes shone with tears, and Jaz put a hand on her shoulder.

Belle shrugged it off. 'I want to be alone.'

Jaz felt she should tell Belle not to be rude, however did not want a bust up this early on in their life together. So she just took a deep breath. 'I'll call you when tea is ready.'

She turned, left the room and shortly afterwards the door slammed shut behind her. Sighing, she found Mikey still jumping on the new mattress. She realised the slatted bed would probably break if he carried on like that.

Mikey stopped when he saw Jaz. 'Thank you for my toys and TV.'

Jaz smiled. At least he noticed. Belle hadn't commented on hers, or on the comfy mattresses, fresh new bed linen and soft carpet.

'Do you want to stay up here? Or come and help me with dinner?'

'With you.' Mikey jumped from the bed. 'Pow,' he said making a super-hero pose, then followed Jaz down the stairs.

In the kitchen, Jaz opened the freezer. She had stocked it with pizza, breaded chicken, fish fingers and chips. Looking at the list Pauline had given her, she realised she would have to up her game in the kitchen department and cook much healthier meals.

'So, how does teddies, chips and beans sound?' she asked her brother.

Mikey jumped up and down. 'Yes, yes, yes.' He looked at the back door.

'I've had the garden tidied. Do you want to go out and play?'

Mikey nodded.

'Get your shoes on, then.'

Jaz unlocked the back door and looked into the garden. Her phone vibrated with a call. As she answered it, Mikey whizzed past her.

'Hi, Holly,' Jaz said.

'How's it going? Do they love it?'

Jaz watched Mikey climbing up the steps to his slide. 'Mikey seems chuffed, but Belle, not so.'

'Why not?'

Jaz stepped onto the path in her slippers, strolled up the garden and lowered her voice. 'She didn't appreciate me throwing out the stuff in her room.'

'Did you explain it was manky, full of fleas and there were two dead mice in there?'

'No, not in that much detail. She looked as if she was going to explode.'

'So, you've given her space?'

Jaz looked up at Belle's room to see her at the window. 'Yes.' She smiled at Belle.

Belle pulled the curtains closed.

'I don't think she likes me anymore.'

'You hate anyone touching your stuff, Jaz. So, it's no surprise.'

'True. I couldn't bear the thought of people going into my apartment when I first let it out. But I love new things and I thought she'd go crazy for them. It's all designer.'

Holly laughed. 'This could be interesting. I hope she calms down.'

'Me too. I don't want to have to discipline her.'

JAZ FELT Mikey was watching her every move as they stood in the kitchen. He hadn't left her side since they came in from the garden. She pulled two trays from the oven and distributed the breaded chicken across three plates, then added chips. She opened the microwave, removing a jug of heated baked beans, which she poured in dollops on the plates.

Mikey had morphed from being a mouse into a chatterbox.

'How many chips have we got each?'

'I haven't counted them.'

'Why not?'

'Because I'm just guessing.'

'We need to have the same to make it fair.'

'Well, if you think I've more than you. Take some off my plate.'

Jaz took the meals into the dining room, placing them on the new placemats she had bought. 'Mikey, can you let Belle know dinner's ready?'

After Mikey swiped a couple of chips from her plate, he bounded up the stairs.

She heard Belle's voice. 'I'm not hungry.'

Mikey came down. 'She said —'

'I heard. Sit down and start yours, else it'll go cold.'

Jaz climbed the stairs and tapped on Belle's door. *Here goes,* she thought and opened the door.

'I said I'm not hungry.' Belle laid on the top bunk, tapping away at her phone.

Jaz leaned on the frame. 'Come on, chick, give me a chance. I'm not pretending I know how to look after you two properly. I'm totally rubbish at this and can't even cook you a decent meal and I'm serving up chicken teddies.'

Belle looked up and caught her eye. A small smile appeared on her face and she leaned over, giving Jaz a hug. 'Sorry – I just felt like all my stuff had gone.'

'I should've explained before you came in. I wanted it to be a surprise. To be honest, I probably would have reacted in exactly the same way.'

Belle moved back onto her bed. 'I just showed Lissa my room on Facetime, and she said she wants to come for a sleepover.'

'Who's Lissa?'

'She lives down the road.'

Jaz hadn't considered sleep overs.

'Me, Lissa, Elsa and Bronte go to the same school.'

'I thought you didn't like anyone at school?'

'We're in the show together.'

'So they gave you a part?'

'One singer isn't there for the show. They're going on holiday instead. So Miss Grove gave me the part.'

'That's great news.'

'So can I have a sleepover then?'

'Once we're settled in. Maybe.'

'Yay.' Belle texted frantically on her phone.

'I said maybe.'

'Everyone knows, maybe means yes.'

Jaz shook her head, realising she had a lot to learn about parenting. 'Come on then, our food is getting cold.'

IT WAS HALF-PAST NINE. Jaz stood at the foot of the stairs, hearing the televisions. She didn't realise bedtime would be such a palaver. And she'd had to explain to Mikey that he was starting school the next day. Which had clearly unsettled him. When she had looked after them before, there was no school, so bedtime had not been an issue. But she didn't want them yawning throughout the day. She realised that televisions in the bedrooms had been a bad move.

Flopping down on the sofa, Jaz reached for the list which Pauline had given her and transferred the details into her smartphone. She had to think about doing a proper food shop. The most adventurous Jaz had been with cooking was a stir-fry or salad. She was a meal in minutes type of person. In contrast, her taste as a diner was varied, considering the amount of times she had eaten out.

Looking at the timings of school and clubs and the two parties Belle was invited to, she groaned. She realised she would have to find childcare if she was going to be able to fit these around a job. Belle was okay. She could look after herself for a while – although she was not sure she would want to leave her alone in the house for too long, especially if she would invite her friends over. She drifted off to sleep on the sofa.

Waking at midnight, Jaz climbed the stairs to bed.

CHAPTER 26

'Belle, are you ready?' Jaz shouted up the stairs, then headed for the kitchen to finish the lunch boxes.

Mikey followed and watched as she made them up.

'One ham, one cheese, crisps and an apple,' she said as she closed the lids.

Mikey clutched at her arm. While he had seemed to accept that he was starting school when she had explained the previous evening, he didn't appear too agreeable this morning. And had spoken little.

'Have you finished your cereal?'

He shook his head.

'Go on then. Up at the table and eat.' She watched him slope through the door into the lounge.

Belle appeared at the door and frowned. 'What's that?'

'Your lunch box.'

'Lunch box? I'm not five, you know. O-M-G - it's got *Pinky Kitty* on it.'

'I thought you liked cats?'

'Not that one.'

'Fine – stick it in a carrier bag.'

'I don't eat during the day.'

'What?'

'Mum didn't mind.'

'Well, Mrs Jackson made you lunch.'

Belle rolled her eyes and shook her head.

'If you don't eat, you could pass out.'

'And what's that big bottle?'

'Your water.'

'I normally have an energy drink at lunch.'

'Er, no. They're not for kids, Belle.' Jaz held out Belle's lunch, which was now in a carrier bag.

Bell crossed her arms. 'That won't fit in my bag.'

'Of course, it will ...' Jaz trailed off, noticing the small bag Belle had slung over her shoulder. 'Where's your backpack?'

'Urgh, I'm not using that for school!'

'It might not be to your taste, hun, but everything fits into it. Go get it.'

'You're not my mum.'

Jaz looked up to the ceiling, then back at Belle. 'Don't start this, Belle. I certainly am not your mother. I'm Jaz and I'm doing the right thing by you two. I've given up my whole life to come down here.'

'Yeah. We know. You already said.'

'Get your bag.' Jaz heard her own voice come out as a growl. She felt herself shake, and she guessed by the way Belle sped up the stairs, she may have sounded harsh. *This is not going well,* she thought. She wanted to get her point across, but the last thing she wanted to do was scare the kids. Considering how fragile they were.

Jaz put her hand to her forehead and walked into the lounge. Mikey sat at the dining table, drinking the left-over milk from his coco cereal, straight from his bowl. Putting the bowl down, he grinned at her with a big chocolate ring around his cheeks and across his forehead.

Jaz smiled. Reaching for the kitchen paper, she tore off a sheet and handed it to him. 'Here wipe.'

He shook his head, so she tried to do it herself, as he screamed.

'What are you doing to him?' Belle shouted.

'Calm down. As you can see, I'm wiping chocolate milk off his face.' She handed Mikey the paper towel. 'Go to the bathroom and do it yourself, matey.'

'I'm off.' Belle walked towards the door with the backpack flung over her shoulder.

'Don't forget your ...'

Belle slammed the front door.

'... lunch.' Jaz let out a long sigh and watched Mikey scrubbing his face at the sink in the downstairs toilet. 'I'll pop it into the school later. Come on, monster, are you ready for your big day?'

FIFTEEN MINUTES LATER, a few yards from the school, Jaz opened the passenger door of her car. They had left it too late to walk. 'Come on, Mikey, let's get out of the car. Quickly we're in the way.'

A woman tutted as she struggled past the Audi with a double pushchair.

'Now,' Jaz said.

Mikey stuck out his bottom lip. It quivered, and tears tumbled down his cheeks as he got out of the car.

Jaz softened her voice. 'Let's go on the swings first.' She decided to take him over to the play area, across the road from the school, until he had calmed down. 'Then we'll go in when the crowds have gone.' It was a busy school. She guessed he wasn't used to so many people.

Mikey nodded and wiped his nose on his sleeve. Jaz reached for the wet wipes which Holly had suggested she kept permanently in her hand bag and scrubbed at his messy sleeve. She didn't want him looking grubby on his first day. She wished she had taken a picture at home instead of leaving it. The first day at school photo could be a talking point between her and Stacey if they had to meet.

Mikey cheered up after a short while on the swing. And Jaz even managed to get a cute picture of him in his uniform, which was a navy-blue sweatshirt and grey shorts. Jaz looked at her phone. They were now ten minutes late. 'Come on, monster, time to go.'

'No.'

She walked over to him, taking his hand. He tugged hard against her. *I should have just taken him straight in,* Jaz thought as she realised she was making mistake after mistake, with her attempts at parenting.

By the time they reached the school's reception, they were twenty minutes late and Mikey was having a meltdown.

The receptionist looked up. 'I'll call Mr Hooper.'

You're kidding me? Jaz thought. Mr Hooper was the head-master when she was at the school. *I hope it's not the same one.*

It was.

Mr Hooper opened the door and frowned.

'Miss Swift, I see your timekeeping hasn't improved?'

'Hello, Mr Hooper. So, you're still here?'

'Correct.'

Mikey's grip around her legs tightened.

'I understand you're the current guardian for Michael. If you could do your best to get him here on time in future.' Mr Hooper looked around Jaz's legs and flared his nostrils. 'Especially if it's going to take him a while to settle in.'

Mikey continued to scream.

'It's much better to get him in early, rather than late. He will now disrupt the entire class when they have already started their morning learning activity.'

'I'm sorry. He was upset, and I thought I'd try to calm him down before I brought him in.'

'I suggest you adhere to the school timetable. He has a lot of catching up to do. Being a late starter.'

'My mother is sick.'

'I know the background, Miss Swift. I can assure you I've read the report from his social worker, in full.'

Mr Hooper spoke to the woman at the reception desk. 'Beverly, can you call Dawn to reception?' He turned back to Jaz. 'As Michael is late to order his school meal, I take it you've prepared a packed lunch?'

'Yes. I have.' Jaz looked down at Mikey's bag. 'Oh, sorry, I forgot to put it in. I'll pop home and get it. I have one for Belle, too.'

A woman entered the reception.

Mr Hooper gestured towards her. 'This is Mrs Withers, the welfare officer. She'll settle Michael in today. Please ensure he's fully equipped and on time tomorrow.' He turned and left.

Mikey clutched onto Jaz.

Mrs Withers bent down to his level. 'Hello Michael, I'm Mrs Withers.'

'He likes to be called Mikey.'

'That's a nice name. Come on, Mikey.' She outstretched her hand.

Jaz pushed him gently forward. He screamed louder.

'It's fine for you to leave now. A lot of this will be for your benefit – to tug at your heartstrings. He'll be fine.'

*J*az checked the time on her phone. It was two thirty in the afternoon. *Where's the day gone?* she thought. It was only twenty minutes until she had to leave the house to pick the kids up. Looking down at her jeans and t-shirt, she decided to dress up for the school run. Ten minutes later, she checked her reflection. She wore a cream shift dress with a red bag and high heels. Picking up her handbag she donned her sunglasses. *That's better,* she told herself. *Older sister, picking up siblings.*

She swore under her breath as she looked for a parking space outside the school. Eventually she parked so far from the school gates, she may as well have walked from home. Smoothing her hair, she checked her reflection in the rearview mirror. *Here goes.*

She trotted towards the school, hoping she would not be late. Stepping into the school grounds on time, she immediately noticed a huddle of women. One of them looked over and raised her hand. Jaz looked away. With sunglasses on, she hadn't caught the woman's eye. She found a remote space, away from the crowd. Looking around the playground her tummy lurched, remembering being there herself, and the them-and-us between the Eversley Burrows kids and those from the village. And then Holly on the periphery of both groups. Holly wasn't part of Eversley Burrows, or part of the village. She was the little rich girl from the garden nursery and Jaz was her proclaimed protector. Jaz sighed. She didn't like the tribal thing then, and she certainly didn't want to get into it again. *I'll keep myself to myself,* she thought.

Jaz jumped as she felt a tap on her shoulder.

'Excuse me.'

She spun around. 'Hello?'

A woman about her height, with curly black hair in a sports brand hoodie with matching leggings, smiled at her. 'It's not Jaz Swift, is it?'

Jaz lowered her sunglasses, so she could get a better look at the woman. 'Yes.'

The woman turned around and shouted at the crowd of parents. 'It is her.' She spun back around. 'I said to Mel, it was you. It's me, Sian. Tina said you were staying at Stacey's place looking after the kids. Wow! You look well-nice.'

'Thanks,' Jaz said, aware of the eyes on her, and not just from the Eversley Burrows crowd.

'Have you just come from work?' Sian asked, looking her up and down.

Jaz did not want to admit that this was her school-run outfit. 'I'm looking for a job.'

'Oh, I see.' She gestured behind her. 'Do you wanna stand with us?'

The sound of excited children reached their ears. 'Oh, I'd better find Mikey now.'

'Okay. We'll catch up tomorrow then?'

Jaz smiled and walked towards the classroom. It seemed

weird to her to be on the grounds of this school and for someone other than Holly to want to be friends with her. She remembered that Sian and Mel, had been less than nice to her, when they had attended Eversley Primary together.

As she walked towards the school building, she realised she had no clue which classroom Mikey would be in. *Maybe I should ask at reception?* she thought.

'Hi there.'

Jaz turned around, and a woman smiled at her. With her hair, long and tonged, she wore full makeup.

'I'm Bobby. You look lost? I haven't seen you here before.'

'It's my first day and I've no idea where the reception class is. And my name is Jaz.' She just stopped herself from retrieving a business card from her handbag. It was second nature for her to network and this woman was just the sort she was used to selling cars to. But what was the use of networking? She didn't even have a job.

'Follow me, that's where I'm headed,' Bobby said as she slipped an arm in Jaz's.

Jaz felt herself stiffen. *Be nice,* she thought.

She extracted her arm as soon as they reached the classroom and Mikey came out smiling.

Thank heaven for that, she thought.

He rushed up to Jaz and gave her a hug.

'Alright, matey? Did you have a nice day?'

Mikey nodded. Jaz looked up as she heard a woman speaking to her.

'Hi, I'm Mrs Goodhand, Mikey's teacher.' She carried a folder. 'We have parents' evening next week to update on the child's progress over the year. We'll use it to go over the catch-up material for the six-week holiday period, so he isn't so behind next year.'

Jaz nodded. 'That's a great idea.'

'I'll focus on assessment and settle him in this term. But on first impressions, he's as bright as a button, his maths skills are fine. I'm hopeful he'll catch up with his reading quickly.'

'That's good news.' Jaz looked down at Mikey. 'What a clever boy you are.'

'And we'll focus on his social skills.'

'Thank you.' Jaz took Mikey by the hand. 'Come on, monster, let's see if we can find our sister.'

Jaz walked around the playground looking for Belle, then remembered the main school did not empty for another ten minutes.

As she reached the school gate, there was a group of parents that turned as she approached.

Bobby, now holding hands with a little girl with blonde pigtails, smiled at her. 'Everyone say hi to the new mum.'

A blonde woman in front swung around. It was Kimberly. 'Oh – it's you.'

'Do you two know each other?' Bobby looked from Jaz to Kimberly.

Kimberly nodded. 'Jaz used to go out with Julian.'

'Awkward,' a red-haired woman said.

Jaz smiled. 'Not at all. Julian and I split up a year ago and I'm not a mum, Mikey is my brother.'

'So, you've been living in Eversley for ages, then?' Bobby said. 'I moved here six months ago.'

'I moved to Cheshire last year and I'm back to take care of my siblings, while their mother is in hospital.'

Mikey tugged on Jaz's arm.

Bobby smiled. 'We'll have to add you to our mum's WhatsApp group.'

'But I told you, I'm not actually a mum,' Jaz said, not wanting to get sucked in.

Bobby laughed. 'We'll make you an honorary member.'

Great, she thought.

'Here they come,' Kimberly said. 'Max. Noah.' She waved at the boys as the primary school emptied.

Jaz watched the sea of kids flowing out.

Noah walked over to Kimberly, not noticing Jaz. 'Where's Dad?'

'He asked me to pick you up. He's got a meeting.'

'Okay.' Noah looked in Jaz's direction. 'Jaz.' He grinned.

'Hey,' Jaz said. Noah looked so much like Julian. She smiled with a warmth she felt bubbling to the surface.

'Come on, boys. Let's get you home,' Kimberly said, ushering them away.

Bobby handed Jaz a slip of paper. 'This is my number, text me and I'll get them to add you to the chat.'

THE NEXT DAY, Jaz opened the front door to let Holly in.

'How are you?' Holly said as she crossed the threshold.

'I'm well and truly knackered, hun.' Jaz closed the door and they headed for the kitchen.

'How was the drop off this morning?' Holly asked.

'We got there early. Mikey was upset again when I left him, but at least I didn't get a rollicking off Hooper.'

Holly laughed. 'I forgot to mention to you that he's still there. He must be about one hundred now.'

'Honestly, chick, he looks the same. He probably looked older than his years when we were there.' She filled the kettle at the sink.

'Have you spoken to Stacey yet?' Holly placed a paper bag on the worktop.

Jaz shook her head. 'She knows I'm here. Donna had to

tell her. But I have to see her as I've a pile of post.' She pointed out of the room towards the dining table where a neat pile of letters was placed. 'I need to get her permission to open it and deal with any bills.'

'When are you going in to see her?'

'Friday.'

'I picked up some lemon drizzle cake from Wells this morning.' She pointed to the bag she had placed on the worktop.

'Hun – you're addicted to that stuff.' Jaz laughed as she poured hot water into two mugs.

'What are you going to do about work?' Holly asked.

'It's tricky, what with the kids. I think I'm going to have to work part-time,' Jaz said.

'Will that be enough to live off?'

'If I find a job with good commission rates, I should be able to earn enough. After all, it's only short-term. Hopefully in six months to a year, Stacey will be back on her feet. Of course, I'll still be a part of the kids' lives, but I won't be their sole carer.'

'There's so much to consider.'

'My mind is churning like a flipping washing machine, hun. Do you think I've made a mistake taking all of this on?'

'Of course not. You went with your heart – that's always the right thing to do.'

'I feel like I've thrown my career away.' Jaz removed the tea bags from the mugs.

'Nonsense, you'll end up achieving your goals, it might just take a little longer. What's your next step?' Holly opened the fridge and took out the milk and passed it to Jaz.

'I said I'd look for a car for Julian. I thought I'd visit the local showrooms and suss them out before I decide who to approach for a job.'

'There's no point in going without him. He'll want to choose it.' Holly pushed Jaz's phone towards her along the worktop. 'You'd better text him.'

'I hope this isn't you matchmaking again? Kimberly and him are pretty close – she even picks Noah up from school.'

'I'm not matchmaking. I'm being practical.'

After taking their teas to the dining table in the lounge, Jaz texted Julian. Jaz noticed the time. 'It'll be time to pick them up in half an hour. The day goes by so quickly. Hopefully, I'll dodge the other parents today.'

'Why dodge them?' Holly asked. 'Some of them could help you out with childcare.'

'When we were there, they hated us. I've still got a scar on my knee from where Mel pushed me over.'

'I'm sure you must have left her with a scar or two.' Holly laughed. 'Many of the parents come over to the arts hub. They're all really friendly and are nothing like they were as kids.'

Jaz was not convinced.

After seeing Holly off, Jaz changed into three quarter length lemon cotton trousers and wore white dolly shoes and a white lace top. Donning her sunglasses, she looked in the mirror. 'Here goes.'

As she left the estate and walked onto the Eversley Road, she heard a familiar voice from behind her. 'Jaz.'

She stopped and watched Julian jog up the road, noticing how her heart began to beat at a faster pace.

He grinned as he reached her. 'Thanks for your text. That's a great idea about looking around the showrooms.' He smiled at her. 'So, how are you finding family life?'

'I'm no natural, as you know. There's so much to think of. And I'm a rubbish cook. Holly gave me some ideas today, though.'

'Don't worry, I've been cooking my whole life, it's easy, you just follow the recipe.'

Jaz remembered the times Julian used to cook for her.

'What have you tried so far?' he asked.

'Sausage and mash.'

Julian laughed loudly.

The sound of his laugh brought a warmth to Jaz. She missed it. 'The potato went gloopy, but there were still lumps in it.'

'Ah, it's all down to buying the right type of spud,' he said. 'How's the job hunt going?'

'I've not had time to look yet. When we are looking for your new car, I can suss the showrooms out.'

'Don't worry, something will turn up. You're amazing at what you do, and everyone loves you.'

The L word seemed to echo around Jaz's head. Remembering the first time he'd said it. And realising he was the only man she'd ever said it back to.

As they reached the gates, she could see the two groups – the mums from the estate and Bobby's crowd. She groaned.

'I take it you don't like school pick up?' Julian chuckled.

'It's like being back here again. I don't feel I fit in.'

'Everyone's really friendly.'

'Yes to you – because you're a good-looking guy.'

'Am I?'

Jaz blushed and looked away.

As they arrived, Kimberly stepped forward and gave Julian a kiss. With nowhere else to go, Jaz edged away towards the Eversley Burrows parents.

Sian's face lit up as she reached them. 'You look amazing, again.'

'Thanks,' Jaz said.

Sian nodded towards Julian. 'So, your ex is going out with one of the plastic lot?'

Everyone knows everyone's business here, Jaz thought.

'They really reckon themselves,' Sian said. 'They've taken over the PTA and the school fair. Every year we've organised it. Sausage on a stick and beer ain't good enough for them. No. They want hog roast and a champagne bar. Stupid, if you ask me.'

Jaz groaned. *Some things never change,* she thought. Them-and-us was alive and kicking at Eversley Primary. She remembered she had not checked the messages on the WhatsApp group yet. It had pinged so often she had turned the notifications off. There was no way she wanted to get roped into organising the fair. She looked over at Bobby and her group. She had been selling cars to that type of client for years. She'd better stay on their good side, though. She saw no point in jeopardising any future sales.

Sian continued. 'We used to hold our meetings in the *Dog and Horn*, but now they hold it at one of their posh houses and you need a car to get there. How's your Mum?'

Jaz licked her lips. 'I'm off to see her Friday. It's going to be a slow process.' She had been putting it to the back of her mind but knew she had to prepare herself and face the fact that she needed to at least communicate with her mother.

CHAPTER 28

*A*fter dropping the children at school on Friday, Jaz set off for the hospital. The roads were busy as she travelled through the back end of the morning rush. Her nerves were tense as she sat in traffic. The feeling of dread heightened the closer she got.

After parking her car and walking through the hospital, she approached the ward desk and the nurse smiled. 'Mum is out of the danger zone now. We may even be able to release her.'

'Are you sure?' Jaz said. This was a lot sooner than she was expecting. She was sure they had said it would take about six months for her to be independent. Maybe the desk nurse had got Stacey confused with someone else?

'I told the occupational health team that you were coming in, as we need to have a meeting with you about Mum's care.'

Jaz frowned as she reached Stacey's bed. Her mother looked a lot brighter, but in no way was she capable of looking after herself, let alone the kids. *Surely, they must be mistaken*, she thought.

'Love, I don't know what to say. I'm so grateful for you looking after the kids.'

Jaz took a deep breath. She had already rehearsed what she was going to say. Her main objective was to divert the conversation from anything personal.

'It's no bother,' Jaz said and then pulled out the pictures she had printed and letters and paintings the children had prepared. 'The kids are coming to see you next week.'

She prompted to tell Stacey all about Mikey's progress and gave her the picture of his first day at school. She could tell that Stacey was trying her best to hold it together, she periodically wiped tears from her cheeks.

After ten minutes, the nurse called Jaz, and she left the pictures and letters with Stacey as she was directed to an office. Inside, Dr Raj was sitting at a table with two women.

'Hi, Jasmine, this is Clare and Liz,' Dr Raj said. 'We need to discuss the next steps. We do not want to put you in an awkward position.'

'What's the situation?' Jaz asked.

'Is it possible for you to care for your mother at home?' Liz asked.

'What? Me? As well as the kids?' Jaz's heart thumped. 'No. It's not possible.'

'We understand,' Clare said picking up a pack of papers. 'We are looking at placing Mum in a nursing home until she's strong enough to go home.'

'Can't she stay here?' Jaz asked.

'I'm afraid not. Her care needs have changed. It's a case of time, while she rehabilitates but she will continue to receive her therapy as an outpatient.'

Clare handed Jaz a sheet of paper. 'Here's a list of the recommended nursing homes in your area. Stacey qualifies for free care but only in a few of the homes. They are indicated with a star.'

Jaz looked at the list in her hand but her eyes could not focus. Hopefully, the homes would be okay. She wasn't working and knew that the prices of private nursing homes were extortionate. One of her previous work colleagues had to place his father in care and found the costs were more than his monthly wage.

'We suggest you narrow it down to two or three and then allow Stacey to make the final choice. It's important that she feels involved in the decision making process.'

Jaz sighed. 'Okay.' Things seemed to get more and more complicated, and she felt a searing pain in her temple as she rubbed her forehead.

Back at Stacey's bed, she found her mother asleep. She sat down quietly in the chair beside her. The team had told her it could be up to a year before Stacey was strong enough to care for herself, let alone look after the kids. Jaz did not want to ponder on the future, or the prospect of Stacey living in a care home indefinitely. Jaz told herself to calm down, she needed to take each day, and crisis, one step at a time.

She heard a murmur beside her and turned to see Stacey had her eyes open.

'Hi,' Jaz said, still finding herself unable to call Stacey 'Mum'.

Stacey's eyes brightened. 'Have they told you I need to move to a different place?'

Jaz nodded. 'I'm looking into it for you.'

Stacey tapped her hand. 'You're a good girl.'

Jaz shut her eyes, in an effort to blot out her emotions while feeling that she was falling deeper and deeper into a hole.

· · ·

AFTER SCHOOL, Jaz had taken Belle and Mikey to the farmhouse, where they had eaten their evening meal with Holly, Mitch and their staff. Val and Len had also joined them. The kids were playing snakes and ladders with Val and Len at the far end of the table. Jaz sipped a glass of sparkling water, as Mitch and his staff cleared away the table.

'Shall I come with you on Monday?' Holly asked. 'To check the homes out?'

'A home?' Belle asked with her eyes wide open, from the other end of the table.

'A nursing home for Mum,' Jaz said. 'Not for you. Somewhere she can go to get stronger so she can come back to live with you.'

'With us, you mean.' Belle returned to her game as Val cheered then moved a counter up the longest ladder on the board.

Jaz turned to Holly. 'I have a list to go through. I might be able to reject some, by looking at the details on-line rather than visiting them.'

'I'll get my laptop.'

After half an hour, they had whittled it down to five and Holly had insisted on going along with her.

'Are you sure?' Jaz glanced at Holly's bump.

Holly nodded. 'I can't fit in your car, though.' She laughed. 'You'll have to drive the van.'

THE FOLLOWING WEEK, Jaz and Holly embarked on their trip around the nursing homes. It was raining as Jaz drove Holly's van up to the first place. Most of those on the list were dotted around Wells. From the outside, it looked like a budget hotel, concrete, grey and lifeless but was her first choice, due to its location.

As soon as they walked in, Jaz was hit by the smell — a pungent mix of overcooked vegetables and air freshener.

A woman answered the door to them. 'Please sign in.' She gestured to a book on the reception desk.

Jaz gulped as they were led down a corridor. There were elderly people everywhere, and no-one of Stacey's age.

'Do you have any younger residents?' Holly asked the receptionist, as if she had read Jaz's mind.

'Some are younger, but most people here are severely ill.'

'My mother will be convalescing. She's not terminally ill,' Jaz said as she looked around the overcrowded lounge at the residents.

'I'll show you the room that's currently vacant.'

Jaz shook her head. 'Actually, I don't think this is appropriate for my mother, but thank you for your help.'

Outside, she took deep gulps of air. 'I can't put Stacey in there. It's like a waiting room for death.'

'Residential homes are much nicer, but Stacey needs the care.' Holly put her arm around Jaz. 'Let's try the next place.'

However, at the next two homes, it was the same story.

'Let's get the other two done,' Holly said. 'Then maybe we should go back to the first place again and have a better look.'

Two hours later, at the farmhouse kitchen table, Jaz nursed a cup of tea. 'What two do you think I should shortlist? Stacey can't afford the paid options and whilst they looked nice from the outside, and were in prettier locations, they seemed much the same on the inside. If maybe a little less crowded.'

Holly bit her lip. 'It's difficult.'

'I feel so guilty, hun. I can't look after Stacey and the kids. I'd never be able to get a job. I'm not even sure I want a relationship with her. The plan was that she wasn't going to come home until she was well enough. I just assumed she'd be at the hospital, not in a nursing home.'

'How long is it until she's going to be discharged?' Holly took a sip of her tea.

'As soon as her care has been finalised. I'm not going to be able to think about anything else.'

Holly touched Jaz's arm. 'Just sleep on it. Maybe the places won't seem so bad when you visit with Stacey. You have our cottage warming on Saturday to look forward to. That will take your mind off it.'

'Who's coming?'

'Val and Len, All Lovelands' staff, Nina, Ethan, David Bunning and Florrie. I invited Julian, but he's working. Mitch's family can't come as they'll be taking time off when the babies arrive.' She rubbed her bump.

'Can I bring the kids?'

'Of course, I expected them to come. It's an afternoon party. I'm too tired for late nights.'

*J*ulian drove along the road to Sophie's house. He was glad there was no animosity between them. They had always been a solid team behind Noah, who seemed to think it was perfectly normal for his parents never to have been together. In fact, he'd never asked Julian about it. Looking across at Noah, Julian thought he appeared especially keen to go to his mother's house. He guessed Sophie had something planned.

'What are you doing with Mum this weekend?'

'I don't know yet.'

'You seem to be looking forward to it?'

'Yes ...' Noah looked out of the window.

'So, you want a break from me, is that it?' Julian said with a chuckle, wondering whether he had been hard on his lad that past week.

'No, Dad. It's just nice not to have to see Max.'

'Oh, Noah. I'm sorry, does he get on your nerves?'

'He isn't always nice.'

'What has he done?'

'He's nasty about other people.'

They had arrived at Sophie's house.

'Right here we are, son.' He decided to quiz Noah further when he picked him up. He might need to have a quiet word with Kimberly.

They both got out of the car.

Noah walked around to the boot as Julian opened it. 'Dad, next week can we see Jaz? I like Jaz.'

Julian raised his eyebrows. 'I didn't think you were keen on her brother and sister?'

'They're okay. The boy seems fine. And Belle just ignores me. At least she doesn't tell me what to do all the time.'

Sophie opened the front door and waved at them.

'We'll talk about this when I pick you up.'

'So, can we see Jaz?'

'I don't know, son. I'm friends with Kimberly now.'

'Are you going to marry her?'

'Let's talk about it after the weekend.'

BACK AT THE PUB, Julian found Simon behind the bar.

'You can get off now,' Julian said. 'And get ready for your day out.'

'She's cried off,' Simon said.

'Sorry, mate.'

'She's got a cold, so an afternoon kayaking probably isn't a great idea. You can go off to Holly's party this afternoon. I'll hold the fort here.'

'Are you sure?' Julian felt a surge of energy. It would be a chance to chat to Jaz. He realised the urge he had to see Jaz meant it was time to cool it with Kimberly. Regardless of whether Jaz was interested or not, he was feeling near elated at the thought of seeing her. Since he'd discovered Jaz was single, he could not stop thoughts of her coming to mind and the hope for a reunion was becoming stronger every day.

The door swung open, and Kimberly walked in. 'Mum's watching over Max, so I thought I'd pop in for an afternoon drink.'

'You're in luck,' Simon said. 'Your man is free to take you to the party today.'

Julian flashed Simon a look as his mood plummeted.

Simon frowned. Julian realised his disappointment was shown on his face, but Simon wasn't to know why.

'Oh?' Kimberly asked.

'I got stood up so I'm working,' Simon said, his eyes darting to Julian.

Julian slapped on a smile.

'What party is this?' Kimberly asked Julian.

'It's a small housewarming, but I already told Holly I couldn't make it.' The last thing he wanted to do was turn up with Kimberly.

'I'm dying to see her cottage. It looks divine from the outside. Come on Jules, we can take a bottle and some snacks from behind the bar, it won't matter that she hasn't catered for us.'

JULIAN WALKED across the village green with Kimberly holding his left arm, while he carried a bag with refreshments in his right. He would not be drinking alcohol himself as he was expecting a full house at the bistro that evening.

'I can't wait to see inside,' Kimberly said as they walked along the winding path, which meandered through a freshly sown lawn with lush green blades, already poking through the soil. The cottage had new windows, and the scorched stone walls had been cleaned and looked fresh with new mortar and a smart red roof.

Kimberly lifted the old-fashioned iron door knocker on the varnished front door.

The door opened, and Julian found Jaz at the entrance. She grinned at him, but then frowned as she looked in Kimberly's direction. He got the feeling that Jaz did not like Kimberly much – which was no surprise; they had little in common and there had been the confrontation over at Digger World.

'Come in,' Jaz said. 'I didn't realise you were coming.'

'Nor did I,' Julian said. 'Simon offered to cover the pub.' He stepped aside to let Kimberly in and followed them both through the cottage. The space was warm and homely. It had a newness about it, with the faint smell of paint. They headed for the kitchen. He had visited a few times before the fire had decimated the place. They had extended the kitchen to include a dining area with a corner sofa, creating a beautiful living space and family home.

Holly approached them. 'I'm so pleased you're here.'

Julian placed the drink and snacks on the large oak table, and Holly gave him an enormous hug. He could feel her bump press up against him.

'Hi Kimberly,' Holly said, smiling.

'Your place is divine and you look so happy,' Kimberly said.

Mitch joined them. 'It's great, you could make it. What do you think?' he asked Julian.

'It's a brilliant family home, Mitch. Congratulations on all fronts, I'm so pleased for you both.' And he was. His eyes moved to the right, and he could see Jaz scowling out of the periphery of his vision. He smiled to himself, feeling a pang of sadness mixed with a warmth. He knew she cared. There was nothing he could do about his feelings. He turned to smile at the woman he loved, the good and the bad. She caught his eye, and he found himself locked in her gaze.

Kimberly put an arm in his and Jaz turned away.

'Julian, my man.' David Bunning slapped him on the back.

Julian noticed David was swaying slightly. He knew he was having business troubles. He'd been in the Eversley arms offloading his woes, as folks often did.

'Have you shifted those motorhomes yet?' Julian asked.

David sighed. 'I'm trying to forget about them today. I've locked the place up. I can't face looking at them.'

Julian gestured towards Jaz, who was filling a glass with wine. 'Why don't you speak to Jaz? That woman can sell anything.'

Kimberly slipped her arm away and joined in a conversation with Holly and Mitch.

David looked over to Jaz. 'Isn't she working in Cheshire?'

'She's moved back to look after her brother and sister.'

David raised his eyebrows. 'Thanks for the tip-off,' he said before meandering around the kitchen table in Jaz's direction.

Mitch approached Julian. 'Do you want a tour of the cottage?'

'Yes, please. That would be amazing,' Kimberly said, holding onto Julian's arm again.

'I'll start here,' Mitch said. 'This, of course, is the kitchen-diner-family room. We've space for children to play in, so we can keep an eye on them when cooking. We've already bought a huge playpen.'

'Oh, how sweet. Are you planning on a big family?'

Julian noticed a flicker in Mitch's eye. He knew they were

having twins and it seemed that Holly still wanted to keep that quiet.

'Two would be ideal,' Mitch said, leading them out of the room. 'This is our sitting room,' he led them into a cosy lounge with a wood burner in an inglenook.

'This is dreamy,' Kimberly said. 'I'd love to live in a place like this.'

Julian felt her squeeze his arm before they climbed the stairs.

'We've three bedrooms up here and a family bathroom. All decor designed by my artistic wife, with a floral theme.' He gestured at a bedroom. 'This is the nursery. I have yet to put the cot together.' Mitch looked content. Julian wished he could feel that way, instead of the knot that was in his stomach.

Julian knew he would have to end it with Kimberly. As wonderful as she was, they did not share that spark. He realised he should have gone with his gut in the first place instead of forcing a relationship. He looked at her smile at him and the guilt sat on his chest — he was going to let her down. He had to tread carefully, but it was never going to work, and he knew why. It was because being with anyone other than Jaz, felt wrong.

CHAPTER 30

*J*az clenched her teeth, as Kimberley returned to the kitchen draped over Julian. Jaz wished they didn't look so perfect together. She turned away to find David Bunning approaching. her, he had refilled her glass with white wine.

'Let's go outside,' she said to him, not wanting Kimberly in her eye-line. The kids were also out the back playing with Trixy, and she wanted to check they were okay.

Once in the walled garden, she found Belle and Mikey training Trixy to sit, with a bowl of cocktail sausages. She laughed, knowing that Trixy had been trained by Holly to do all manner of tricks. It was more likely that Trixy was training the children to give her sausages.

Jaz turned to David. 'Is Florrie okay?'

David motioned to an up-cycled bench, which had been gifted to Holly by one of the artists from the hub. 'She's away,' he said. 'The company she works for, asked her to start a week early on a Caribbean cruise.' He sighed as he sat down. 'I won't see much of her this summer. I was planning to do a couple of two-week trips with her at sea. But I've got myself into a bit of a situation with the business.'

Jaz's ears pricked up as she sat beside him. She sensed he was going to ask her for advice. It would be great to think about business for a while instead of her domestic issues.

'I have stock I need to shift and it's not moving.' He looked into her eyes. 'I wanted to make you a business proposition.'

Act cool, Jaz told herself donning her poker face. She was desperate for a job which would work around her new responsibilities, but didn't want David to know how keen she was, if she was about to negotiate a contract with him. 'What sort of stock?'

David sighed and took a gulp of red wine. 'I was at an auction and got carried away.'

'It's easily done,' Jaz said, having seen her ex-boss in a similar position after he bought a job lot of cars which had been used in the 2012 Olympics to chauffeur the athletes between the sporting locations. Ten white BMWs had been plonked on the forecourt and no-one was buying them. Until she saved the day.

'They're RV motorhomes. Large ones. Very large, in fact everyone says they're too large and too expensive. It seems us Brits prefer smaller motorhomes or large tow caravans, which are much cheaper and can be kept on one site for the season. But I'm hoping, with your reputation?'

'What price are they?'

She noticed David swallow. 'I've bought four, for an amount that makes me nauseous. I raised the funds via a high interest bridging loan. I thought I'd pay it off quickly. I can't afford the next payment. I need to sell at least one by the end of next month otherwise I'm in big trouble.' He sat back in his seat. 'I'll have to re-mortgage my house, but that will only push the can down the road.' He wiped his brow. 'I've done so well to build my business and now I'm going to potentially lose it all after one stupid mistake. And not only that, I run the risk of being considered not fit-and-proper to be a Councillor. I fear I'll lose everything.'

No wonder he looks stressed, Jaz thought. 'Can't you sell them at auction and break even?'

He shook his head. 'I paid over the odds, I realise that now. No-one wants them. They do well in the States but I can't ship them there.'

'And you want my advice?' Jaz said playing it cool as she took a sip of her drink. David clearly wanted her to shift them for him.

'I want you to work for me. I'll match the salary you had at the local car showroom. I'm sure I can't afford your Cheshire salary.'

Jaz felt the knot which had been present inside her chest relax slightly. 'I'll come to your office on Monday afternoon, if you like?' That would give her something to look forward to, because she was moving Stacey to the home first thing Monday morning.

David smiled. 'So, you're interested?'

'I am.'

They clinked glasses.

Jaz's heart pounded as she dropped Belle and Mikey at school. Stacey had left it to Jaz to choose the nursing home, saying she trusted her judgement.

'See you at Holly's tonight.' Jaz waved the children off. Val and Len were collecting them from school and taking the kids to the farmhouse for tea as Jaz expected to be with David Bunning negotiating her contract.

As Jaz drove towards Wells, she wondered how Stacey was going to react to her temporary home. The thought of spending time with her, just the two of them, was giving Jaz palpitations. It would be the first time she had been alone with her mother, since the day she left home. Memories she wanted to forget flooded her mind, as suppressed emotions bubbled to the surface. *Forgive and forget,* she repeated to herself.

The hospital had arranged for Stacey to be taken to the nursing home by ambulance. There was no way Stacey could get in and out of Jaz's car. As Jaz reached the home, an ambulance followed her in. Her stomach lurched as she parked her car. She approached the entrance pulling a wheeled case, which she had filled with new undies, night and lounge wear. As she reached the entrance, Stacey was being brought out of the ambulance in a wheelchair and then transferred to another belonging to the home. As soon as Stacey noticed Jaz, her face brightened.

'Hi,' Jaz said.

'Sweet, I'm so pleased you came.'

Jaz realised Stacey must have worried that she would not show up. Looking at her in regular clothes and out of the hospital, Stacey appeared so much younger. Certainly, too young to be going into a home where most of the residents were elderly.

'I'll just drop your case inside,' Jaz said to her mother. She took a deep breath telling herself she would be home in an hour.

As she returned to the ambulance the driver was bidding Stacey farewell.

'Good luck, Stacey, I might see you when you go for your next check-up at the hospital.' He returned to his vehicle.

Jaz took hold of the wheelchair handles.

'Before we go in, sweet, I just want to say how sorry I am for what happened between us.' Stacey's voice cracked.

The last thing Jaz wanted was a big heart to heart. 'Let's get inside,' she said in a brusque voice.

As they entered, Jaz felt the same awful feeling she had the first time she was in the home, which had been the initial one Holly and herself had looked at. Whilst it was sterile, it had appeared the cleanest and was in the best location.

A woman dressed in a lilac uniform approached them. 'Welcome, Stacey. I'm Corrine, I'll show you to your room.'

Corrine placed the case in the lift before exiting to allow enough space for Jaz to push Stacey inside. 'I'll take the stairs and meet you on the second floor.'

Jaz stared at the indicator lights of the lift as it travelled.

As the lift door opened Corrine smiled at them. 'This way.'

Jaz pushed the chair onto the landing and followed Corrine along the corridor.

Stacey remained silent.

'Here you are,' Corrine said as they entered a small room with a dark red carpet and a hospital style bed. The room smelled of strong detergent, which Jaz guessed was coming from the en-suite wet room.

Jaz wheeled Stacey up to the bed.

'I'll let you settle in,' Corrine said, placing Stacey's case next to a chair.

Jaz avoided Stacey's gaze. 'I'll help you unpack,' she said as she lifted the case and placed it on the bed before unzipping it.

'You don't have to, sweet, you've done so much already. I'm sure you're busy. The last thing I want to do is be any bother.'

'It's fine. I've time.' Jaz wasn't due to see David Bunning for another couple of hours. She opened a drawer and placed the clothes inside.

'I know we've not spoken sweet, but I'm ever so proud of you.'

Jaz made no comment and quickly filled the drawers with the rest of the clothes. There wasn't anything in the case which would need hanging up in the wardrobe.

She turned around once she had finished. Stacey had tears in her eyes. Jaz felt she had to get out of there. Yet, she felt awful, leaving her mother alone in the place. It didn't seem right. Stacey had a home, the one in Eversley Burrows. The nursing home was fine. It was clean, Corrine had seemed nice, but it just didn't feel appropriate. Not for someone so young.

Corrine knocked on the door and entered the room, breaking the silence. 'I'll take you down for lunch, Stacey.' She turned to Jaz. 'Do you want to come too, as we settle Mum in?'

No, she didn't, but still nodded in agreement and followed them out. This time Jaz took the stairs and Corrine took Stacey down in the small lift. Jaz felt sick to the core as she descended the stairs, trying to keep her emotions in check. She reached the ground floor before them and waited.

As the lift opened, she saw Stacey wiping her eyes with a tissue. As soon as she noticed Jaz, she gave a breezy smile. Jaz gulped and smiled back. As their eyes met, she felt a connection, the one she had been avoiding. Dragging her gaze away, she took a deep breath. She'd experienced an emotion she'd forgotten. A link between herself and this person who had let her down all those years ago, but somewhere, at some point, she had been someone she had felt attached to. Close to. A bond. A love.

Keep it together, Jaz told herself, as she followed Corrine along the corridor.

When they reached the dining hall, it was, as Jaz expected, full of elderly patients. While they did not look unhappy, it felt a mismatch.

Jaz put a hand to her mouth. 'I, I'm sorry, I need to go.' She stumbled along the corridor towards the exit.

Once outside, she took in huge gulps of air as she walked towards her car; the tears choked her as she reached into her pocket for her keys. She pulled open the door of the Audi and climbed in. Resting her hands on the steering wheel, she pressed her head against them and cried out. Sobbing seventeen years' worth of tears. It was the young girl inside, the little girl let down by a mummy who wasn't always there to look after her. The angry teenager neglected by a mum who was forever drunk. And the grown-up Jaz, who'd lost her career because of a mother she had no relationship with.

Jaz looked up at the home through bleary eyes, wiping her face with the back of her hand. She knew that no matter what Stacey had done to her — her mother still loved her. She had seen it in her eyes and felt it in the very core of her heart. Regardless of their history, she could not leave her there. She reached for a tissue in her glove compartment, wiped her eyes, blew her nose, and composed herself.

As Jaz redid her make-up in the mirror, she took deep breaths realising that as soon as she opened the car door, she had to move forward, and to be able to do that, she must forgive her mother.

CHAPTER 31

Julian trimmed his beard and applied aftershave, as if this was a part of his usual daily routine, which, of course, it wasn't. It was because Jaz had asked him to meet her at the showroom she used to work at. She said she was building bridges and her old boss, Rick, would source his car. She asked him to meet her there, although did not explain why they could not travel together. He had glimpsed her on the school run but had not been able to chat. He did not need to trade in his BMW for a four-door family affair. He knew he was only going as an excuse to see Jaz and it would be an ideal opportunity to slip into the conversation that he had no future with Kimberly. And to gauge Jaz's reaction.

Kimberly had been understanding when he had told her he wasn't ready to progress to the next stage, but she said not to tell the boys, or broadcast the fact, until after the school jamboree. She did not want Max to feel upset or for there to be any awkwardness between them. She suggested they made the camping trip as enjoyable as possible. Although she had added that maybe they might find a spark, he was certain that would not happen and had repeated to her — it was not right for him. He had no intention of stringing her along and made it crystal clear — it was over.

As he reached the garage, Jaz was standing by her Audi with her old boss who was looking under the hood of her sporty red car. *Surely not,* he thought as Rick appeared to be assessing the car. *She's not selling it?* Jaz without the Audi was like a game of rugby without mud. Julian parked up and approached Jaz.

'Are you upgrading your Audi?' he said as he reached her side.

'I wouldn't call it an upgrade, as such,' she said with a sigh.

He was sure he could see a tear in her eye before she looked away. He couldn't imagine Jaz crying. Her usual displays of emotion were masked by anger. *Mind you,* he thought. *She would cry if she sold that car.*

'I need something I can put a wheelchair in.'

'A wheelchair?' he asked.

'My mother's in a nursing home and it's not right for her in there. She's only late forties, so I'm going to look after her at her house, until she's back on her feet.'

Julian was momentarily stunned. Jaz taking of the kids was unbelievable enough, but caring for her estranged mother as well? 'But you love that car,' he said.

Jaz fell silent.

Julian chastened himself. *Idiot.* 'Sorry, I'm not making this any easier for you, am I?'

Rick approached Jaz. 'I can give you ten. It's got some miles on it.' He nodded at a large blue people carrier in the corner. 'It'll mean I only need three from you. I've already got someone interested in the Audi.'

Jaz remained silent and nodded. Lifting her keys, she handed them to Rick. 'Can your sort Julian out?'

Julian looked over at the people carrier. It wasn't something he'd want to drive.

'He's a family of four,' she said.

'I ...' Julian stopped, not knowing what to say. He wanted to tell Jaz that he had cooled it with Kimberly, but with the revelation she had given about her mother, he guessed romance was far from her mind. It seemed inappropriate. *Poor Jaz,* he thought. One thing was for sure, he would definitely be there as support.

Rick led Julian over to a Mazda and gave him the lowdown, and then they looked over a Mercedes. Jaz joined them, half-heartedly giving her opinion. She didn't look right, and he didn't want to keep her there any longer, dragging out the experience of giving up her beloved car.

'Thanks Rick, you've given me food for thought,' he said. 'And thank you for pricing up my BMW. I'd like to involve my lad in the decision, if you don't mind. So I'll be in touch.'

He watched on as Jaz signed the paperwork for the exchange of cars. Walking out of the showroom, she took one last look at her prized red Audi TT as Rick told her he would arrange for her private plates to be returned. Julian accompanied her to the people-carrier and heard her take in a breath, which sounded like a stifled sob.

He placed a hand on her shoulder. 'You're doing a noble thing, Jazzy. Times will turn around. I'm sure of it.'

'I hope so, Ju,' she said, opening the door of the blue car, which Julian thought looked like a small school bus, especially with Jaz being so petite.

He smiled at her. 'You're one in a million.'

She sat in the driver's seat and turned on the engine, which did not growl like the Audi, it rumbled like a bus.

'Thanks, Ju, for coming. Sorry you didn't find your ideal car. See you around.'

Julian watched her drive out of the car park and decided he would certainly see her around. He had loved her from the first time the punky teen enter his parent's pub. He had hated not having Jaz in Eversley and it might not be the right time for romance, but he would wait until that time came, because he could not imagine his future life, without Jaz in it. He turned back, he had business to do with Rick.

CHAPTER 32

*J*az drove towards the nursing home with tears streaming down her cheeks. The red Audi had been an extension of her, a symbol of her success, the first expensive thing she had bought once she had 'made it' in car sales. Rick had let her have the red sports car at cost and deducted the payments from her salary, which had not taken long to repay, as she was the best salesperson the firm had ever had. And now it was gone.

She was grateful that Rick had let bygones be bygones and helped her out with the people carrier, he had come through for her and she knew she had been given a good deal. She only hoped that the person who bought the red Audi, lived nowhere near Eversley. She would hate to see someone else at the wheel. It was as if she had given away her childhood teddy bear. Funnily enough, she mused, she never had a particular teddy during her childhood that she had been attached to.

After stopping in a lay-by and reapplying her make-up, she arrived at the nursing home. Stacey was already outside, waiting. Her face lit up as she saw Jaz draw up. Jaz got out and went to the rear of the vehicle to work the mechanism which would allow her to get Stacey on board. Once it was set for its passenger, Jaz approached her mother.

'I don't know what to say, love. I don't deserve you, sweet – I know that.'

Jaz swallowed away the lump in her throat. 'Come on, let's get you home.'

AFTER A WEEK of parenting duties and being a full-time carer, Jaz was in a routine. The care team was brilliant, so she didn't have to do much in the way of personal care, she only had to help Stacey to the toilet about three times a day, and Stacey was getting about using a frame. The care team moved her upstairs at night and down in the morning, so there was thankfully no need for a bed in the lounge.

Jaz had messaged the WhatsApp group to say she could not possibly help with organising the school fair due to family commitments. *Every cloud has a silver lining,* she thought. Following that, she had received a few friendly messages of support and Bobby urged her to join them on a night out, to let her hair down as a break from it all. But she had declined the invitation.

A string of neighbours had visited including Sian, who, she guessed, was coming to visit her rather than Stacey. One neighbour was a mobile hairdresser and Stacey was looking so much brighter with a fresh cut and colour. A couple of neighbours had brought pots of cooked food covered in aluminium foil, which Jaz always welcomed.

'We need to go through your paperwork, Stacey,' Jaz said

as she cleared away after the evening meal, still feeling too uncomfortable to add the 'Mum' tag.

'I know, sweet.'

She knew she was brusque with her mother. Not rude or resentful, but very matter of fact. She found viewing her new role as a job made it easier to cope with and extracted the emotion from the situation.

Jaz softened her voice. 'I'll open it all, fish out the junk, then we'll go through the important things and pay the bills. I've your hospital paperwork at hand, so I'll try to get any late charges reversed, under the circumstances.'

'You're such a good girl,' Stacey said.

'I'll stick the TV on for you.' Jaz reached for the remote and selected a soap Stacey enjoyed. The house was quiet as the children were in bed, watching TV before sleep.

Jaz spent an hour at the dining table, opening the post and placing it into piles.

'Right. I've found the bills, but no bank statements. Everything has been paid by direct debit. There are no reminders. How do you view your bank records?' She assumed Darren had paid into the account and covered the bills. With the guy in mind, she picked up a handwritten letter.

Stacey shook her head. 'I don't have statements. I do it online, sweet. On my phone.'

Jaz approached Stacey. 'I didn't open this one. It's from France.' She knew this wasn't a letter she should read — it was clearly personal. She handed it to her mother, guessing it was from Darren. It had come the day before.

Stacey blinked rapidly but did not open it.

Jaz realised her mother needed some privacy. 'I'll make tea,' she said and went to the kitchen.

As she boiled the kettle, she peeked through the serving

hatch and watched Stacey put a shaky hand to her mouth. Jaz felt an instant shot of fear in her chest and stepped back. Taking deep breaths, Jaz reminded herself that just because Stacey was upset, she was not going to get drunk. Tina had said Stacey had not drunk for years. Apart from that, there was no alcohol in the house. Jaz left it a good ten minutes before she walked in with a cup of tea for herself and one for her mother.

Stacey looked up and smiled at her. 'If you get my phone, I'll check my bank account to make sure I'm not in the red. And thanks for sorting it all out for me.' She paused. 'And then later, sweet. I need to tell you something important. About your dad.'

Jaz nearly spilt her tea. 'My dad?'

'I've not told you about him.'

Jaz shook her head. 'No. I've got enough to cope with, with you and the kids.' She gave a nervous laugh. 'I can't cope with another relative.'

'But there's something you need to know.'

'I can't hack it now. It doesn't matter. It can wait. Honestly, Mum.'

And there it was.

I said Mum, she thought.

Stacey's eyes filled with water, clearly registering the affection.

Jaz went over and kissed her on the cheek. 'I'm not going anywhere, so you can tell me another time. Give me a few weeks to adjust. Honestly, it's fine.'

'I love you so much, my Jasmine. My beautiful girl.'

Jaz hugged her mother as Stacey clung onto her, sobbing, only stopping when the carers arrived to help her to bed.

Jaz laid on her bed, which was no longer in the double

bedroom. She was on the bottom bunk in Belle's room. At least her sister had agreed to take the top bunk, because Belle could see the TV from up there. Jaz laid back and did her best to put Stacey's words out of her head. But she constantly asked herself questions. What was it Stacey wanted to tell her about her father? Was he still in Australia? Did he want to see her? Was he dead? But it really would have to wait.

'I can't take any more,' she whispered to herself.

'But everyone in the class is going,' Belle said with a whine at the farmhouse.

Jaz had taken the kids to Holly's for dinner. Tina, from next door, was sitting with Stacey for a couple of hours until the carers showed up.

'I thought you hated everyone?' Jaz said to Belle.

'Well, they all like me now.'

'Why's that?'

'Don't know.'

'Probably because you've bothered to turn up!' Holly said as Mitch collected the empty plates with the help of three student staff members who had joined them for dinner.

'But we can't go to the Jamboree,' Jaz said.

'What's a jamboree?' Mikey asked before he shovelled a spoonful of apple crumble and custard into his mouth.

Belle jumped in before Jaz could answer. 'It's a cool trip where you get to camp with your friends, play games, make fires, toast marshmallows and eat midnight snacks.'

'I wanna go,' Mikey said.

'Belle, I wouldn't have thought it was your sort of thing,' Jaz said. 'But anyway, we can't go because of Mum.'

Belle crossed her arms. 'That's not fair.'

'And we haven't got a tent.'

'Lissa's mum and dad are going in their caravan. Maybe we can fit in there.'

'You could borrow one from David Bunning,' Holly said.

Jaz frowned at Holly. 'But I let him down. I didn't even turn up for the meeting, let alone accept his job offer.' She didn't want to go on the stupid camp, but then a small smile appeared on her face. 'Maybe …'

'Yay,' Mikey said

Jaz laughed, realising she had used the M-word again. She picked up her mobile phone. 'I'm just popping out to make a call.'

CHAPTER 33

'This is going to be so much fun,' Kimberley said.

Julian had not seen Kimberly, other than during the school run since they split. He lifted her tent into the back of her hatchback car. 'I'll see you at the site.'

He returned to his BMW which was full of their clothes, snacks and drinks. 'Off we go,' he said to an excited Noah who sat in the back seat as they drove away.

It was his first trip to the Jamboree as Sophie had taken Noah before. A local campsite owner who'd had children at Eversley Primary years before, allowed the school to book the entire site for the weekend at reasonable rates. It had begun as a one-off, but had since turned into an annual event, even though the owner's children were now at college.

Julian drove along the Wells Road towards the campsite. He was brought from his thoughts by a large hoot from what sounded like a bus. Looking in his rear-view mirror, all Julian could see was the radiator vent of a large vehicle. He pressed his foot on the accelerator of the BMW and sped away until he could see a huge RV motorhome in his rear-view mirror.

'Some people around here must be loaded to afford one of those,' he said to Noah, wondering if David Bunning had got a lucky sale.

Noah swung around. 'It's Jaz, Dad, it's Jaz.' He pulled his seatbelt off his shoulder and sat facing out the back window.

Julian laughed. 'Of course, it is. Now put that belt back on and face front.' Julian felt a little brighter about the weekend.

SETTING up the tent was a painless exercise. Kimberley read the instructions, and Julian placed the poles where they needed to go, as the boys held them in place. The tent was up within minutes and he was pleased to note that there were distinct separate pods, which would separate the two small families.

'We make such a good team,' Kimberly said.

He looked around the field. Some parents had already descended into arguments over pitching. 'I think I'll lend a hand,' he said, gesturing at a couple who were regulars in the pub, as they wagged their fingers at each other. 'Noah, can you help Kimberly get our things into the tent before you go off to play with your mates?'

After ten minutes, Julian was joined by Noah, who helped him with the tent pitching. After erecting a third tent, Julian looked out for anyone else struggling, when he spotted Belle walking by, arm in arm with a friend.

'Hi there, Belle, I see you've come in style?' He pointed to the RV.

'Yes, it's amazing. It's so comfortable and easy to hook

up. It's ideal for a family holiday, and at a reasonable price, too.'

Julian threw his head back and laughed. 'Jaz has got you in training, I see?'

Belle let go of her friend who continued on, and approached him, lowering her voice. 'Jaz said if she sells it we can all go on a proper holiday.'

'I bet she did,' he said with a chuckle.

'Why don't you come and see? You might like to buy one? I'm sure Jaz would love to show *you* around.' She smiled at him sweetly.

Julian laughed and let her drag him along with Noah in tow. As he approached the RV, it seemed even bigger than it looked on the road as the sides were extended out to make the internal space even wider. He climbed up the steps and was hit by the smell of new leather, reminding him of when he bought his BMW from Jaz. At the entrance was a cream leather driving seat.

'This is what you call luxury,' he said.

Jaz swung around and smiled. 'What's it like out on the field?'

'We're in a tent with Max and Kimberly,' Noah said.

'Urgh,' Belle said. 'She's so stuck up.'

'Belle, let's not be nasty. I'm sure Kimberly has many qualities we don't know about.' She gave Julian a wide smile.

He looked around. There was a passenger seat, again in cream leather and along the side ran a plush leather sofa. 'What's the price tag?' he asked.

It depends on the customer. You can have it at cost,' she laughed. 'But I have to sell it for a minimum of one hundred grand.'

Julian gave a low whistle. 'Bunning really is in trouble.'

'Did he tell you about it?'

'He sure did.' Julian admired the cupboard space made from oak. 'That's some kitchen,' he said. 'It even has a double sink.'

'And here,' Jaz said, pulling a lever. 'Extra worktop slides out.'

As he moved through the RV, Julian reached a dining area. 'Very smart.'

Belle passed him. 'And come through here.' She opened a door which led to a plush bedroom dressed in bedclothes worthy of a display at Selfridges. 'There's enough room for you and Jaz in here.'

'Belle,' Jaz said slowly.

'Why do you want to stay in a tent when there's enough room in here with us? There are two bedrooms.' She pointed to another door. 'I can sleep on the sofa and Noah can sleep in the bunk bed with Mikey.'

'Yeah,' Noah and Mikey said in unison.

Julian laughed. 'I thought you were supposed to be selling me the motorhome, not a bed for the night. But yes, it's a lot more comfortable in here than in the tent.' He smiled at Jaz.

'Hello,' Kimberly called from outside.

'You're wanted,' Jaz said.

He left the bedroom and went to the door.

'I can't seem to inflate our air bed,' Kimberly called. 'I'd try to blow it up myself, but it's a non-starter, with it being a huge double.'

'See you later,' Jaz said, gesturing for him to leave.

Julian shook his head. He could see what Kimberly was trying to do. Yes, she had a double airbed, but she was sharing it with Max, not him. He had brought camping mats for himself and Noah to sleep on, and he was not looking forward to it. He looked back at the RV, remembering the comfortable bed and imagining himself in it.

'Sorry, I wasn't interrupting something, was I?' Kimberly said.

'Belle asked me to look at the motorhome, it's quite impressive.'

'It's not really camping though, is it?'

Julian remained silent, truth be known he wasn't a fan of camping, it didn't suit him, he was too tall for sleeping bags, and camp beds and he had broken more than a couple of camping chairs in his lifetime.

'Once we've got the airbeds set up, I thought we'd open a bottle of wine before going over to the food trucks.'

Julian looked over to the RV knowing where he would rather be.

CHAPTER 34

*J*az smoothed the covers of the bed in the RV, remembering how nice it felt when Julian and Noah were in the motorhome, the five of them together. It seemed relaxed, jovial, and right, until that girl-friend of his showed up. Belle was right Kimberly was stuck up. Jaz sighed and told herself off, knowing Kimberly had had a hard time of it. Bobby had filled her in on Kimberly's marriage break-up, at the school gates.

'Let's face it, Jaz,' she said to herself. 'You're just plain jealous.'

After calling Tina to make sure Stacey was okay, she looked around the motorhome, realising she needed to make it look a million dollars if she was going to convince anyone to buy it. Thankfully, the site had electric and water hook-ups — they were well equipped for visitors with motorhomes. She also made sure she and the kids looked great. They had to sell this as a happy family holiday. She decided to take pictures and post them to the private social media page that the school had set up for the event.

Later, she chose a picture showing the crate of bubbly

she had brought. Underneath, she wrote. *Fancy some fizz in my motorhome? All are welcome.* Followed by a picture of herself in front of the RV sipping from a flute of champagne. Although, it wasn't champagne — it was a five-pound bottle of Prosecco from the supermarket.

'Can my friends come too?' Belle had asked.

'Of course. If they bring their parents,' Jaz said.

By seven o'clock, the RV was filled with the WhatsApp mums and when it was too crowded, others had brought their camping chairs over.

Mel's husband shouted. 'We're in the cheap seats,' as Jaz laughed and filled his camping mug with bubbly.

After a while, the revellers went to fetch their own drink as the bottles of fizz ran low. Someone lit a campfire in the closest fire pit and the kids sat around, toasting marsh-mallows.

Jaz plonked herself outside the RV on a camping chair. Her legs ached. She had been around the inside and outside of the motorhome with every member of the Mums' WhatsApp group. Apart from Kimberly, of course who was notably missing. Jaz had shown her prospective clients how easy it was to hook up the electricity and water, and remove the sewage. A couple of them already owned motorhomes, but none like the RV. She did point out that no-one was to use her facilities, as the home was a show item and put a 'no entry' sign on the toilet door. The only liquid allowed down the pipes was clean water during her demonstrations. It was also 'shoes-off' inside.

Bobby lead everyone in a rendition of 'for she's a jolly good fellow,' as they emptied the last bottle of bubbly.

Jaz looked around as the night turned dark, noticing everyone was laughing with her, not at her. It was as if her rotten school days had been erased from her history.

One dad whipped out his guitar, and they had a sing-song. Jaz felt a buzz, a bit like the buzz she got when she sold a car. She crossed her fingers, hoping she could shift the RV.

THE NEXT MORNING, Jaz and the kids brushed their teeth in the shower block.

'Why can't we do this in the motorhome? There's a shower in there,' Belle said.

'I've told you, it's not ours. We have to keep it super clean. Someone here might buy it.'

'Like who?'

'The group that were inside the van.'

'The ones with all the jewellery, make-up and dresses on?'

'That's them. They live in big houses and have pots of money.'

'You wear a lot of jewellery. Have you got pots of money?' Mikey asked.

Jaz laughed. 'Nowhere near as much as they have."

'Mum says that money can't buy you happiness,' Belle said.

'True,' Jaz said, putting her toothbrush in her bag. 'But it makes life a whole lot easier. And I'd rather be unhappily rich than unhappily poor. That's why you need to concentrate on your studies so you can find a good job. Now come on, there are lots of activities to do. Let's go.'

As they exited the shower block, Jaz noticed Julian striding over with Kimberly, who promptly put her arm in his.

'Looks like you had some party last night?' Julian said, disentangling himself from Kimberly.

'It was amazing,' Belle said. 'You should have come along.'

'We had an early night.' Kimberly smiled sweetly at Jaz.

'That's boring,' Belle said.

Julian laughed, shaking his head. 'Are you going over to the activities? They're just about to start the kite making.'

Belle and Mikey dumped their toiletry bags on Jaz and ran off.

'I'd better get back to the motorhome and clean it. See you around,' Jaz said.

The day was a hive of activity, and Jaz was especially pleased when Holly and Mitch popped over with Trixy. Two artists from the arts hub were providing free activities for the children, with the hope of promoting their classes and picking up new customers.

'This looks amazing in here,' Holly said, looking around the RV. 'It puts my caravan to shame.'

'Your caravan is lovely,' Jaz said. 'It's got character. Sorry you've had to keep Trixy outside.'

'She's fine. Mitch has taken her to see the kids.' Holly sat down and winced.

'Not long now, chick.' Jaz smiled.

'I'm getting a little nervous. I'm trying not to think about the actual birth. We're staying in the cottage for the first time tonight.' Holly glanced around the RV. 'Have you had any interest from potential buyers?'

'Yes, from the incomers, I'm banking on them. I can see in their eyes they want it. But these RVs are high ticket. David was right, he made a mistake buying them.'

'Well, if anyone can sell them, you can. And I just saw Julian.'

'Holly, no matchmaking, remember?'

Holly smiled at her. 'Okay. But I just want to say Jaz, you deserve some happiness because you are a total saint taking on the family and looking after Stacey. I just can't believe it.'

Jaz laughed. 'Me neither. I feel like I've crossed over to some sort of parallel universe.'

'Well, as long as I'm a part of your universe I'll be forever happy.'

Jaz stood up and gave her best friend a hug.

A WEEK PASSED since the Jamboree and Jaz had not sold any of the RVs. She didn't want to push too hard. David was getting stressed, and she had seen him in the Eversley Arms and assured him she was doing her best. But family life had been good. Stacey was looking so much brighter. Just being out of hospital and in a familiar environment had made a huge difference. She had even cooked a meal with Jaz's help. Jaz kept a diary of her gradual improvement for Dr Raj and he had been especially pleased when he had seen Stacey at the outpatient clinic.

Jaz was clearing the dinner table with the help of her siblings when the doorbell rang.

'Great,' Jaz said. 'I'm expecting a delivery.' Following parents' evening at the school, she had ordered books for Mikey to help with his reading. Opening the door, she stood transfixed. Standing before her was a man, a very tanned man. About five foot nine, in his late forties, she guessed. But he wasn't a delivery driver, he wasn't holding a parcel, he had a case. She knew instantly who he was. Although she had never met him before.

She opened her mouth to speak, but no words came out.

Jaz blinked and said nothing as she studied the man's face. His dark hair, his warm brown eyes, and above them. His eyebrows.

Jaz felt her blood run cold.

He stared at her for what seemed like ages. 'Are you Jaz?' he asked with a frown.

She gave a silent nod.

'I never expected to see you here. You look so much like Belle. I'm Darren.'

Jaz stepped outside and Darren moved backwards.

'It's not a good idea,' she said in a measured tone. *Does he know?* She asked herself.

'I need to see Stacey. I don't care what she says.'

'You shouldn't have deserted her then, should you?' She crossed her arms.

'Is that what she told you?' He shook his head. 'It wasn't like that.'

'You do know she's sick, right?'

'No? What's wrong?'

'Who is it?' Jaz heard Belle shout.

'Just a delivery,' she called out then put her finger to her mouth.

Darren shook his head. 'That's my daughter in there. I need to know what's going on. Let me in.'

Jaz stared into his eyes. Did this man not know what was clearly obvious to her? 'You'll have to wait,' she said, shaking. 'I'll make sure Mum is okay with it. We can't afford to put her blood pressure up. Go next door, Tina's in, she'll explain.'

Closing the door behind her, Jaz's heart raced, as she touched her eyebrow and the space where the hair didn't grow.

'Who was that love?' Stacey asked, smiling.

Jaz took a deep breath and approached her, looking into her mother's blue eyes and wondered why it had not occurred to her that Stacey didn't share the same eyes that she, Belle and Mikey had, or the same eyebrow.

'That discussion you wanted to have with me about my father?'

Sharon raised her eyebrows. 'You want to talk about it now?'

Jaz took a deep breath. 'He's outside.'

'What, Darren?'

Jaz nodded, as she looked through the serving hatch to see the kids were busy with the washing up.

'I ... I ...' Stacey's hand shook as she held it to her mouth.

Jaz's heart beat at a pace. Why had Stacey told her that her father had emigrated to Australia when he had been living in the Burrows for years. She took a deep breath and let it out slowly. 'Mum, calm down. I'm not going to get angry with you.' And at the same time, she told herself to calm down. She could not afford to raise Stacey's blood pressure. 'I've sent him next door while I speak to you.' She sat beside Stacey on the sofa.

Stacey placed her hands on her lap and stared at them. 'I've been waiting for this. Waiting for you to notice how much you and Belle look alike and that neither of you look much like me.'

'We share the same father?'

Stacey nodded her head and cried. 'When you were born, I didn't know who the dad was.'

'So why didn't you just say that?'

'I wanted the best for you. I was scared. Your granny was sick and had no money, and Darren's family was poor and his dad was inside.'

'Inside? As in prison?' Jaz said.

Stacey nodded. 'You could have been Pete's baby.'

'The guy that moved away to Australia?'

'His family lived in a big house. It was easier to say you were his. And I thought you were too. I worked out the dates, and it was more likely, so I convinced myself you were definitely his.'

'Why were you with this, Pete?'

'Me and Daz, had an argument. Pete was a rebound. A one night thing.'

'But why didn't you tell Darren later?'

'He went away. And by the time he got out of the army, you had moved out. Anyway, it wasn't until Belle was about three when her hair was so dark and she looked so much like you, and when everyone was saying she had her daddy's looks. It wasn't til then that I knew for sure. But me and Daz had agreed never to discuss the past, to look forward. If me and you were speaking, of course I'd have said something to him and you.'

Jaz shook her head.

'I'm a rubbish mother and you're the best daughter I ...' Stacey choked on her tears. 'I don't deserve you and if you hate me ...'

Jaz sat back as her heartbeat slowed. 'You were only five years older than Belle is now, when you had me. I can't imagine what that was like for you. We all make mistakes. All you need to do now is to get well. You've two beautiful children that need you.'

'I've three beautiful children. And the kids had a dad here who loved them and I told him not to come back, because I was scared he was leaving me for good. I ruin everything.'

Jaz heard the front door open behind her.

'Sorry, but I'm not waiting outside my own house,'

Darren said, and upon seeing Stacey on the sofa he rushed over. 'Stace.'

Belle screamed. 'Daddy.'

Mikey followed her from the kitchen.

Jaz moved from the sofa as the family hugged. All of them were in tears. She watched on — from the outside.

Jaz went to Belle's room and packed a bag, as Mikey showed Darren his bedroom. They had helped Stacey up the stairs.

Listening to the excited chatter, Jaz quietly left the house, wondering whether they had even noticed her go. It was not until she reached the end of the close that she allowed herself to cry.

CHAPTER 35

*J*ulian looked at the clock. *Where the heck is Adam?* He was not answering his phone. The prep wasn't done and the restaurant would open in an hour. Julian had been out all day at a meeting, so didn't realise Adam was not around until he got back at five. He had ten customers booked in, and no doubt more would show up — they usually did. He didn't want to let anyone down. Walking into the bar, he wondered whether Adam had left a message.

'Simon, have you heard anything from Adam?'

'No, boss. He's not answering my calls. Maybe you should ask his parents?'

'I've already called them. They haven't seen him since first thing. They said he had a bit of business to attend to.'

'What? So he's not sleeping somewhere, he's gone AWOL? Don't you open in an hour?'

'Yes.' Julian felt panic rising up his body. 'I don't want to let anyone down.'

'I can't cook to Bistro standard and there's only me in tonight.'

Julian went outside to see if he could see Adam approaching. As he looked out across the green, he spotted Jaz stomping across the grass. He waved at her, if a little frantically. She hesitated, then stared at him.

He jogged over to her and as he got closer, saw that she was crying. 'What't wrong?'

She smiled at him. 'You look like I feel, Ju. It's just family stuff. And I can't talk about it now. I need to calm down first,' she said in a stilted voice. She took a deep breath. 'Are you okay?'

'I've got a crisis on my hands, so if you need a distraction, come with me to the Bistro.' He pointed across to his restaurant. 'It will definitely take your mind off it.'

'Okay.'

'But if you want to talk about it later – you know I'm here to listen.'

'Thanks, Ju. You're a great friend.'

His heart dropped at the term *friend*. Especially as he had broken it off with Kimberley once and for all. And Jaz had not been near him since the jamboree.

Inside the bistro, Jaz turned to him. 'So, what's the big crisis?'

'Adam's gone AWOL.'

'And you're opening tonight?'

Julian nodded as they reached the kitchen. 'I've got ten bookings.'

'Have you found anyone to cook in his absence?'

He picked an apron from a hook and handed it to her. 'Yes, I have.'

'Wait, what? I can't cook.' Her brown eyes widened.

'You're about to learn.'

'Ju – you're joking, right?'

'No, we'll limit the menu to pies, which are already

prepared and the fish, chicken and steaks. Everything with new potatoes.'

'But what about the sauces?'

He handed her his phone. 'Your job is to google the recipes.'

Jaz laughed. 'You're a nutcase Julian Webster'

NATALIE CAME in with the first orders. 'Luckily, tables two and three only want mains. Two beef and ale pies and two seared salmon. Table three is one steak, medium rare with peppercorn sauce, another salmon, and two chicken and mushroom pies. But the guy on table one wants a starter, the scallops, plus a steak with Diane sauce.'

'Okay,' Julian said.

'You've got this,' Jaz flashed her phone. 'The recipes are here. I'll start lining up the ingredients.' She looked at the larder.

'And I don't want to worry you ...' Natalie trailed off.

'What?' Julian asked.

'The guy on table one has red hair and a notebook.'

'Not the food critic?' Julian asked, feeling his jaw tense.

'He fits the description Adam gave us.' Natalie gestured behind her.

'I'm done for,' Julian said.

'Shh, not too loud,' Jaz whispered. 'He might hear you. And anyway, you've been cooking in the pub for years. You can do this.'

'Not to award standard?' Julian looked up to the ceiling. 'I'm finished before I've even begun.' He looked back at Jaz to witness her sucking in her lips to stop herself from smiling, as her eyes danced.

'It's not funny,' he said, although at the same time, he

was pleased he was improving her mood, even if it was at his own expense.

'I know – I know. But it's only one critic. Your regulars won't take any notice. We can do this. I've been sitting with Stacey for weeks watching cooking shows back-to-back. You need a lot of butter in the pan and scallops have to be golden on the outside and not overcooked. Look, chuck one over here and I'll do a tester.'

Julian gazed at Jaz, she made everything less painful. And while she was not taking it too seriously, she made up for that with her energy and self-belief. *That's why I love her so much*, he thought as he shook his head. *Love?* He knew he had never stopped loving her.

Fetching a scallop, he passed it to Jaz.

She turned up her nose. 'It's still in the shell.'

'Keeps it fresh,' he said.

'No worries.' She fiddled about with her phone. 'There's a video for everything.'

Julian laughed as Jaz turned a crisis into a fun evening. As they worked, he remembered other times they had laughed together, how everything seemed amusing, even when it wasn't.

Natalie had been great at apologising for the delay.

'Nat, how's it going with the food critic?' Julian asked as she entered the kitchen.

'He said he enjoyed his food. He certainly ate it all.' She lifted an empty plate. And he's been smiling at me a lot, and writing in his book.'

'Do you think I should check him out?' Jaz asked.

'No,' Julian said.

'You go out there and see him then!' Jaz said. He felt her push him in the back. 'You're supposed to be front-of-house. It's your restaurant.'

'You're normally out there,' Natalie added. 'The customers will wonder where you are.'

He knew they were right. He removed the apron he was wearing and unrolled his sleeves. With a smile, he walked into the restaurant and was immediately complimented by a couple he knew from rugby training. He noticed the red-haired guy, sat on a table alone. His eyes followed Natalie across the room and he appeared to be writing in his book. He wished he could see what the guy was putting down on paper.

'Hello, did you enjoy your meal?' Julian asked the red-haired man.

'Oh, yes,' he said, shutting his notebook. 'It was great.'

'I haven't seen you here before. Is this your first time?'

'Yes, I'm staying in the area. I'm an artist. Holly Loveland recommended this place.'

Julian relaxed. 'Oh, I see.' Looking at the man's book, he saw it was a sketch pad. 'I hope you come back and visit us again.' He turned away, masking his smile.

CHAPTER 36

*J*az slumped at a table in the empty restaurant. 'Wow. That's even harder work than looking after the kids.'

'I'll be off then,' Natalie said.

'Thanks for helping with the clearing up,' Julian said.

'No worries, I enjoyed this evening.' She laughed and pointed at Jaz. 'You're a fab cook.'

'Honestly, at home it's freezer food most of the time.'

'You should cook more, Jaz. You're a natural,' Natalie said.

'Julian did most of the actual cooking,' Jaz said.

'But you told me to add more seasoning, checked the steaks and dressed the plates,' he said.

'I've eaten out a lot. I know what it should look and taste like.'

'Exactly,' Julian said. 'You know a lot about presentation. The meals looked great. In fact, you sent them out on the plate as well as Adam does.'

'Better I'd say,' Natalie added.

'Hey, don't get carried away. He's the Michelin Star guy,'

Jaz said with a laugh. She felt happy in that moment, Julian was a great tonic and her mood had totally changed from how she had felt leaving Eversley Burrows earlier that evening.

Natalie waved as she went out. 'Seriously, this has been the best day at work I've ever had.' She closed the door behind her.

'I'll second that.' Julian smiled at Jaz as he sat opposite her. 'Although, Adam didn't win any Michelin Stars tonight.'

'Have you heard from him?' Jaz asked as she sipped a coffee.

'A brief apology. He's in London but says he'll be back on Friday.' Julian shook his head. 'Opening on a Tuesday as a trial was his idea, and it seems he forgot about it. I'm worried he's gone on a bender.'

'Is he an alcoholic?'

'It's not alcohol, but don't repeat that, as his parents don't even know.'

Jaz sat back in her seat and groaned. 'You know how useless I am at keeping secrets, Ju.'

He laughed. 'Don't worry, if Adam carries on like this, the whole of Eversley will find out. That's why he came back from London. I found him in a right state and offered him a new start.'

'You've been great to him.'

'Hopefully, it was a genuine oversight.'

Jaz's heartbeat quickened, as Julian stared into her eyes.

He moved his hand across the table and took hers. 'This was my favourite night in the restaurant yet.'

She sat motionless, not knowing what to say. He massaged her hand, as he enveloped it in his own. Her breathing was heavy. As if in slow motion, he pulled her to him, then leaned across the table and kissed her. She shut her eyes at the sensation of his lips against hers. Igniting a closeness that was reserved for them. He pulled away and like lightning, he moved around the table until he held her completely in his arms. She put her hands on his shoulders as he swept her up. His powerful arms held her close, as he kissed her again. She felt the thud of his heart as the kiss turned passionate. His need was apparent, and it matched hers in an equal measure of intensity. She moved hard against him, letting him know her desire was as strong as his.

'I've missed you,' he whispered into her ear, which sent tingles to all her nerve endings. She ached within as he ran his hand down her back and then squeezed her so close, it took her breath away. She felt as if they were in their own world, protected from the outside, within a snatched piece of heaven, in the centre of her uncertain world.

He moaned into her ear. 'Shall we take this upstairs?'

'Yes,' she whispered.

He carried her towards the back door of the restaurant, still kissing her.

The front door of the bistro banged open behind them.

Julian spun around with Jaz still in his arms until she saw Kimberly standing in the doorway with her hands on her hips.

'So this is why our relationship wasn't working out,' Kimberly said.

Jaz was pulled out of the intimate haze, as if she had walked into an icy rain.

Julian lowered her to the floor, but placed himself between her and Kimberly.

'That wasn't the reason.'

Jaz felt hot. A different type of heat from what she had been feeling. Her chest felt heavy. The one thing she had always been proud of, was that she had never hit on another woman's man. Never broken the girl-code. Infidelity was not in her DNA, having seen how it had destroyed Stacey, leading her to drink.

'I'm so sorry,' Jaz said. 'I'll get out of here.' She scooted around Julian.

'Jaz, stop.' Julian called. 'You've nothing to feel sorry about.'

'Of course, I have,' she said as she grabbed her bag and scooted around Kimberly, mumbling another apology.

Once outside, the hot tears stung her eyes as she ran alongside the green toward the Eversley Burrows estate– when all she wanted to do was run to Holly. But it was late and Holly needed her rest. The babies were due the following week.

How could Jaz have forgotten about Kimberly? Everything in her life was weird. Stacey and the kids, living in Eversley Burrow. Holly was huge – she'd always been slim. Okay, so she was pregnant, but still looked so different. And meeting her father for the first time? Then running away, not being able to cope with yet another thing. Her whole world was upside down, but with Julian she had felt herself again. Julian was the same. The same man. The same warmth. The exact same love, as if she had never been away. And she had felt good, exceptionally good, in his arms. She slowed her pace as a sob caught in her throat. She looked back at the bistro. Julian was still in there with Kimberly. She felt an intense surge of loneliness.

'What was he doing?' she asked herself as she stomped back towards Eversley Burrows and then stopped, realising that while her whole family was there, she wasn't needed. Darren was back and while she was undoubtably their blood relative, she felt she did not belong. She pulled her keys from her bag. *Yes*, she still had the key to Holly's caravan. She spun around and walked across the dark village green, alone.

JAZ'S HEAD thumped as her mobile phone vibrated with a text. She was probably dehydrated from crying. At least she didn't have any alcohol, although if she had, maybe she could have blamed the kiss with Julian on too much booze. She rolled over and groaned. She had been stunned by the intensity of that kiss, the closeness, and the acute sense of togetherness. They had been like magnets, clamping together. She reached for her phone, which she had turned on silent the night before, after Julian had called her repeatedly. After refusing his calls, he had finally sent her a message which said:

We need to talk. It's over with Kimberly.

'Well, of course it is,' Jaz had said aloud in the empty caravan. 'She caught you kissing me.' It certainly had not made her feel any better about breaking the girl-code.

Glancing at her phone she saw there were a few missed calls and messages, but she first opened one from Mitch. She blinked as she read it.

Holly's in labour. We're at St Michaels.

Jaz jumped out of the bed, pulled on her jeans and a fresh, if somewhat creased, top from her bag. She rushed out of the caravan and when she reached the green, sped across and didn't stop running until she reached Eversley Burrows. Approaching the people carrier parked up on Stacey's drive, she looked up as the front door swung open and Belle called to her.

'Jaz, where've you been? We've been calling you.'

'I was out late, so stayed at the caravan.'

'Can you take us to school?'

'I can't, chick. Holly's having her babies right now. Your dad can take you.'

Darren appeared at the door. 'Hey. There you are. We've been so worried about you, Come in/", love. We need to have a proper chat.' He took a step towards her. Stacey had clearly broken the news to Darren that he was, in fact, a father of three.

Jaz took a step backwards. 'I can't now. My best friend is in labour, and I need the car.' Without waiting for a reply, she jumped in the motor, wrenched the car into gear and reversed off the drive. Darren put his arm around Belle's shoulders as Belle waved Jaz goodbye.

WHEN JAZ REACHED THE HOSPITAL, she followed the signs to the maternity unit. She had texted Mitch to let him know she was there.

He appeared with his hair sticking up, and had dark bristles on his face where he had not shaved. 'Hey.'

'Has she had them?' Jaz asked.

'Not yet. I'm so pleased you're here. The contractions have stopped.' He yawned.

'Can I go in?'

'Yes, of course. I need to get some food. I'll take you in first.' He gestured towards the maternity ward.

Jaz followed him into the room and found a tired-looking Holly.

'I'm so pleased you're here.' Holly gave a watery smile.

'I'll be off for a while,' Mitch said.

Holly nodded. 'Get some food and try to sleep somewhere. It may be some time yet. I'll text you if something starts happening.'

'Sorry, I only just got Mitch's message,' Jaz said to Holly as Mitch left the room.

'No need to apologise. What were you up to?'

'I had a bit of a mare last night. But you don't want to hear about that. You should get some sleep too, hun.'

'Trust me, Jaz. That's just what I need, something to take my mind off it. I can't believe two little people are soon going to join us. But they're causing me a bit of pain.'

Jaz sat on the chair next to the bed. 'Does it hurt a lot?'

'It's a dragging sensation. It's pretty painful, so yes, it hurts. But it's not a frightening pain. Not like I'm sick. But I'm grateful for this little rest, to get my strength up. I don't want a caesarean, otherwise it'll be weeks before I can lift, drive and go about my business. Especially with twins.'

'I'll be around to help, hun.'

'But you've got Stacey and the kids to look after.'

'As it happens, the kid's dad is back.'

'Really? What's he like?'

Jaz breathed out. 'It turns out he's also my biological father.'

'Oh, my, goodness. I don't know what to say.'

'Yeah, it's a shocker.'

'How did you find out?'

'I could tell just by looking at him, then Stacey confirmed it. I left before she broke the news to him, but he knows now. He wanted a chat this morning when I picked up the people carrier.'

'How do you feel about it?' Holly said holding her hand, after Jaz had relayed the conversation she'd had with Stacey.

'Honestly, I don't know. I'm not ready to think about it. I had to get out of there, I felt suffocated.' Her voice broke.

'I'm sorry. I've not been there when you needed me.'

Jaz laughed. 'Your priorities are in the right place, Holly. Look, I'm here for you, not the other way around.'

'Honestly, this is taking my mind off. Keep talking.'

'I was over at the Bistro standing in for Adam because he didn't show up.'

'Hang on, it must be the drugs, I thought you said you were standing in for Adam at the bistro.' Holly laughed. 'Ouch.' She paused. 'Maybe laughing isn't such a good idea.' She took a gulp of gas and air and panted for a few seconds as Jaz held her hand.

'Go on,' Holly said.

'Hun, I did. Adam was nowhere to be seen, so Julian and me did the service. Luckily, there were only ten people in.' Jaz smiled. 'We had such a laugh, Julian thought that a red-haired guy you sent over, was a food critic.'

'What Freddy, the portrait artist?'

'Yeah, we thought he was making notes about the food, but he was actually doing a sneaky sketch of Natalie. He left the picture of her on the table with his phone number.'

Holly grinned. 'Smooth. So, what was the problem?'

'We were alone, talking one minute, then we were all over each other. We kinda got lost in the moment. Then Kimberly walked in on us.'

Holly took a sharp intake of breath. 'No way. What happened next?'

'She was obviously not impressed. I apologised and left. I feel awful. It was like me and Julian and nothing else in the world existed. I totally forgot he was with her.'

Holly clutched her hand. 'As much as it was wrong, what's done is done. I said you were made for each other. So, what now?'

'I hate infidelity and he went behind her back.'

'It was only a kiss.'

'It would have been much more, trust me – if she hadn't barged in.'

'But you and Julian have history. Let him work it out.'

'He sent me a text to say it is over with Kimberly, but it's bound to be, after what she saw.'

Holly yawned.

'You need to sleep, hun. I won't go anywhere. Just have a snooze.'

Holly nodded and drifted off to sleep.

Jaz smiled as she held Holly's hand. Talking things over with her best friend had helped. It always did.

Later, Holly woke and moaned. 'Hand me the gas,' she gasped.

'I'll get Mitch,' Jaz said as the midwife checked Holly over.

'No, I want you with me. It could be hours until the babies arrive. Mitch needs his rest. I could be at this all day and you've been with me through thick and thin. Let's do this together.'

Jaz felt calm as she held Holly's hand.

Eventually, she'd taken it in shifts with Mitch throughout the day, giving each other a rest to catch some shuteye in the waiting room.

'They're coming,' Holly screamed as it approached midnight. 'I need to push.'

Jaz felt exhausted, and the door swung open as Mitch appeared. Wide-eyed.

Jaz walked down the corridor. She had loved being by Holly's side, but knew it was Mitch that needed to be with her now. She decided to stay in the waiting room until the babies were born. There was no point in going home. She didn't even have a home. Her apartment in Wells was filled with tenants. Eversley Burrows was full of a family she was a part of, yet felt disconnected from. And the caravan was hardly home. She leaned her head back on the wall and fell asleep.

'Jaz?'

She stirred to find a nurse from the maternity ward smiling at her.

'Holly wants you.'

'Is she alright?'

'Of course, and the babies.'

'Thank goodness for that,' Jaz said.

As she entered the room, her eyes were drawn to the new additions. Mitch held one of the babies, smiling into her eyes, and a nurse handed the other to Jaz. All wrapped up in a yellow blanket.

Jaz felt a tear run down her cheek 'She's beautiful.'

'That's Daisy and Mitch has Poppy,' Holly said.

'They're so cute. Well done. I'm so proud of you, hun. And you, Mitch.'

'I'm glad they waited until after midnight,' Holly said.

Jaz made no comment, but she knew what Holly was getting at. It was Jaz's birthday.

CHAPTER 37

*J*az had travelled back to Eversley in the early hours. Having dropped the car back to Rosemead Close, she had returned to the caravan, and finally got to sleep at about four.

She awoke at one o'clock in the afternoon and had received a text from Belle.

Can you pick us up from school? Dad is taking Mum out. Miss you xx <3

Jaz groaned, it was too late to text back and say no, considering Belle would now be at school and not have her phone with her. Belle was more than capable of walking Mikey home from school. She knew her sister just wanted to see her. But she also realised it was time to show her face. And having seen Holly in labour – she could not imagine how Stacey had felt, a sixteen-year-old girl going through that ordeal. One thing was for sure, Jaz had definitely not changed her mind about having children.

It was not the only text she received. Tyrone had sent her a picture of himself in the Lamborghini with Crystal who was wearing a huge diamond ring with the words. *She said yes, we are on a road-trip to celebrate.* Jaz smiled remembering when she and Tyrone were at a charity event and he was too shy to ask Crystal out for a date. She had literally dragged him over. She sighed, the life she had in Cheshire seemed a million miles away, as if it had never really happened.

JAZ APPROACHED THE SCHOOL GATES, and saw a few members of the WhatsApp mums huddled together, throwing her distasteful looks. One of them put an arm around Kimberly's shoulder. A kiss had catapulted her from the top of the popularity charts to zero. David Bunning had been calling her for daily updates and she had let today's call go to voicemail. The likelihood of getting any RV sales from the WhatsApp mums was also zero.

Bobby tapped her on the shoulder. 'If it isn't the scarlet woman.'

Jaz spun around to see Bobby's grin. She obviously found the whole situation amusing. Jaz pulled her sunglasses down so she could look into her eyes. 'Look, I feel bad for Kimberly. I shouldn't have kissed him. I don't know what came over me. We've got history.' She flipped her glasses back up.

'All's fair in love and war, that's what I say.' Bobby looked over at Kimberly. 'It's not like they were married and trust me, a few of that group have done a lot worse.'

'It's not something I'm proud of.'

'He wasn't that into her, everyone knows that. Anyway.' She paused. 'They might be giving you daggers, but they're not talking about you. There's a crisis. They've been let down by Portia Lane.' Bobby shook her head slowly and pouted.

'The reality TV star?' Jaz asked.

'Yes, she was opening the school fair. She's got a better offer, some modelling gig in Crete, so she ditched them.'

Jaz didn't seem to think that was a bad thing. The show Portia was famous for wasn't appropriate for primary school children.

'Didn't you see from the WhatsApp group?'

Jaz checked her phone, then flashed it at Bobby. 'I've been removed from the chat.'

Bobby laughed. 'You really have been left out in the cold.'

'So what's your next move?'

'It's a mess. They've got nothing sorted for the catering, just a handful of stalls, so I'm asking you, very nicely, to take it on.'

'I told you ...'

'I know you're busy, but think of the children, all excited with no fair to go to. And the school need the fundraising to resurface the playground.'

Jaz smiled at Bobby, she knew when she was being sold to.

Bobby shrugged. 'I've got time on my hands, so just tell me what to do and I'll get it done. We've got just over a week.'

'Ok, but we have a new team. Not with them.' Jaz nodded across the playground.

Bobby stuck her hand out. 'Deal.' She looked over Jaz's shoulder. 'Oops, here comes your man. I'll pop off.'

Jaz moved away as well. There was no way she wanted to be standing beside Julian with an audience. She made a beeline for the Eversley Burrows crowd. And stood between Sian and Mel.

'Right, you lot. I need help. We've taken over the PTA and are organising the fair.'

'You utter legend,' Sian said.

'Count me in,' Mel added, as did the rest of the group.

'I guess you have more time on your hands, now your dad's back,' Sian said.

Jaz laughed as she shook her head. 'News travels fast in Eversley Burrows.'

'Can I help?' she heard Julian say from behind, realising he had followed her over.

She spun around. 'We need a beer gazebo, with half the profits going to the school.'

'I'll give all the proceeds to the school.' He smiled at her.

She gulped and felt a warmth as she smiled back.

'Shall we have a meeting tonight?' Sian said. 'At the Dog and Horn?'

'I'm up for that,' Julian replied. 'But my bistro isn't open this evening, so why don't we hold it there?'

'Ooh. I hear it gets hot in that place,' Mel said as the others laughed.

'Let's keep it clean,' another mum said.

Jaz crossed her arms, and the titters dwindled.

Julian's face was tinged red above his beard, but his eyes were smiling. 'I take it eight is good with you all, after the kids are in bed?'

Jaz nodded. 'I have family stuff to attend to but should be there by then.' She realised she could not put it off any longer. She had to go home.

As they entered Rosemead Close, Jaz saw that the front door was open. Darren and Stacey were clearly back from their trip, as the car was parked on the drive. Belle ran ahead and Mikey followed.

Jaz slowed her pace, her heart beating harder. It had not

passed her notice that today was exactly seventeen years since she had left home. With every step, an extra tear filled her eye, but she knew she could not run away.

By the time she crossed the threshold, tears were spilling down her cheeks.

'Surprise!' her family shouted.

Blinking away the tears, she was taken aback as she looked around at the birthday banners, balloons and wrapped gifts. A large cake sat upon the dining table surrounded by a small buffet. Her eyes widened. Belle and Mikey looked so excited, her mother stood with her arm in her father's.

Darren coughed. 'I've missed all your birthdays, Jaz, so we're having a small family party.' He put his arm around his younger daughter. 'It was Belle's idea.'

'You've got thirty-two presents,' Belle said, near screaming with excitement.

Stacey shuffled over and her whole family followed, giving Jaz hugs and kisses. And she did not hold back the tears.

'We'll have a proper chat later, love,' Darren said. 'But let's have tea.'

Jaz nodded at him, realising he must have had a shock too.

'Are you going to open your presents?' Mikey asked.

She nodded. 'Do you want to help?'

'Yeah.' He pulled at her hand.

Jaz picked up the first one. *To our daughter, all our love, Mum and Dad.*

It took some time to open the gifts, including photographs, toiletries, and a heart-shaped locket with pictures of the children in.

'Thank you, so much.' She wondered whether they

realised she had not celebrated her birthday since she was fifteen.

Jaz relaxed as they ate the party food and showed them pictures of the babies on her phone, which were coming in from Holly, thick and fast.

'Come on, kids, help me clear up in the kitchen,' Stacey said shuffling along on her frame.

Darren smiled once they were out of the way. 'You look so much like Belle. I'm sorry, I should have known as soon as I saw you.'

She touched her eyebrow as she looked at him.

Darren put his hand across the table and held hers. 'I've just found out that I have the most amazing daughter.' His eyes welled up with tears. 'You're so successful. I can't believe you're mine.'

'So, you've been to France?'

He released her hand and sat back in his seat. 'Money had been tight as I was out of work. I took a three-month contract. Stacey thought it would only be for three months, considering that's what I promised her. When I told her I had to extend it, she freaked out and told me never to come back.' He ran his hand over his cheek. 'I should have returned straight away but wanted to settle our debts. I hadn't read the small print about an automatic extension if the job wasn't completed. With there being a retainer, if I'd left, I'd have forfeited fifty per cent of what I'd earned so far.' He looked to the kitchen. 'I thought Stacey would calm down.' He shook his head. 'I've been in the forces I'm used to going away and coming back. It's normal for me. I should have thought it through. And the kids ...' He cleared his throat. 'I've made more in those six months than I have over the past four years. If I'd known Stace was sick ...' He paused. 'I keep blaming myself for her getting sick, because

I stressed her out. And that must have affected her blood pressure. And I let the kids down.'

'We sometimes make wrong judgments. None of us is perfect. Certainly not me or Mum. You made a sensible decision. It did make financial sense.' She looked through the kitchen hatch at Stacey with the kids, washing up. 'It seems you two have made up. Just look forward now, to the future.'

He smiled. 'I've enough money to see us through for a while. We've always had a simple life here. I was hoping to buy a house, and for us to get married. But that can wait until your mother is stronger. I'm taking time off work to look after her. It's not right for you to have to take it all on. You've got your own life to lead. You're a saint.'

Jaz laughed, guessing that the label 'saint' wasn't the one being brandished around by the WhatsApp group.

'I want to hear everything you've done. We've got a lot of catching up to do.'

Jaz smiled. 'We've loads of time for that. I'll be staying in the area, seeing as I now have big sister and aunty duties.' She glanced at the time on her phone. 'But I've got to go right now, as I have a school fair to organise.'

*J*az watched Julian set up the beer tent on the school playground. It wasn't a marquee like the one they had at the village fair — it was set up underneath a pop-up gazebo, provided by a local brewery with its logo emblazoned upon it. She smiled. Julian had been a great help, he had been promoting the fair all week and had personally recruited five extra stall holders. He was giving her space, the whole village had been gossiping about Jaz discovering who her real dad was, and of course many suggested they knew all along.

Jaz and Julian had not discussed the kiss. After the planning meeting at the Bistro he had told her he wanted them to have a chat, but she said she needed to spend the week getting to know her father, and planning the fair. Not forgetting she was doing her best to sell the RVs for David. She did not want to speak to Julian, until they both had space to breath. Her mind had been clouded, and she wanted to be able to give him her full attention.

Word had got around that Julian had broken it off with

Kimberly, before his kiss with Jaz. And that had made Jaz feel a whole lot better and polished away the tarnish from her reputation.

Jaz decided to have a walk around the stalls to see how the set up was going. She waved at Holly who had the twins in a double pram. She had brought art kits for sale, and was running a raffle for free art sessions at the hub. She had enlisted the help of her student staff. Next to her was a stall with Mitch's students from the farm selling vegetables and promoting the box scheme.

Holly approached her, with the pram and Jaz smiled at the sleeping babies covered with floral blankets.

'How are you feeling?' Holly asked.

'The nerves are setting in, hun.' Jaz glanced over the playground at the school railings, through which she could see a large group of people waiting for the opening address from the surprise celebrity guest. For once she had learned to keep a secret. Mel and her husband were on the door. No-one would be getting passed Mel without handing over their entrance fee. She had given them the heads up on their expected guest as she needed them to direct the car to the designated parking space. She was sure she saw Mel blush. Jaz guessed Mel was a massive fan.

Jaz gave Holly a hug. 'Wish me luck, I'll check on the rest of the stalls to take my mind off it, it's still half an hour until the gates open.'

'It's going to be an amazing day,' Holly said.

Jaz wandered around the rest of the school field. There were many traditional stalls, like tombola, guess the name of the teddy and the coconut shy. Bobby had The WhatsApp mums organised, overseeing the hair braiding and face painting stalls. It was all very amicable, and Jaz was back in favour. Even Mr Hooper had thanked her for her help, which she thought was praise indeed. She had certainly not earned any compliments from the headmaster while she had been a pupil. Sian and her husband were running the sausage stall and he was firing up the barbecue. A trestle table was filled with rolls, napkins and condiments, which their children were sorting out

As she made her way back to the exit she saw Kimberly approaching her.

Jaz cleared her throat. 'I'm sorry, Kimberley.'

'There's no need to apologise. Nothing really happened between myself and Julian. We didn't have the same connection that you two clearly have.' She raised her eyebrows.

Jaz had a flashback to the heated encounter in the bistro. 'We've known each other for a long time,' she said.

'I was reading too much into my friendship with him. To be honest, I need space to get over my ex. I was rushing in head first.' She gestured around the field. 'And well done. You've achieved a lot in a week.' She leaned forward and gave Jaz a hug. 'I don't want any awkwardness between us. Julian is lucky to have you.' She stepped back. 'Good luck.'

Jaz watched Kimberly walk away and let out a sigh of relief before heading to the entrance.

Everyone wanted to know who the surprise celebrity was that Jaz had arranged. Truth was, she didn't want to say who it was in case there was a no show. She looked at her phone, it was approaching twelve, she relaxed as soon as she heard the vroom of the Lamborghini as it swept into the school carpark, and gave a sigh of relief. Mel guided him to a cordoned off area of the car park as her husband watched on, with his mouth agape, as if he doubted it was really going to happen.

Jaz hurried over and reached the car.

Tyrone got out and stretched. 'Hi, Jaz.' He walked around the car and gave her a hug then opened the door and helped Crystal out, who flashed Jaz the rock on her finger, which glinted in the sun.

'It's Tyrone Hart,' someone squealed, and Tyrone waved. Jaz was sure there were screams not only from the kids, but from a few of the dads.

Jaz gestured to a small platform erected at the entrance. 'This way, Ty. And thanks so much for coming, you'll make some dreams come true today.'

When they reached the small stage, Jaz handed him a card and a cordless microphone. 'It'd be great if you could read this out and then I'll take you both over to the RV I've got set up, for the signings.' She waved at a couple of the dads she had recruited as security. They were standing, motionless, staring, clearly star struck.

'Oh, I love this,' Crystal giggled as she tottered along. 'What a bunch of loves.'

Tyrone stepped onto the platform and helped Crystal up, as a reporter from the Gazette took pictures of them. The crowd hushed as he looked at the card Jaz had given him, then put it in his pocket.

He looked out to the crowd and lifted the microphone. 'I couldn't say no when Jaz asked me to come to her old school, because she's great.' He gestured to Jaz. 'Come up here.'

Jaz looked across at the audience and standing at the front, were her parents. Darren was behind with Stacey who sat in a wheelchair and an excited Mikey hugged their mother as Belle grinned beside them.

Tyrone clearly wasn't following the speech she had

prepared for him on the index card. She took his hand as he hoisted her up.

'Everyone thinks because you're famous you're like this confident person,' Tyrone said. 'But I had no confidence at all. And Jaz here made me feel better about myself. She told me to hold my head up and "it doesn't matter where you're from," she said, "all that matters is where you're heading." I hear this was her old school and I'm sure this must be the best school in the country, if the kids turn out like her.'

The reporter for the Gazette stepped forward and took a couple of pictures of Jaz.

'I've got a stack of photos with me to sign and all the money raised will go to the school.'

Everyone cheered.

When the applause had calmed down, Jaz took the microphone from Tyrone. 'If you could all make an orderly queue at the RV.' She pointed to where she had pitched up, on the school field. 'Tyrone will start in half an hour.'

JAZ SHOWED Tyrone and Crystal into the RV. 'Help your-selves to refreshments and have a rest before coming down to sign. My sister will be taking the money for the photographs.' She pointed at Belle sitting at the table in front of the motorhome. 'And the guys down there will be making sure no-one gets too close.'

'This is great,' Tyrone said looking around the RV. 'I came down to Somerset with me Mam and Step-Dad, when I was little. We went to a camp site, it was the best holiday I ever had. But the caravan was nothing like this.'

'It's not mine, I'm selling it.'

'I love it,' Crystal said touching the leather upholstery.

'How much does one of these set you back?' Tyrone

asked. 'I've been thinking of something to get my parents. As a thank you present.'

'We could borrow it and go all over the place,' Crystal said. 'It would look great on my vlog.'

Jaz looked out of the window at the WhatsApp mum's lining up.

'They go for one hundred and thirty thousand, but if you buy it today and tell everyone, you can have it for one hundred.'

'Deal.' Ty shook her hand.

Jaz considered that the Eversley Burrows parents made a great team, as the last of the litter had been picked up. Tyrone and Crystal had headed off. Jaz had called David Bunning who had hot-footed it over to the fair. He had arranged for them to stay at an exclusive spa hotel for the night while he arranged the paperwork for the RV. Jaz had made appointments for three other couples to look around the remaining RVs at the showroom, the following day. David had given her such a tight hug before he left, he near winded her. He also said he was looking for a partner in his business.

Belle and Mikey had gone home with her parents, she could see her whole family were proud, not least because they had told her so, throughout the day. She guessed Stacey would feel tired. She had suggested she went back to the house a couple of times but Stacey said she didn't want to miss out.

Sian and Mel approached Jaz.

'You came through today, girlfriend.' Sian gave her a high five.

Mel laughed. 'I nearly wet myself waiting for Tyrone to

show up and blubbed when he got here. My Dad's a massive United fan. He was so made up. You made his year.'

'Well, it wasn't me that sat there signing my name until my hand nearly fell off. Good job he doesn't play in goal, he's probably got a repetitive strain injury in his right hand.'

'Jaz, take the credit,' Sian said. 'Tyrone Hart thinks you're well cool, and so do we. We're off down the Dog and Horn if you want a few drinks?'

Jaz looked over their shoulders as Julian walked across the field towards her. 'I'm having tea over at the Eversley Arms.' Julian still had the personal number plates that Rick had given him to pass on to her, when she had traded her car in. He had invited her over to pick them up. She suspected he had other motives for asking her over to his place, and she hoped she was right.

'Have fun,' Sian said in a suggestive voice as they left.

Jaz waited for Julian to reach her.

'No Noah?' she asked, remembering how the lad had rushed up to her at the fair and flung his arms around her telling her she was the best. And as she had held him, she had felt her eyes well up. She realised she had let him down, when she left.

'He's gone to a birthday sleep-over. I pity the parents. The kids are hyped up after the celebrity visitor and fair.'

'Noah looked happy with his autograph.'

Julian laughed. 'He thinks you're best mates with Tyrone and asked when he was coming over for dinner. Well done, you're one in a million. It couldn't have gone any better, could it?'

'I feel good about it, Ju. David has an interesting business proposal for me. For the first time in weeks, I'm excited about the future.'

'You certainly saved Bunning's bacon. Everything you touch turns to gold.'

'I don't know about that.'

'Come on.' He offered her his hand and she grabbed it.

They laughed and joked about the day and reminisced as they walked to the Eversley Arms. Jaz felt the whole way that she wanted to stop, to hug him and kiss him, but she resisted. She wanted to wait until they were alone. She felt there was nothing in her way, and an unspoken under-standing about what they would do once they were behind closed doors.

Once they reached the pub, Julian walked her around the back of the building. 'They're in the garage.'

As he opened the heavy doors, she felt her whole body flush hot, as she put both hands to her cheeks. Inside were her personal number plates, as she expected, the surprise was that they were still attached to her gleaming red Audi TT.

Julian pulled the car keys from his pocket. 'A gift from me.'

She looked up into his eyes. 'I don't believe it.'

'You're just not my Jaz without the Audi.' He moved closer and kissed her tenderly.

She wrapped her arms as far as they would go around his strong torso, not wanting ever to be parted from him again.

He enveloped her. 'I couldn't be happier you know that right?' he whispered into her ear.

'I do.'

Julian released her but clutched onto her hand. 'Now I have you here, I'm not letting you go home tonight.'

She grinned. 'I need to tell my parents if I'm staying out for the night.'

They laughed as they walked hand in hand to the pub entrance. When they reached the door, Julian picked her up and whisked her over the threshold to the cheers of the locals. He carried her through the bar, straight up the stairs and to the bedroom.

'Welcome home, he said as he eased her onto the bed. It's not just for tonight, though, it's forever.'

She pulled him close and as she kissed him, Jaz knew she was back, in the very heart of Eversley Village, for good.

A NOTE FROM SUZANNE.

Do you want more? Would you like to spend Christmas in Eversley Village?

Grace Bunning left Eversley Village for London, under a cloud, with a reputation she was not proud of. She has since graduated from University and has a glowing career in the charity sector.

Grace returns to Eversley, to spend Christmas with her father in his country home, just outside of the village. She plans to surprise him, but when she arrives, she finds her father is away for the festive season, and that his scary business partner, Jaz is house-sitting with her family. The only space free for her to sleep, is on the sofa.

Sitting in The Eversley Arms with all eyes on her, recently widowed Helen Kelly asks Grace for help with her Christmas Charity auction. Her eldest son is in town and romantic sparks fly between him and Grace. But he is off limits.

Can Grace prove to the village that she has grown up and changed? Or is this going to be the worst Christmas ever?

Order, *Christmas Wishes in Eversley Village* to find out.

REVIEWS ARE REALLY helpful to an author. So please leave one if you have a few moments.

PLEASE VISIT www.suzannefox.co.uk to join my mailing list.

ACKNOWLEDGMENTS

I started this series way back in 2018 when I wrote the first three chapters as part of my Open University degree with the help of my tutor, Rosemary Dun who helped some more, after I joined a couple of her short courses. I also had help from Jenny Kane in her 'novel in a year' course. And help from an anonymous author through the Romantic Novelists' Association's new writer's scheme, who gave it two read throughs. And Alison Knight. And my lovely beta readers Callie Hill, Claire O'Connor, Jenny Treasure, Shell Rice Mutimer and Tara Starling. I mainly publish cozy mysteries under a pen name, however wanted to publish this trilogy and have other ideas in the pipeline for this genre.

Thanks also goes to the rest of my friends in the writing community, to my husband, for putting up with me tapping away at the keyboard 24/7. And to my daughter Lottie for her marketing assistance, which helps people to find my books.

Made in United States
North Haven, CT
26 September 2025

80142013R00171